Travels and Travails Of Small Minds

BY
Daniel Falatko

The Ardent Writer Press
Brownsboro, Alabama

Visit Daniel Falatko's Author Page at
www.ArdentWriterPress.com

For general information about publishing with The Ardent Writer Press contact *steve@ardentwriterpress.com* or forward mail to:
The Ardent Writer Press,
Box 25
Brownsboro, Alabama 35741.

This is a second edition of Daniel Falatko's *One Thin Dime*, revised significantly from the self-published first edition (2009) and retitled as *Travels and Travails of Small Minds*. All rights reserved by Daniel Falatko, Brooklyn, N.Y. Excerpts of text may be posted online only for a noncommercial use, provided quotations do not exceed a total of over three hundred (300) words.

Cover composition by Steve Gierhart, The Ardent Writer Press, using Photoshop techniques. Comic characters are from the book and were developed using work for hire from illustrator Byron Elliott, Indianapolis, Indiana. The revised brownstone building for the cover was created using Photoshop techniques and the public domain photo of a building in Brooklyn taken by Joel Dabu, webmaster of BedStuyGateway.com (included on Wikipedia). Composition of cover and interior artwork and colorization are covered by the same grant for noncommercial use noted above. Author photo by David McDade.

Interior illustrations by work for hire illustrator Byron Elliott, Indianapolis, Indiana. Office Icon made by Freepik from www.flaticon.com.

Library of Congress Cataloging-in-Publication Data

Daniel Falatko, Brooklyn, N.Y.

Travels and Travails of Small Minds

p. cm. (Ardent Writer Press -2017) ISBN 978-1-938667-69-5 (paperback); ISBN 978-1-938667-72-5 (hardback); ISBN 978-1-938667-73-2 (MOBI eBook); 978-1-938667-74-9 (ePub eBook)

Library of Congress Control Number 2017938935
- FICTION
- FICTION / Humorous.
- Humor
- HUMOR (BISAC)
- FICTION / Absurdist (BISAC)
- FICTION / Humorous / General (BISAC)

Second Edition (© 2017; First Edition One Thin Dime © 2009)

CONTENTS

ONE YEAR LATER	1
JULY 31ST	9
AUGUST 1ST	29
ONE YEAR LATER – PART TWO	48
AUGUST 2ND	55
AUGUST 3RD	95
AUGUST 4TH	107
ONE YEAR LATER – PART THREE	140
AUGUST 5TH	145
ONE YEAR LATER – PART FOUR	177
AUGUST 6TH	181
AUGUST 7TH	207
AUGUST 8TH	221
DECEMBER 13TH	239
ONE YEAR LATER - EPILOGUE	241

The Pash scares the trash while Mariska watches the vodka

ONE YEAR LATER

SLAVA. This is the word that every Russian ex-military member or former prisoner has tattooed somewhere on their pale, muscled bodies. In most cases the word is etched unevenly onto the forearm or the upper-shoulder, relegating its public appearances to the strangely tropical summers that clamp down on Moscow, when the sleeveless Ts and fake platinum chains that make up this type's standard hot weather uniform come out on full display. It is never good to lock eyes with these men on the streets, not due to fear of being attacked, but because they are likely to beg you mercilessly for a cigarette. Best to stare straight ahead, focused on a point a thousand yards into the distance, though from the corner of your eye you can never help but catch a glimpse of those foreign block letters in blue or black ink, peeking at you from atop a skull with flaming eyes or a crooked knife with a snake wrapped around it. *Slava.* I've been told it means "Glory."

I'm Nathan and aside from these men's army dorm and jailhouse tats, my life is presently devoid of any glory, directly lacking the essential tools from which to milk it. Just a grey flat with wood-grain-patterned wallpaper and floorboards that sag and squeak violently with my footsteps. Mice the size of rats

Travels and Travails of Small Minds by Daniel Falatko

gorge themselves on the generic brand Pop Tarts I found at the open-air market, no matter how high up in the cupboards I place them. I could hang the box from the ceiling and the acrobatic little bastards would still find a way to gnaw on them before they reached my plate. The flat is unrelentingly hot in the summers, a box-like oven. Sleep is impossible and sweat covers the body in a draining, constant soak. In the winters, which are impossibly long and unfathomably cold, steady gusts of pure wind find their way through the walls, rendering the space heaters useless fire hazards.

Directly outside the flat's lone, film-encrusted window, on the corner of the barely paved outer-district street, lies a small yet insanely bustling business hawking pirated DVDs and computer software burned onto blank discs. I've seen titles on the store's shelves a full year before their official Hollywood release dates. Often, the queue up to the front door stretches down the poplar-lined boulevard and out of sight, dozens of men in fake black leather jackets and buzz cuts sucking greedily on unfiltered cigarettes as their teenage-looking girlfriends appear bored-to-death on their arms, all straight blond hair and leopard-print skirts and penetrating, almost Asian eyes. Like the majority of Russian businesses, the store also sells vodka; from top-shelf Stoli to unlabeled "Spirits" bottles that cost very little and taste like turpentine. Unlike the DVD/Computer Software section, which is made up of open shelves for browsing, the vodka stash is locked down and protected 24/7. Glass that appears to be bulletproof encases the selections. Bottles are passed to customers through a secured slit like the one utilized by Hannibal Lecter's guards in *Silence of the Lambs*. Many a drunk has attempted to shatter that glass, using empty bottles, rocks, boards, beating upon the panes with their fists, begging for a bottle, sobbing uncontrollably. These are the nights when Mariska, the blond, leopard-print-skirt-clad teenager who works the night shift, yawns disinterestedly and hits the speed dial for Pasha, the store's owner and my landlord who resides on the

One Year Later

next block. This will inevitably bring The Pash screeching up in front of the store in his road-salt-streaked Lada, brandishing a baseball bat or, on special occasions, a gun to chase the drunks away. The Pash, who speaks exclusively in a nearly impenetrable storm of Russian slang, is built like a grizzly bear, complete with sweaty tufts of neck hair and club-like hands with fingernails so long they resemble claws. One of his forearms is easily the size of my head. A tenant on the next floor, an addict named Maldo with yellow jaundiced skin and a surprising but rudimentary grasp of English, tells me it is rumored that The Pash had, many years ago, murdered his own father with an axe. I always make sure to pay the bi-weekly rent far in advance.

It boggles the mind how quickly $25,000 can vanish in Eastern Europe. Last year it was coach compartments aboard the Eurail, mid-tier hotel rooms with coarse carpets and angular-pattern mock-designer curtains, a year's sublet on a small but cozy furnished apartment with a partial view of the Moscow River and the factories pumping black liquid that bursts through long pipes into the icy waters. It was many a night indoors, safe from the cold, up early for a brisk run over the ice and hard-packed snow, breath steaming and wheezing from a newly developed minor smoking habit, down through the underground walkways that stank like frozen urine, past babushkas selling potatoes from cardboard boxes and small children peddling Ritalin pills for two Euros each. It was breakfasts at the Black Earth Diner, hypnotized by the English language papers, huge cups of coffee and bronze busts of soldiers with demented eyes outside the double-paned windows. It was *Learn Russian in 90 Days!* books and countless hours of pirated DVDs (how I first met The Pash) with English subtitles. It was all a smokescreen, an attempt to blend, to become invisible, far from the reach of Dr. Behr or whatever ghosts had taken his place. It was turning off my mind completely, coasting along on autopilot, not just ignoring all of the facts that had led me to this isolation but relegating them to a place where they didn't exist at all. It was just a year in the cold with nothing to do.

Travels and Travails of Small Minds by Daniel Falatko

An expensive year, as it turned out. Life's basic necessities, things such as food, drink, shelter, smokes, reading materials, DVDs, and especially the dozens of bribes handed over to various members of the *militsiya* when stopped on the street with an expired passport, did not come cheap in Moscow that year. They suctioned themselves to the money satchel stashed in the tank of the apartment's toilet and, by the time spring rolled back around and the snow thawed into black rivers of toxic sludge on the eight-lane streets and the student came back from Nizhny Novgorod to re-claim her apartment, they had successfully drained a good chunk of the $270,000 I had to my name. Large stashes of money tend to become albatrosses when their possessors have no income whatsoever, just sitting there unprotected while a little more gets chipped away as each day ticks to a close.

It is time to scale back, to conserve as much as possible, to live off the fat of the land. With no foreseeable source of income, this 110 grand will have to last for years, if not the rest of my life. So here I find myself with two shirts in a tiny closet, nibbled Pop Tarts and my rodent friends, four plates, two glasses, and a poster left tacked to the dirty wall by the previous tenant, some Russian hair metal band named Gorky Park. Each day brings with it the possibility of arrest and detainment by any one of the dozens of agencies, sister agencies, or satellite agencies that make up the impossibly complicated web of authority. There is the UAK, the PAC, the ULB, the UGK, the LESA, the MCM, even the AKUKESB, any one of whom could kick in the door or snatch me off the street at any moment. My passport is long expired. I have no visa. The Pash warmly refers to me as "The Invalid." I only leave the building at night, out of fear of attracting *militsiya* attention in the daytime. No longer am I willing to cough up the cash for bribes. I would be cuffed with the plastic links utilized by the Moscow *militsiya* (steel handcuffs must be far out of their budget), marched into the back of a beat-up van, endure a bumpy ride with all the drunkards and gypsies and Chechens also rounded up that day, taken out into the forest far beyond

One Year Later

the outer rings and, after a swift but severe beating, left to be swallowed into the savage provinces. Even worse would be the foreigner's prison in the Center where all those unfortunate enough to not have their papers in order when being arrested for drug possession or homelessness languish for years with no legal counsel, no trial, no phone calls, fifty to a cell while tuberculosis breeds in the moistness on the cinder walls.

    This is why I no longer leave the building during the days. Around noon each day The Pash will stop by from overseeing the shop, bearing a bottle of vodka for his "little invalid" that he will proceed to drink most of himself. After one or two shots I start feeling sick to my stomach and have to bow out, The Pash laughing at me while draining glass-after-glass, his "little lightweight invalid."

    After The Pash sways out the door, I am left with the television, an old Japanese model that picks up a single station with the aid of tinfoil rabbit ears. The most interesting program comes on at 3:00, a show in which they pluck local teenagers off the streets and allow them the opportunity to win complicated-looking video game systems. But first they must get through a terrifying gauntlet which includes men in leather face masks rolling what appear to be solid metal balls at their legs. The metal balls rarely miss, sending the participants sailing head over heels into vats of steaming slime which, you can tell by the way the participants squint and gasp in near-agony, burns the eyes and irritates the throat if swallowed. Often times the participant will fall when escaping one metal roller, only to be hit full-on in the head by the next one. One day a girl with green hair and daisy duke shorts takes a hit so hard the metallic ping is audible over the static-prone TV speakers. The audience gasps. Before panning away, the camera catches the girl's legs go limp. Only once have I witnessed a contestant make it past the masked men and their metal rollers, a fourteen-year-old named Vital with hair like Keith Richards circa 1971, who was immediately cast into a chaotic realm of dry ice and strobe lights. Temporarily blinded, his mouth

Travels and Travails of Small Minds by Daniel Falatko

hanging open in horror, pierced tongue wagging, he was almost immediately taken out by a swinging contraption, a mechanical spider arm that swept him into a river of purple sludge, only his hand visible above the surface as he was swept away toward a huge whirlpool. Most of the kids picked for the show are of the squatter speed addict variety, their pupils huge under the studio lights during the introductions, wiping their noses with nervous smiles plastered across skeletal faces. The host, a man in his 40s with blinding white teeth and eyes that gleam every time another kid gets smashed with a ball or swept away by slime, mostly shouts repeated catch phrases while sweating heavily. The skin shows through the open top buttons of his shirt, which is drenched by the end of the show. The video game systems remain in their glass cases. At night the station broadcasts the matches of a soccer team clad in dark red uniforms with half-crescent moons on the back whose fans are fond of wearing fake fangs and lobbing smoke bombs onto the pitch. The matches are often paused to clear out the smoke or because of mass rioting, during which the station runs advertisements for Shadow Hours, a local strip club, with a tagline I can roughly translate as "Get behind the Shadow."

    Late in the night is when I take my walks. When I lived near the river, the long, circular night hikes were a glorious path to wander. Kremlin lights could be seen, Red Square ghostly illuminated and strangely empty, the streets of Novy Arbat alive with neon and posh shopping malls and beautiful mink-coated women with their mobster boyfriends, the streets crawling with Mercedes and Bentleys, ominous black government vehicles with flashing blue lights cutting through the traffic, huge cathedrals with domed towers rising into the black clouds of congested night skies.

    Out on the outer rings the scenery has changed. There are muddy vacant lots through which wild dogs run. There are dozens and dozens of identical cement tenement blocks stretching as far as the eye can see, their many windows illuminated with dim

One Year Later

yellow lighting that gives the buildings a hovering, transcendent feel, like a pod settlement on an otherwise empty and forlorn planet. Groups of teenagers gather in the building's courtyards at night, staring at me menacingly as I pass. An old billboard on the side of an abandoned *apteka* off the far end of my street, an advertisement for a grocery store that I have never been able to locate, features a woman with high cheekbones and calm green eyes that remind me of Amy's, but I try to put it out of my mind. The sense of isolation in these parts is thorough and complete. Carved up pine and birches surround each of the tenement blocks. Gone is the cell phone chatter of cream-skinned blonds and the controlled hum of black SUVs, left now to walk amongst shards of colored glass from smashed soft drink machines, listening to the gnashing of my own teeth.

A grunting Dr. Behr hovers over Nathan in their dusty and disheveled office as Edward snoops

JULY 31st

"ARE YOU GETTING OUT of there any time soon?" asked my girlfriend, Amy.

Her voice had the uncanny ability to sound both annoyed and hopeful in the same instant, teasing yet deadly serious, nagging my eardrum through the receiver of the black office phone. Fresh home from L.O.L. Publications, I could make out the sound of her Aldo boots on the hardwood in her tiny, messy efficiency located a little too far up into Harlem. She was pacing. Admittedly, she did have a point. It was well past 5 o'clock, verging on 6, and Dr. Behr had yet to issue the distinctive grunt that always signaled he was finished for the day, a phlegm-tinged guttural outburst that made the grey nose hairs protruding from the rims of his nostrils ebb and flow with the exhale. The grunt usually sounded between 4:30 and 5:00, emanating through the open door of the cluttered, dust-choked closet he called an office, letting co-worker and friend Edward and I know that he had officially lost interest in reading and re-reading the heavily notated documents which outlined the specific terms and conditions of the properties his father had left him in his will.

Pushing 80, Dr. Behr had never touched a computer and refused to purchase any for his two-man staff. Edward, who had

Travels and Travails of Small Minds by Daniel Falatko

been working for Dr. Behr for nearly 15 years, was fond of telling a story about the time he came back to the office from a long lunch with his boyfriend, Michael, to find Dr. Behr hovering over his desk, closely examining his calculator, picking it up and poking at it like a primate who had just discovered fire. At only 300 square feet, the two-room office on Broome Street was impossibly cramped even with only 3 occupants, and it was always a relief when Dr. Behr took one of his twice-yearly week-long vacations when a friend and former Columbia colleague we only knew as the Oxford Man from England would come visit him in the city. The old linoleum floor was perfect for collecting dust and dirt, which was a problem since Dr. Behr had fired the cleaning staff in 1978 when, in a story he still told with some regularity, he thought he smelled pot smoke when he stopped by the office while they were cleaning one evening. A large metal filing cabinet took up most of the front room, leaning dangerously, loaded with yellowed deed notes from the 80s.

    Edward and I occupied the tiny remaining space, our desks crammed against the scuffed walls, the surfaces and drawers overflowing with newer deeds and tenant contracts that would eventually find their way to join the yellowing masses in the metal filing tomb. The rare visitor would have to stand sideways between our desks if he wanted to fit. Dr. Behr's "office," directly behind Edward, was like something from a pack rat case study. Boxes of papers and manila folders were stacked to the ceiling, forming columns that I was always afraid would one day buckle and engulf Dr. Behr in a deadly avalanche of decades-old documents. A trail through the stacks led to his desk, which could not be seen due to the buildup of paper sediment. Dozens of stacks covered the surface, their outer layers spilling onto the floor. The tiles between the paper columns were covered in a dust surface broken up by the footprints left by Dr. Behr's slipper-clad feet. Stacks of *New Yorkers*, some from the days before color pictures, melted into one another against the far wall below a poster of Hemingway, caked with grime and threatening to break free of the thumb tacks that held it in place. A chipped Columbia mug lay sideways between two evil-looking African masks on an antique half-table. Anything you touched in the office would cause an explosion of dust. Whenever a ray of light came through the lone window it would illuminate a dust haze, thousands of particles that hung over the office like an ancient mist.

Within the dust cloud, for hours each day, Dr. Behr would read and re-read the only yellowing document in the office that meant much of anything, the will signed by his father in 1968 that left the former literature professor 10 rundown buildings on the now-chic Lower East Side before dying relatively young from liver complications. As someone who could dissect Faulkner more easily than ingest the specifics of a basic expense report, Dr. Behr was understandably wobbly when plunged into the alien world of high finance. He would read over that will each day, even inspecting the blank backs of the papers, eyebrows wrinkled and nose hairs prickling, as if he still didn't believe it after over 35 years, as if it was all inevitably going to disappear, as if suddenly after all these decades, he was finally going to find the catch.

For a man sitting on some of the most potentially lucrative property in Lower Manhattan, you would never know it by looking at Dr. Behr. His main stylistic reference point seemed to be the homeless men that hung around the Bowery, not the schizophrenic crackhead variety but instead the semi-sophisticated-burnt-out-old-hippie philosophers, with their ancient stained khakis, moth-eaten button downs, and wild head of Einstein-grey hair jutting out in all directions as if pulsed by electric current. Crooked Carlos the Jackal glasses shielded his eyes, giving them a kaleidoscopic effect. Coarse grey hairs protruded from his upper cheeks and chin in a manner that Edward pointed out as resembling Michael J. Fox's mutation in *Teen Wolf*. Dr. Behr rode public transportation. He wore an old North Face backpack always jammed with papers and

Travels and Travails of Small Minds by Daniel Falatko

battered hardcovers. Edward claimed that he still lived in the rent-controlled studio off the Columbia campus that he rented back when he was employed there in the mid-60s. He had never been married, though he did boast a surprising amount of friends, mostly retired Lit professors who would call the office constantly, me saying "Hello, Dr. Behr's office" and them replying, "Oh, hi Edward," before I buzzed them through without correcting them. Some days Dr. Behr would tell me not to let any calls through other than the Oxford Man, whose voice I came to recognize as a low bubbling rumble, unfailingly polite and genteel yet nonetheless creepy, inquiring as to whether Dr. Behr was in the office. He called at least seven times a week and they would speak for hours, the red light which indicated Dr. Behr's busy line blinking furiously. On the rare occasion that Dr. Behr would be out of the office when the Oxford Man phoned, upon being informed of the bad news, he would say, "Dear boy, do tell him I called" in a voice that sounded like he had gargled with Southern Comfort and sand that morning, low and just barely audible over the international connection. Dr. Behr preferred a custom brand of coffee called "Moonlight Mile" that they only sold at Solid Ground in Midtown, and I would be sent to retrieve it. By the time I got back to the office it would be cold, and Dr. Behr would voice his disappointment by smacking his lips together in a sour manner and pointing at the cup as the source of his agony. The office did not have a coffee machine or a microwave.

    Real money people, those who were accountants or real-estate developers or brokers, all seemed to systematically hate Dr. Behr. He didn't speak their language. He didn't follow their ways. But what really infuriated them was that this was clearly not an affected stance or a calculated strategy. He was genuinely aloof in a way they had never previously encountered. They treated him as if his brain had halted development at five years of age, completely baffled that this freak held any cards whatsoever. He was so utterly alien to their way of operating that they couldn't even rob from him. Dr. Behr's complete and utter lack of business training or skill with money matters inadvertently rendered his empire air-tight. There was a simple low-interest savings account and an attached free checking account like any family in America would have with their local bank. There were minimal investments and no high-risk stock portfolios. His buildings were crammed with rent-controlled apartments in which his mostly Chinese tenants had been living for decades. Unlike myself, who had only slightly more business/real estate knowledge than Dr. Behr, Edward had done a year as a Business Major before switching to Experimental Psych at UNY New Paltz and would tell me, in a hushed awe, that Dr. Behr's eccentric exterior masked a meticulously barbed business sense almost in spite of itself.

 Edward, who actually knew what he was doing and had been jammed in the office with Dr. Behr long enough to be common law, held the most dignified position of our two-man staff, that of glorified secretary and confidant. Edward was trusted with filing and keeping track of the all-important tenant contracts, reviewing bank statements and arranging for the sneak-apartment inspections that Dr. Behr was fond of.

 As a lowly long term temp, I was only trusted with the Midtown coffee runs, answering the phone when one of his aging academic cronies would ring, compiling office supply needs lists which would ultimately be ignored, or journeying to the Upper West Side duplex where his truly ancient mother, who was bed-bound but miraculously still breathing, would wheeze at me about how the 24-hour nurse was stealing her orthopedic socks, the veins in her neck blue and pulsing. I never quite grasped the reasons for being sent. These missions were never defined. I was given no items to take to her, nothing to check on or report back. The entire building was filled with old women, all of them living in apartments people in that neighborhood would kill for. One woman, hunched and shriveled with long red hair hanging to the middle of her waist, would wander the halls outside Dr. Behr's mother's apartment with the aid of a robotic mega-

Travels and Travails of Small Minds by Daniel Falatko

walker, moaning a long diatribe of which I could only make out one word: "Beatniks." I always assumed a man with a beret and goatee had stolen her purse in the late 50s. I would be ordered there once every several months, listen to Dr. Behr's mother's rasping about the orthopedic sock thefts in a voice similar to her son's, watching her neck veins pulse, reaching out to me with a swollen arm, me backing away in terror. Edward, who used to have to make the mother runs before I started as a temp, said she used to tell him that her son hadn't been by to visit her for over 10 years. Another time she had motioned for me to lean close, and in a conspiratorial whisper warned him, "His hands are like splinters."

After two-and-a-half years, I was more than ready to move on.

"**I WOULD HOPE** that it would be sometime soon, yes," I told her, cradling the phone limply against my collarbone and re-shuffling the same sheath of wrinkled mystery papers I had been shuffling for the past three hours, not even bothering to lower my voice to avoid the hairy eardrums of Dr. Behr. "Because if it isn't sometime soon, my dear, I'm going to retrieve the nail gun the maintenance guys left in the hallway and put one through my frontal lobes to end this misery."

"Well try to hit your target, drama queen," she yawned, a radio tuned in to a classic rock station in the background, a soulful voice belting, "The juices of love, the juices of love, lick from your fingers the juices of love!" over dueling guitars. "Because if you miss and put one through your nerve center, I must tell you I'm not willing to have a drooling paraplegic as a boyfriend. A lobotomized human zombie, yes. A twitching wheelchair-bound jelly man, no."

I wasn't paying attention to her because I thought I had heard the Grunt, dropping the receiver and listening hopefully for some movement from Dr. Behr's office, the oncoming patter of slipper-clad feet, the click of the lock on the tiny safe (key code 5543) where he kept the near-disintegrated, well-read will document, but alas there was nothing but dry dust silence emanating from Dr. Behr's cell. I realized that what I had mistaken for the day-ending Grunt was only Edward attempting to open or close one of the rusty drawers on his ancient metal desk. He was now slumped in his chair, staring a little too interestedly at the ceiling tiles, clearly wishing the Bic pen clenched in his teeth was a Parliament Light. Please, Dr. Behr, set your children free.

"I'm losing you, dear boy." Amy's voice came crashing back into focus. "Not sure if you're still there or not… perhaps you had an emergency coffee run to attend to, but if you can still hear me then please know that you better blow that joint and blow it quick, because I will be at your apartment at six and if you aren't there to let me in after I've traveled all those harrowing miles on the L, my dearest Nathan, then I will be PISSED."

Before I could say anything she had hung up with a click like an exclamation point, and I could envision her tossing the cell back into her purse with an effortless flick of her bone-thin wrist. I didn't bother to phone her back. Amy hanging up on me was a regular occurrence. When she was finished talking, she was finished talking. Period. A small desk plant lay dying before me, wilting in its cheap green plastic pot, starved for light and coated in the weird dark dust that shrouded the office and made the insides of your nose tingle, whirling in circular patterns from the small white fan that Edward kept fastened to the end of his desk. Decades worth of dust. Dust from the depths of the 70s. I wondered why I had purchased this plant, what strange whim had possessed me on that day to believe some type of life could possibly sustain itself within such a fossilized death vacuum.

Tentatively returning the phone to its cradle, I turned back to the yellowed papers that Dr. Behr had placed upon my desk nine weeks previous without a hint of instruction. He hadn't even looked at me, just placed the papers deliberately before me

Travels and Travails of Small Minds by Daniel Falatko

while shuffling by, his nostrils whistling loudly with each intake of air. I had stared at the papers for a long time, stunned, and was about to place them into a drawer, never to be touched again, when I noticed they had been elaborately fastened together with a tiny silver-colored clip. Organization was not a huge buzzword around the office, as could be attested by the pounds of mixed-up paper sediment that covered every available surface. The sediment had begun spilling onto the floors at a rate that would soon make movement impossible without treading over layers of ancient leases and maintenance invoices from 1981. But here were a sheath of papers that not only appeared to be in order, but were actually fastened together in a manner entirely unprecedented in the office's history. Add to this the fact that Dr. Behr had gone through the considerable trouble to sidestep the four gigantic crumbling boxes of papers that served as a divide between my area and Edward's, crossing the threshold to place an assignment upon my desk for the first time in all of the time I had worked for him. Adding all of those unusual factors together in my mind, there could only have been one conclusion: Those crumbling, time-stained papers, the mystery assignment that lay hidden within their wording, must have been pretty fucking important. The fact that the whole thing had been handed to me, merely a disinterested interloper, as opposed to trusted lackey Edward, was a source of great pride.

    I spent weeks pouring over those papers in between coffee runs, holding them up to the light, turning them upside down, tossing them in the air and letting them float down onto my desk, hoping to shake something loose from their crusty folds that would explain what they meant, what they were trying to tell me. I took to carrying the silver clip around in my pocket on the weekends, taking it out from time-to-time and holding it up to the sun, hoping the glint would spell out a secret message that would guide me toward cracking the assignment. The wording typed onto the papers seemed to be of little significance, just a minor confusion within a mirrored hall of mysteries. It looked

July 31st

to be a standard property deed for a building on Avenue B, near Tompkins Square Park, dated from 1972. The only interesting aspect of the entire document was the fact that the building had been purchased for a grand total of $75,000. Alphabet City in 1972 must have been a vastly different place from the NYU bars and ethnic restaurants that now choked its streets. I didn't know a single person who could afford to live there.

When shown the address, Amy shrugged and commented, "Isn't that where Jim Hendrix or one of those hippie losers choked on his own vomit or something similarly culturally groundbreaking?"

A thorough sweep through the files of Wikipedia failed to confirm this theory and I was back to where I had started, holding the papers under lights in attempts to uncover secret imprints or telltale stains. Edward refused to speak to me for three straight business days, chewing sullenly on the end of a ballpoint pen and avoiding my eyes. My lone co-worker's initial resentment eventually broke when he could no longer contain his curiosity. Soon he was hovering around my desk, grilling me extensively on the exact details behind Dr. Behr's handing over of the papers that day. Had he grunted or spoken? Had he made eye contact? Did he gesture at the papers with his veiny, deteriorating hands? Edward read and re-read the papers, finding it to be the simplest of deeds, just one of many thousands of similar documents scattered through every free space in the office, jammed into multiple drawers, towering menacingly in stacks over our heads as we spoke. Edward developed a theory that every third or fourth letter within the document synched up to spell out a hidden message. Having examined the papers for countless hours, breaking no such codes, I was fully incredulous of this theory.

"This is how gangs send messages to inmates," he told me. "I saw a documentary on A&E." He offered to lend his assistance, spending four obsessive days searching for patterns within the letters, secret codes, backwards spellings, hidden watermarks,

Travels and Travails of Small Minds by Daniel Falatko

finally giving up but still in firm belief that the answer lay encoded within.

The thought crossed both of our minds that perhaps Dr. Behr had meant nothing by his actions. Perhaps this was not an assignment at all and was instead the initial onslaught of full-on dementia.

This theory had been proven wrong two days previous when I was awoken from a mid-morning trance by a shadow falling across my desk, fearfully looking up to find Dr. Behr hovering over me, eyes uncharacteristically clear behind the tinted lenses, arms folded before him like the ghost of an ancient sentry. Our eyes met. He nodded toward the papers, which I had arranged into an inverted pentagram covering the desk's surface in hopes that the devil could assist me in deciphering what was supposed to be done, and let loose a demanding, angry-sounding grunt from somewhere deep within his dust-choked lungs. Before I could react he had pulled an about-face and was shuffling in his slippers toward the dark safety of his office. Edward had halted whatever he was doing and was looking at me, mouth open and face going pale. I considered marching into Dr. Behr's office and demanding to know the exact nature of the assignment, what the papers signified, why this dump on Avenue B was of any more importance than any of his other dilapidated tenements in high rent areas. "Go ahead," Edward had laughed. "Cross the threshold if you dare." Entering Dr. Behr's office, the dust in the air grew thicker, stinging my eyeballs as I tried to adjust them to the murk, easily twice as dark as the outer office area. The Hemingway poster loomed on the cinderblock wall overhead, his confident, glimmering eyes seeming to warn me away. Dr. Behr was slumped at his desk, itself just a mountain of papers, the dust forming a sort of halo around the matted grey tufts of his head. He was asleep, the sacred will papers clutched in his hands. His snores were more like giggles, breaking into full-scale laughter as I drew near. He began to murmur, softly at first, building into a full-blown repeated chant. "They were brazen. They were dead. They were brazen. They were dead." From behind his wall of sleep, he broke into full-scale laughter. Shuddering, I turned around and walked out.

The office was silent save for the clicking of Edward's pen as he tapped it against his teeth, a habit that had long ago lost its ability to annoy me. He was reclining in his chair, designer-sneaker-clad feet thrown over the desk, staring off into the murky gloom that always hung over our quarters in the late afternoons. I had my head in my hands, lightly massaging my temples with the tips of my thumbs, watching the dust shift and settle over my work area. The papers had been tossed aside, still a mystery, taunting me from the end of the desk. I looked over at Edward and nodded my head in the direction of Dr. Behr's office, tapped a finger against the part of my wrist where a watch would have been had I owned one.

"Perhaps he finally died back there?" Edward said to me, a tinge of hope detectable in his voice. Swinging his feet around, his knee joints cracking audibly as he rose. "No grunt yet? This is ridiculous. I'm going in." He stretched his arms, preparing himself. "If I'm not back in five minutes, well...run." Slow and tentative, as if walking upon a tightrope, Edward approached the darkness of Dr. Behr's office. He paused for a moment when he reached the doorway where a shadow fell from the layer beyond, where dark met dark, as divisive a border as there has ever been. He glanced back at me worriedly. I motioned for him to go on. I desperately wanted out, watching as Edward slowly, cautiously, took a step into the shadow threshold. My heart had been awakened, kick-starting from its usual dull murmur to a serious level of blood-pumping ferocity, breath coming in phlegm-clogged rasps, in full admiration of Edward's bravery. I had forgotten what it felt like to be inspired. He was almost completely engulfed in the darkness now, vanishing into the inner-dust rings that shielded Dr. Behr from harm. One last time he turned to glance in my direction. The next step would engulf him completely. Our eyes met.

Travels and Travails of Small Minds by Daniel Falatko

No matter how long you waited for the Grunt, the signal from the deck of SS *Behr* announcing his soldiers were free to run amok onshore, no matter how badly you yearned for it, it always seemed to catch you off guard when it actually happened. That afternoon was no exception. Edward had made it no further than the doorway when, from the depths of the office beyond, a low, guttural rumble could be heard, quickly roaring into a full throttle Grunt straight from the decrepit, dusty lungs of Dr. Behr. Startled, Edward backed into a trash can overflowing with discarded invoices and went sprawling onto the floor. Dr. Behr appeared in the doorway, windbreaker zipped up to his chin in preparation for the 92-degree summer day outside, giving Edward a quizzical look as he scrambled to get up off the floor amongst the avalanching invoices. The slightest hint of a smile crossed Behr's colorless lips.

"**THE OLD FUCK** was laughing at me." Edward was still flustered as we dodged roving packs of Chinese teenagers in public school uniforms on Grand St. "He's been laughing at me for fifteen years. If only just once he would let out a real laugh, out loud and in my face, then at least I could prove it. But no, the spacey old kook laughs at me with his eyes. So infuriating!"

The smell of rotten fish, decaying in the late afternoon sun on the maze of seafood carts lining the streets, was nearly overwhelming but it still couldn't stop Edward's rant. This was a tangent I had heard many times before. "We live within a large metropolis," I would tell him. "There are literally hundreds upon hundreds of other jobs." But on that day I just didn't possess the energy to utter even the vaguest reassurances. We parted ways at the subway station, Edward heading in the direction of the F Train uptown. I said goodbye to him, moving toward the JMZ, told him to not take it personal. "Oh, honey, I'm over it already,"

July 31st

he assured me, pausing in front of a Chinese man playing a flute for change and suddenly breaking into a wild dance. "The tunnels are alive with the sounds of music!"

Someone had etched the words *FALSETTO FASHION* into the train's dirty window in thick block lettering with extra emphasis on the *H*. The train struggled through the tunnel, creaking and groaning with the effort. I kept my face close to the window, attempting to read the graffiti on the tunnel walls as the dim lights shone through the scratched glass windows, throwing moving shadows at my feet.

Descending the green stairs to the street, stinging dots of sweat had formed on my eyelids due to the cruelly un-air conditioned environment of the train. I had to duck under a green vintage bicycle, complete with rainbow streamers and handlebar basket, being hoisted up the steps by one of those breed of artists one only sees within the Bushwick section of Brooklyn, the kind whose homeless-chic beards, Wooly Mammoth hair and literature-inspired tattoos conjured an image of the art-damaged urban mountain man. He winked at me conspiratorially as he passed.

Though small even by NYC standards, really little more than a tiny room and two microscopic closets, one to hold clothing and the other to barely house a bed, the apartment was far from a rat-hole. Cool-looking lacquered hardwood squares crossed the floor in a vaguely abstract pattern, filling the space with a magisterial glow that was particularly prevalent on sunny early mornings. An antique ceiling fan whirred lazily over a vibey, earth-tone collection of second-hand furniture collected from the dozens of sidewalk and stoop sales that lined the Brooklyn streets on spring and summer weekend days. A kitschy set of cat-face coasters rested atop a glass coffee table straight from the early 70s. A stack of records found their home in the corner next to a complete hi-fi set a junkie was hawking for 40 dollars on the Spanish side of Graham Avenue. A Rolling Stones tongue and lips logo magnet leered from the fridge within the tiniest of

Travels and Travails of Small Minds by Daniel Falatko

kitchenettes. There was a dented bronze coffee pot and a house plant on the counter named Ronnie. The lighting was dim in an intimate way that was cozy and never depressing. The ceilings were high. The faucets never leaked. The rent was 1100 plus electric.

"So I had this dream last night." Amy entered the scene in a whirl of tasteful perfume fumes and a vaguely 80s-inspired dress, a peck on the cheek leaving behind chapstick traces, her forehead glinting angelic with a light sheen of sweat. "Or more of a vision, really, where due to some type of star alignment or strange winds or Devil's calling, all the world's children suddenly had the urge to walk into the sea. Like, en mass. Parents had to lock their children up inside to keep them from joining the Migration. Hundreds of kids. Thousands. Older ones carrying younger ones. All of them heading to the sea."

Reclining in a rather comfortable Ikea chair designed to look like an uncomfortable postmodern piece from the 70s, I held out my hands in exasperation. "And…this was some sort of mass baptism? A return to Atlantis?"

She was now leaning down to take off her left boot. "Oh, no, it was mass suicide. The call of oblivion. Fuck procreation!" She looked up from her foot, pointing at him in an accusing manner. "And how do I have vomit on my new boots already? I tell you that L Train is filth incarnate. And look." She held up her boot for inspection. Something long and grotesquely shiny was hanging from the end of it. "Sick fuck had noodles for lunch. It's disgusting. This whole human race, Nathan. I need to get out for a bit. I'm feeling like Céline today, and that's never a good thing."

LESS THAN 20 MINUTES LATER I watched as a graphically outdated star shooter mowed down row-after-row of particularly evil-looking alien hamburgers. A slow weeknight at the Barcade,

July 31st

the empty warehouse acoustics working to amplify the various blips and bleeps of the old school arcade games lining the walls, light chatter from the bar area, the bartender a college-age girl with duel salt shakers tattooed on her wrists. Amy expressed her displeasure at one of the alien hamburgers that had just taken over her star shooter device, "Fucking motherfucker!" She took a sip of her glowing yellow German beer and a deep breath, went back to playing. I had never enjoyed video games, didn't understand their appeal, and thus was not a huge fan of the Barcade or their ridiculously expensive beer selection. The constant blipping and beeping made me paranoid, like being stuck inside 1988 with huge black bouncers guarding the door. Amy loved it, her eyes growing wide at the mention of the place, always dragging me there every time she was in the borough. She would play games that required aiming huge plastic guns at the screen or beating on buttons that said "Roundhouse Punch!" Video boxers with pixilated faces taunted her mercilessly from inside the machines. She really loved the game *Asteroids*. She said it reminded her of her brother, the one who whacked his head on the side of a swimming pool trying to jump off a roof at his friend's house at 13 and was never the same again. Amy's eyes would fill with tears as she played it.

"Yea, I see her too." Amy nudged me during a pause in her game. "She must really be into salt, huh? Very cute. But do you have to stare? That's never attractive, Nathan." Before I could say anything or even clear my throat she was back at the game, mowing down several rows of alien hamburgers with a gleeful vengeance that was frightening to me.

Out on the street the day's hot haze had lingered into the night, a sizzling mist muffling the streetlights along Grand St., the deluded light giving the sidewalks a wet, alien feel. People's faces passing by were covered in light sheens of sweat. Heavy, wet air descended from above like a jungle haze. Amy was a little drunk, making a show of holding my hand, breaking pace to walk ahead, yanking me forward and speaking excitedly about how if you look real close into the audience during the Madison Square Garden scene in *Gimme Shelter*, you can make out Johnny Thunders and Charles Manson standing right next to one another in the first several rows. She said it looked as if they were holding hands. "I wonder if Charlie would be the 'top' in that relationship," she wondered. "He does always like to be in control."

A 20-something girl in a white dress and matching white headband, her feet bare on the filthy sidewalk and pupils like black dimes, materialized from the heat haze and stopped as we came upon her.

"There is a loft on this street where the walls are wet with tears," she said to us, smiling, then twirled off into the mist.

"A loft on this street would go for 5500 a month," Amy muttered.

"WERE YOU FLIRTING WITH HER?"

Amy had banished me once again to the uncomfortable side of the futon, the side that was so caved-in and lopsided I would sometimes slide off in the middle of the night and become hopelessly tangled in the sheets, waking up panicked in the dark, trapped in a blanket cocoon. The bedside lamp cast a dome-shaped glow over the bed in the otherwise dark room. Amy was paging through a *Time Out New York* magazine that I didn't remember purchasing, white block letters on the front page proclaiming CANARSIE AHOY! EVERYTHING YOU EVER NEEDED TO KNOW ABOUT THE LAST STOP ON THE L TRAIN.

"Flirting with who?"

I was staring at the point where darkness obscured the ceiling, past the illuminated lamp range where it all became murky and unclear. Who was she talking about? That Topanga Canyon-chic hippie girl with the form-fitting yoga pants I did the double

July 31st

take on in the park on Saturday? How could she have seen that? She was browsing around the corner in a store that sold nothing but totally hip toasters. Was she telepathic? Did her roving eye coast on sine waves? Startled momentarily by a shadow on the wall, my body twitched audibly enough to startle Amy, causing her to tear the page as she turned it.

"I mean, she was pretty, Nathan. Don't think I didn't notice it too." She gave me a nudge in the ribs, playful but with force behind it.

"My dearest Amy, may I inquire as to what the fuck you're talking about?"

Ominously, the magazine had dropped to her side. She was now looking at me full-on, her wide eyes devoting unnerving attention on the side of my face.

"The fact that you don't know who I'm speaking about denotes that you most likely flirt with lots of girls over the course of your days," she declared. I couldn't tell if she was playing around or not since her voice remained neutral. "You locked eyes with her for a full ten seconds. You guys were totally in tune with one another, had a little mind fuck. I was walking right next to you. I mean, that was what? Fifteen minutes ago? And already you've forgotten. Love em' and leave em', huh Natey boy?"

My hands had involuntarily clamped themselves to my temples. "Wait, you mean the wall of tears girl? Have your synapses gone haywire? Of course I was looking at her! The girl was rolling so hard her head was practically on backwards, making a complete spectacle of herself in the street!"

Amy was toying with the buttons on the alarm clock, the slump in her shoulders indicating she had already lost interest in a fight that she herself had started, feeling no need to finish off her own battle. Case closed. She yawned.

"I have to set this thing for 6, dear. Forgot to bring my work clothes, and it's a long way out to Harlem."

She shoved the clock at me accusingly, pointing to the red glowing number 6.

Travels and Travails of Small Minds by Daniel Falatko

"Long distance relationships are tough. All this borough-to-borough movement takes its toll." She pouted, put her head on my shoulder, hair ticking my chin. "Especially when your BF gets lured away by girls on the street with knowledge of secret lofts and rivers of tears."

Taking note of my continued bewilderment, she kissed me on the cheek.

"Just playing, my dear. It's cool," she said hesitantly. "I mean, her feet were so dirty it looked like she was wearing shoes, but I guess that Squeaky Fromme look never does go out of style."

She tossed the *Time Out* aside, mentioned that I should renew my subscription. I was in the middle of explaining to her that I never had a subscription and never purchased or stole or borrowed the particular issue she had been reading, that I didn't really even enjoy the magazine at all. She switched off the red lamp, effectively ending my tirade. The room went black.

"I'll get up with you." I kissed her on the collarbone. "I should get in early to figure out this magical mystery assignment before Mr. Borderline Dementia throws a tantrum."

She wriggled away. Amy had ticklish shoulders.

"Mystery assignment? How so very intriguing. You're like the Jason Bourne of personal assistants. Will it be taking you to the far ends of the earth on the wings of rapidly evolving dual-plot sequences?"

I snaked an arm around her torso.

"All I know is that it involves an old apartment on Avenue B that somehow managed to cut through the clutter of Dr. B's mental dustbin to end up on my plate."

She writhed her way out of my loose grasp, complained that the room was hot, that my arm was hot, that everything was hot.

"Why didn't he give it to Edward? Is a torch being passed? When are you going to quit that rat-hole anyway? Just call the temp agency. They basically just dropped you off and left you stranded for what, two years now? They need to bring you back in, Nathan. You've been left behind. Just quit. There are plenty of other jobs out there that aren't so blatantly dead-end."

"Soon, dear. Very soon."

We lay for a while on our backs in the dark. She placed a hand on my torso.

"If you leave your hand there, things may come to life," I told her.

"Hmmm," she teased. "I just wouldn't want your mind to wander, wouldn't want you to start fantasizing about someone else…"

"Look, that Mollied-out out chick was not attractive so please don't…"

"Someone like… oh, I don't know… that kale smoothie bitch I saw you scoping on in the park?" She cut me off.

A short, sharp intake of breath. A sinking of the stomach. Eyes bugging out. Before I could begin stammering, backpedaling, lying, Amy silenced me, placing a tiny hand over my mouth, her other hand running through the hairs of my chest.

"This is for me, not for you."

She rolled on top of me in the dark.

The Oxford Man - Dr. Sneil
"It's like they dug up a corpse and dressed it in Gucci."

AUGUST 1st

BABY IN ONE HAND, cigarette in the other, a small grizzled Chinese man stood on the curb outside the Delancey St. stop, nestled in between a hurriedly parked Saab with a smashed rear-windshield and a black Range Rover with a So, So Fly sticker on the back bumper. The stench of rotting fish in the early morning sun was overwhelming, no longer just a tingling in the nostrils, a mere sensory issue escalated to a physical entity. You could see the dead fish smell in the heat haze, watch it part as you walked through it, feel its particles on your fingers as you wiped the sweat from your forehead. The baby was wailing uncontrollably, shrieking and kicking its feet, waving stubby little arms, its face almost as red as the man's holding him. Switching his cigarette to his mouth, the man held the baby out in front of him. It began urinating, a steady golden arch splashing on the pavement. I turned around just in time to sidestep the torrent, though two small drops got the cuff of my wrinkled dress pants. Shaking my leg disgustedly, I crossed Orchard onto Broome, heading in the general direction of Dr. Behr's office.

The nine o'clock sun barely penetrated our bunker, a weak glow from the lone slit in Dr. Behr's chambers illuminating the dust particles, throwing a thin spotlight over a tangle of blown-

Travels and Travails of Small Minds by Daniel Falatko

out manila folders scattered in a vaguely ritualistic pattern on the floor in the corner. Edward didn't greet me as I entered. He had already assumed position, black designers thrown up onto the metal desk, leaning back in the chair at a precarious angle while flipping disinterestedly through a *Details* magazine.

"Who really gives a shit that fucking Michelle Williams doesn't enjoy carrots?" He yawned. "I mean, if you were to tell me she had a dick shaped like a carrot and that Jake Gyllenhaal sucked it clean on a nightly basis, then perhaps I would be just a tad more interested in this story." He tossed the mag over his shoulder. I didn't hear it hit the floor since the ground behind Edward's desk was covered by a mound of paper sediment so large it threatened to engulf him. The magazine was absorbed, like everything else, into the office vortex.

"Where's the crypt keeper?" I planted myself at my own desk just feet from Edward. "Please tell me his dementia has reached the stage where he forgets where he works."

Staring at the ceiling, cradling a large cup of Au Bon iced coffee, Edward appeared tired, the edges of his eyes rimmed with red, grey hairs visible in his temples, freeing themselves at least temporarily from Just For Men tyranny. His face was not as hard and crisp as usual, skin tone dull and noticeably sagging under the cheeks.

"You look like you got run over by a Molly truck, my friend." I tossed a pen at him. "Rough night for Mr. Ed?"

The pen bounced off his chest, nearly causing him to topple back into the paper mountain. He flailed his arms once, twice, barely managed to regain his balance.

"More like a Percocet and red wine truck," he said solemnly, his nostrils flaring. "You just wait, young buck. You may be able to drink gallons now and wake up bright-eyed and bushy-tailed, but when you get older you have to start paying your dues."

I mimicked his hand movements dismissively.

"Anyway, I have no clue where the old man could be, running a little late I guess. Trouble Velcro-ing the shoes, perhaps? This better not mean The Grunt comes late today. I absolutely refuse to miss my 6:30 facial. I mean, look at me, Nathan! I look like Pete Doherty on a Sunday morning!"

I told him I'd rather not look at his hung-over, craggy face, swiveled into work position with a major creak of the ancient chair, the papers for my special assignment in the same position I had left them the day before. Already a thin dust layer settled on top of the blue folder.

"You better get to work on that," Edward pouted, still jealous. "Perhaps this little workplace power shift can be cited as the cause for my recent pill rampage. Perhaps I'm feeling inadequate?"

I looked up from the folder, hopeful.

"You want it? If so, you can have it. As a matter of fact, take it. Fuck it, here." I shoved the folder toward him. "I don't give a shit. I'll tell him that. I'll say 'Entrust this valuable assignment to the steady hands of Mr. Ed. Let me go back to answering phones. All this mystery is making me sick."

Edward smiled, weary eyes full of old-timer, Yoda-esque knowledge.

"Take the baton and run with it, kid. I'm tired. Oh so very tired. This battalion needs fresh blood, young soldiers. Lift that rifle and charge the brigade. Leave the old on the hill to die."

AFTER 48 MINUTES the blue folder began to expand in my vision, tinting the desk, the walls, the dust, the paper mountains, the filing cabinets, the crusted ceiling tiles all a radiant aqua. It was only by clamping my eyes shut, covering them with my hands and counting to seventeen, sighing deeply and forcing myself to open the folder, that I managed to break out of the blue zone.

The morning melted into dull confusion. It was hot in the office. Edward fell asleep and began snoring. The papers

Travels and Travails of Small Minds by Daniel Falatko

still made no sense, still the same routine deed agreement, though in an entirely unexpected rush of inspiration I dialed information and asked for the phone numbers of the residents of the building. The first operator hung up on me. The second, a man I immediately identified as a non-officious slacker with a distinctively laid back cadence to his speech, offered up not one but all of the resident's land lines, nine in all, with no hesitation. Four of the numbers had been disconnected. Three had no answer and no answering machines. One was picked up by a Spanish woman who screeched at me for a full minute, what sounded like an entire herd of children shrieking along with her in the background, before slamming the phone down. The last number was answered by the chipper voice of a young-sounding girl, a definite 20-something, but I couldn't figure out what to say. I had no plan going into the call, silence on the line and the sweeping chorus of a Teenage Fanclub song in her background, a song which I had loved in 7th grade but had long since forgotten. She hung up after declaring, "Jonathan, please know that I sold all your vinyl. I just couldn't stand to look at it anymore. Goodbye." I added the sloppily-scrawled numbers to the assignment file, a star next to the girl's, made a note to look up this building on Amy's laptop later that evening.

Approaching noon and still no Dr. Behr. Edward had awoken from his nap, departed to fetch more Au Bon. The phone on his desk kept ringing. Then the phone on my desk lit up. The Oxford Man. I could tell even before the craggy voice hit my ears, a familiar sense of stale disconnect in the silence. My shoulders tensed up, as they did each time the man called, even though he was never anything short of polite and gracious. There was just something creepy in that voice, something jagged and shredded that always bled through.

"Dearest Edward," my ear was treated to a brittle, phlegm-induced gurgle. "I would suspect that Dr. Behr is not presently in the office, though if I am correct on this, dear boy, I do hope that you could relay the most important of messages."

August 1st

Pulling off the cap of the pen I had been chewing on, I tore a piece of lined paper from the unused tablet on my desk. "I'd be happy to relay a message for you when Dr. Behr arrives... um... Oxford Man?"

The voice cackled, "Please do call me Dr. Sneil."

"Dr. Sneil" I immediately scrawled on the paper, suddenly at full attention, then drew an equals sign leading to "Oxford Man?????!!!" To my knowledge, the Oxford Man's name had never been previously revealed. Dr. Behr had always, since the day I started, referred to him as either "the Oxford Man" or "my man at Oxford" even though Edward claimed he had retired and lived nowhere near the town. There was never any folder or file associated with this caller. Even Edward didn't know a thing of the man's identity. "Behr refers to people in his life as 'man' or 'woman' preceded by their profession. You know, like, the dude from Con Ed becomes Electric Man or the lady who does the taxes is dubbed Tax Woman. But this Oxford Man... he runs deep. A regular of Behr's social orbit. He's never told me a thing about it."

"Sure thing, Dr. Sneil." I felt clever, sharp as a fresh razor, on the verge of cracking any one of the dozens of mysteries that bound my existence. I let the Oxford Man know that I would be happy to relay any and all messages he had for my esteemed boss.

"Delightful, dear boy. Dee-lightful." Shredded vocal chords struggled to connect in the Oxford Man's throat. "Please do pass this baton of information." He cleared his throat, like sandpaper on skin. "Please tell Dr. Behr that *the trail of worms is open and the slasher boys are free*. Please tell him this the moment he steps in and no later. Apologies if I may sound urgent, but it is absolutely essential that he knows this."

I was silent, in the midst of jotting down the message.

"The trail of worms is open and the slasher boys are free." He repeated.

Travels and Travails of Small Minds by Daniel Falatko

Edward had limped back into the office, his forehead brimming with sweat and an iced latte clutched in his hand. I held up the notebook page to him, pointing to where it said "Oxford Man = Dr. Sneil???!!!" He placed a hand on his mouth, muffled an "oh shit," patted me on the head like a good dog and whipped out his iPhone, presumably to Google a certain Dr. Sneil, former Oxford University professor.

"Ok, got it." Edward was dancing from foot-to-foot, holding out the phone, having apparently made a discovery, motioning for me to end the call. "I will relay the baton the second Dr. B. arrives."

He thanked me, sounding truly appreciative, then crackly silence.

"Oh, Oxford man," my voice squeaked, deciding to test my luck in hopes of killing off another mystery. "I mean, um, Dr. Sneil…" At the mention of the name Edward broke into wild laughter and I ducked under my desk so the Oxford Man wouldn't hear it. "I was wondering if the following address meant anything at all to you. I told him the address on Avenue B. He didn't say anything. I repeated it again. "Think about it," I urged him.

Closing my eyes, I gripped the phone, crossed my fingers, waiting for a response. It was hot under the desk and my temples started to sweat. Edward was still laughing. I waited and waited, wondering if I had crossed some sort of line, listening for the man's raspy engine of a voice to rev up. Silence. The same crackling, eventually drifting into a dial tone. He had hung up already, probably before I had posed the question.

"What are you doing down there, dear boy?" Edward was taunting me with a pitch-perfect Oxford Man impersonation. "Come over here and check out Dr. Sneil!"

Coming out from underneath the desk, panting, I found Edward doubled over with laughter, clutching his side as if he had been stabbed, thrusting the screen into my face.

"He looks exactly like I imagined him!"

I was confronted with a Google Image head shot, probably an old Oxford U. staff photo, a face so craggy it seemed made of indented clay, lines crisscrossing then temporarily separating before twisting to intersect again at even odder angles, a schizophrenic game of tic-tac-toe. Unlike his partner in crime and fellow eccentric old man Dr. Behr, who had a full head of electroshock greys, the Oxford Man's hair was disappearing in heavy clumps, multiple spots of his scalp plainly visible, with sweaty-looking tufts erupting in an oddly synchronized style, the hair so fine and white it was nearly invisible. Black-framed and with seemingly frosted lenses, his glasses were a massive apparatus taking up most of his face, so thick they cast a bizarre house-of-mirrors effect which completely distorted the eyes and rendered the man's prim, chapped-lip smile all the more orchestrated and off-putting. A veiny neck so thin it looked like it would snap in a light breeze, tendons clearly visible and straining with the smile, tapered off into a crisp white shirt and proper tie, a blazer of the type you would not expect the Oxford Man to be wearing, black and sleek, not a hint of tweed in sight.

"Dude, I would totally wear that jacket." Edward had recovered somewhat from his laughing fit, though his voice was shaky and there were tears in the corners of his eyes. "It's like they dug up a corpse and dressed it in Gucci."

I looked harder at the image, sweating profusely now, attempting to make out the man's veiled eyes.

"I can see how those two get along. They most-likely have a lot to talk about, like how much ear hair is too much or how to make a brain continue to function long after the body has died."

CROSSING THE BOWERY, Edward finished his latte' with a long, gurgling slurp and tossed the cup in the general direction of a trash can but missed it by several feet, ice scattering over the sidewalk and disturbing the sleep of a gutter punk couple resting in one another's arms in the shade of a Baptist church. "Fucking

Travels and Travails of Small Minds by Daniel Falatko

faggot-ass-faggot!" the boy screamed, to which Edward replied, "Yup!" We were on a mission in the lunchtime hour, the day now so hot that fighting the sweat dripping into my eyes had become a battle not worth continuing. Edward had agreed to accompany me on this mission only if I would pay for half his lunch, even after I reminded him that he probably made a good ten grand more than me per year. We were on our way to check out the mystery building, an 11-block hike that felt like an essential journey. I needed to get a feel for the place, to allow the mystery to sink into my eyeballs, to face it down in person and breathe in its essence. Perhaps it would talk to me, like the body of a murdered prostitute talks to a seasoned detective, letting me know just from its position what took place and which deranged passions had sparked the slashing.

"Probably just another fucking dump with rats in the basement," Edward assumed, though what we found upon reaching it, our legs stuck to our slacks with sweat, was a charming five story brick affair where the tenants had placed plants upon the fire escapes and many of the windows were covered with what appeared to be decent sets of curtains and blinds. Granted, the building was far left of the stainless steel industrial shininess and ceiling-to-floor windows of the legions of brand new condo monstrosities that are taking over the city, but it was far above the usual Dr. Behr-owned rusty tenement eyesores. Edward whistled at the building the way a construction worker would whistle at a blond on the street. "This may very well be the most glorious piece of property the old bastard owns."

Circling the block, we found it impossible to view the rear end of the building from Avenue C, a locked community garden with many trees and a sculpture of Rihanna blocking our way. "The jealousy has worn off," Edward laughed, lighting a smoke. "I'm glad the old loon gave you this lame-ass assignment. You're on your own, kid. I've got nothing." A girl in crisp, short-sleeve plaid, her hair long and parted down the middle, glided past us in the direction of the building carrying a Key Food shopping bag.

August 1st

She was seemingly immune from the insane heat, not a drop of sweat upon her unwrinkled forehead. She paused at the door, fumbled through her purse for her keys.

"That has to be her," I told Edward. "That has to be the one who sold off Jonathan's vinyl collection."

Edward squinted in the girl's direction, his eyebrows slick with drops of sweat. He blew smoke out the side of his mouth while shaking his head.

"Is Dr. Behr aware that he has given this assignment to a crazy person?" He placed a hand on my shoulder. "Stalking the residents of this building is not the answer, my son. That chick's ex-boyfriend's record collection won't bring you any closer to unlocking this mystery. The mystery most likely lies…" He held his finger in front of my face then pointed to the building, urging my eyes to follow. "…in the building itself, its history, what has taken place in those apartments and hallways, what takes place there now. Perhaps one of those condo companies wants to snatch it up. Perhaps good old Dr. Behr murdered a rival professor many years ago and sealed the body in the walls. Perhaps his father is buried in the basement. Perhaps the bodies speak to the residents at night like that one Kevin Bacon movie where he takes his shirt off."

I was motioning for him to finish his point.

"Look, kid, you'll never figure this shit out. He's deranged. It's a wild goose chase. I'm famished. Let's get somewhere where the AC is fuckin' cranked." He grabbed my arm and yanked me away from the building that the girl with the middle-parted hair had finally disappeared into after spending an inordinate amount of time rummaging for her keys. "Any way you look at it, you're fucked."

The presence of hookahs eliminated the majority of the eateries on Avenues B and C from contention, and we ended up lounging in foldout chairs at a greasy table that wobbled in an establishment on Avenue D. They made us pay before the food was prepared and sneered at our orders even though we only

Travels and Travails of Small Minds by Daniel Falatko

asked for cheeseburgers and fries and cokes. But the AC felt glorious and, with Dr. Behr apparently AWOL for the day, we managed to settle down into a fairly relaxed lunch.

"I feel like we never hang out anymore. Like we've lost touch." Edward's leg was lurching up and down under the table, threatening to upset the ketchup and mustard dispensers. I kicked it to make it stop. "Ouch! You little fuck. You've really developed an attitude to go with all that newfound power."

I asked him to name a single previous instance where we had actually "hung out" in the entire time we had been working together.

"We've done lunch a couple of times, maybe, but not for at least a year. Other than that, all we do is exchange fairly complex hand signals across the office when Behr isn't looking."

Our food, on red cafeteria-style trays, was shoved before us.

"Well, here we are now," he sneered. "Just two more people clinging to reality by their rapidly-splintering fingernails."

WE COULD FEEL Dr. Behr's presence upon our return to the office. There were no real physical signs that he was there, no footprints in the dust, no windbreaker hung upon the hook, silence coming from his chambers. It was a general vibe, a sinking feeling that the party was over, a sense of decay which had not been there that morning. Yes, Dr. Behr was in the building. The laid back smile Edward had been sporting most of the day vanished the instant we came through the door. "He lives another day," he said, his voice full of awe.

We slid into our desks, trying to be as silent as possible, our eyes fixed on the entrance to Dr. Behr's office. "Go back and tell him," Edward hissed at me.

"Tell him what?"

August 1st

"The message, asshole. Sneil wanted you to relay that message."

The trail of worms is open and the slasher boys are free. I could recall it without having to consult the notes in front of me, reverberating through my head like an echo chamber, the Oxford Man's crushed-windpipe voice calling to me from the corners of my synapses. Noise now emanated from Behr's chambers, barely audible over the whirring of Edward's fan, the all-too familiar rustling of his favorite document, his own personal mystery assignment which had been jamming him up for decades. Edward had a point. Dr. Sneil had clearly stated it was absolutely essential to deliver this cryptic missive immediately upon my boss's return to the office. Though not the most noble of trades, the messenger boy will always be needed, will remain employed as long as messages need to be delivered between parties, long after those sending the messages have all been fired or killed. This was my duty.

"Why don't you do it?" I urged Edward.

He smirked at me. "You're the one who received the message, All-Star. That old dude whispered it directly into your ear. Take it and run with it. Quit being such a Barbie."

"Seriously," I rose from my desk, trying to conjure that sense of fearlessness, of complete recklessness, one feels when shooting out the streetlights of a small town with a high-powered BB rifle as a teen. "Fuck off."

Holding the notepad close, more of a prop than anything, I headed off into the dusty outer-rings of Dr. Behr's orbit. "See you later," Edward waved cheerfully, kicking back in his chair, whipping out his phone for a game of Tetris or 3D Pinball. "Sucker."

Edward was in full-scale jealous mode, though this didn't faze me in the least. I had a message to deliver, an exceedingly important message, and my mind was made up to relay it. My nerves had halted their jangling and the bottoms of my soles lifted themselves off the scuffed floor, striding into Dr. Behr's

Travels and Travails of Small Minds by Daniel Falatko

domain with a startling confidence and sense of purpose I wasn't used to.

"Dr. Behr, hi," I addressed the human coma. His head, protected by the grey layer of electric shock split ends, did not rise at my greeting. His eyes beat their constant path through the will document's stilted phrases. I could tell in the way his hunched frame tensed that he had heard me. I had as full attention as I would ever possibly have from him. "A colleague of yours, Dr. Sneil, phoned this morning and asked for me to let you know the following message…"

"My man at Oxford?" Dr. Behr's head had risen at the mention of the Oxford Man's real last name, a cruel puppeteer yanking harshly on a string from above. He fixed me with a watery, half-tranced gaze, his glasses slipping down his nose, leaving a sweat trail across the bridge. He had never looked me in the eyes before. "I was not expecting him to contact me today."

This sounded like a threat, an accusation, his voice channeled straight through his sinuses. He cleared his throat, stammered. The man was obviously struggling. He motioned toward me, exasperated. "Go on. Go on."

I read him the message. Silence. My handwriting upon the yellow note pad looked like that of a six-year-old boy, pinched and studied, no flow to the stiff lettering. Still the silence. I read it again, just for good measure, just because I didn't want to look down at him.

"Nathan," Dr. Behr uttered my name for what may have been the first time, a hint of joy gurgling through to the surface, an emotion so alien to the realm of Dr. Behr that it startled me into carefully studying his face. He was smiling. "Can you be a dear and repeat that one more time?"

I tore out the notebook page and handed it to him. Flinching, he took the paper, eyeing me warily all of a sudden. Dr. Behr did not like bold or unexpected moves. They threw off his whole equilibrium, like the time Edward had blown a New Year's whistle when we were forced to work on New Year's Day and he froze in his chair for so long that we thought he had had a stroke. Dr. Behr studied the words in the detailed fashion he generally reserved for the will documents, only minus the suspicion and trepidation. The smile broke out even further, like a rash across his face, morphing into a full scale mad scientist grin. "This is wonderful news. Just wonderful. Do you know what this means?"

Gazing into Dr. Behr's eyes in that moment, the watery pools magnified scarily by lenses thicker than they had ever made in the 80s, his impish smile made his face appear lopsided like a gunshot wound victim after surgery. I knew then that the world was a non-sequential kaleidoscope of bizarre happenings, that the nightmares we live in are not created through any faults of our own. We just stumble into them.

"I have no clue what that message means."

Still the smile. Still the bead of sweat on the upper lip. Still a spark to the eyes. This was Dr. Behr at his most satisfied.

"It means you have your work cut out for you," he coughed, spittle hitting me on the chin. "It means you may need to take a little, shall we say, business trip."

My hands began shaking, my eyes aching and straining in their sockets.

"If you were thinking of leaving us, and I happen to know that you were, you may want to stick around here for the immediate future." He spasmed into another coughing fit, this one more prolonged. I took a step back, threw up the hands to guard my face and eyes. "Certain opportunities," he gasped, struggling to overcome the onslaught of the coughs, "will present themselves shortly."

He folded the piece of paper over, noticed where I had written "Oxford Man = Dr. Sneil???!!!" He scowled and shook his head. "You two boys are like Tweedledum and Tweedledee, bless you."

Now he was insulting us? This wretched, dusty old man who happened to fall into millions? A man who prided himself on performing sneak apartment inspections on poor Chinese

Travels and Travails of Small Minds by Daniel Falatko

families? Now he was suddenly some sort of all-knowing savant? It was hard to fight the need to start pacing.

"No need to be red in the face." He waved me off, keeping the sheet of paper. "This news you have relayed today is confirmation of something spectacular, something brilliant, cultural, and literary." He looked me dead-on as I backed away toward the relative light of the outer office. "This news is confirmation that certain dimensions remain aligned."

IT WASN'T UNTIL nearly five hours later, over tall glasses of Stella at a bar called Motor Headz, that I finally revealed to Edward what went down in Dr. Behr's office. The day-ending Grunt had come earlier than usual, around 4:30, and we were already half drunk by 5:15. Our boss had spent most of the day on the phone with the door shut, blocking us out, the red light on my phone blinking to signal the line was tied. We both assumed it was the recently revealed Dr. Sneil occupying the line. Edward had attempted many tactics in getting the news from me, including pelting me repeatedly with erasers torn off the end of pencils, threatening me with wet willies, even stooping so low as to offer me his Metro Card which I knew had no rides left on it since he had been cursing about it earlier that morning.

"A business trip?" he spit a sip of the warm, expensive beer onto the bar. "A fucking business trip? For that business? For that office? In all of the years I've slaved my nice little ass off for that moron, I've never been sent further than that geriatric old woman's den of moth balls on 87th Street. And you get sent on a business trip? To where? They have a Solid Ground in Tucson?"

I was watching a face on the television above the bar, the straining neck and bulging eyes of a man with a fake orange tan and frosted blond hair, the backdrop of Hollywood behind him.

August 1st

The TV was on mute so I could not hear what the man was saying, but the words "Mischa Barton, Skulls, Leopards" kept flashing on a banner along the bottom of the screen. "Mischa Barton, Skulls, Leopards."

"What does that mean, Edward?" I pointed at the words. His head was slumped onto the bar, and it seemed to take him a fair amount of effort to look over at me, then at the screen.

"You're just like a little kid." He smiled, mimicking me. "What does that mean, Edward? I'll tell you exactly what that means if you tell me where you're going on your little errand boy business trip."

Sighing, I told him I had no idea, that Behr hadn't mentioned anything specific. "But he did say something about dimensions being aligned."

Edward's mouth was open in an exaggerated "O."

"Oh God, I knew it! He's slipped completely into senility twilight," he screeched, disturbing several rockabilly dudes with rolled jeans, deep into scotch and subdued conversation at the other end of the bar. "Will he forget to keep paying us?"

The banner was still flashing across the bottom of the screen, the man's orange face aglow in the dim studio lighting, flashes of teeth as he spoke silently. "'Mischa Barton, Skulls, Leopards.' What does that mean, Edward?"

Squinting at the screen, his eyes bloodshot and cheeks flushed, the all-too-familiar mischievous smile returned to his lips for the first time since that morning.

"It means the devil has a laundry list that goes on for miles."

NIGHTTIME ON 128th ST. The light from Amy's window was the only illumination on her side of the building, giving the little brick structure a Cyclops-like appearance as we walked away from it toward Clarence Wilson Ezekiel Davidson Sr. Boulevard. I told

Travels and Travails of Small Minds by Daniel Falatko

Amy that she should turn her lights off when leaving the building, if only to save on the electricity bill, and she sounded sad when she said, "There is nothing more depressing than coming home to a dark apartment." The day's heat had not vanished along with the sun. My socks felt soggy and when I placed my hand on Amy's shoulder to guide her around a woman defecating next to a trash can, it came back soaked with sweat. A shirtless man leaning out of a 2nd story window shouted "Beeeeeerthaaaaaaaa!" into the night. Over and over, "Beeeeeeerthaaaaa!" until someone from another window yelled, "Get a phone, motherfucker!"

We were on our way to get ice cream. Amy's place was too hot to sleep in, even after an ice-cold shower. Just the thought of sex or any type of cuddling was enough to make thin rivulets of perspiration ooze from the temples. We recoiled from each other each time accidental contact was made. Amy stepped gingerly over a dead pigeon, seemingly deep in thought. She stopped cold.

"Oh, you have got to be kidding me!"

The ice cream shop was closed. We stood before it, a big metal gate covering the window, our hands in our pockets. The street was empty, hot. We sat down on the curb between a yellow SUV and a large, white 1970s Cadillac.

"Why are you leaving town, Nathan?"

She wasn't looking at me, wasn't looking at anything.

"Amy," I looked away too, noticing that someone had written SUPPORT CHILDREN, KILL COPS on the street sign. "If someone was to say the following to you, what would you make of it? *'The trail of worms is open and the slasher boys are free.'*"

She was fanning herself with her hand. "*The Trail of Worms* and *Slasher Boys* are Thomas Salanack novels." She yawned, threw her head back. "What does that have to do with you leaving town?"

Thomas Salanack. I had never been a fan, though I knew he was popular since people would list his books as their favorites on Facebook and I had overheard many people in many coffee

August 1st

shops whispering about him in hushed, reverential tones. The most out-there of the Beat Movement, estranged even from his experimental peers, I had always been under the impression that his books were nothing more than gross-out chronicles of drug dementia and male prostitution. Still, he had a large following, more than a minor Beat-era footnote, proven by the fact that each year people made the pilgrimage to his grave in New Jersey on the anniversary of his death from intentionally shooting up anti-freeze in the early 80s.

"They are?" I resisted the urge to immediately phone Edward. "Oh shit. Thanks, baby. Oh dear God."

She was looking at me, now interested. "They both suck, in my opinion. Just your typical junkie mythos bullshit. Bugs in the veins, selling yourself to groups of sailors for gang bangs, etc. Just decadence for the sake of decadence. Bo-ring."

Confusion and fear had given way to calm. I felt lucid, suddenly focused.

"So what does that dead old beatnik junkie have to do with you leaving town?" She sounded genuinely intrigued, this bit of mystery touching something off in her voice. For the first time in many days she didn't seem bored to death by my presence. "You gonna' run off and shoot smack in Tangiers or something equally played out and bohemian?"

The thought of Tangiers, of deserts and red brick clay, made the sweat on my forehead spurt like a fountain. "Do you still have those anti-anxiety pills that quack gave you that you didn't like? The ones that made you feel like you were in an elevator passing through water?"

"Oh, those, yea, I think I threw some in the Adderall bottle. Why?"

"This business trip," I told her, the urge to take my shirt off becoming more unbearable by the minute. "It's making me way nervous. Sorry, it's just too fucking hot to even try to explain right now, but I can assure you that strange things are going down."

She was laughing. "A business trip? For that crazy old man? What, he needs you to go on a mission to find a rare type of

Travels and Travails of Small Minds by Daniel Falatko

manila folder? He needs a phone answered in Albuquerque? He needs you to fetch coffee in Canada? That's the most ridiculous thing I've ever heard."

She made a move to touch me, noticed the sweat soaking through the cuffs of my shirt, thought the better of it. "I mean, let's face it. You aren't handling accounts for Morgan Stanley or anything. Jesus, that place is like a hall of mirrors."

Someone tossed a large bag of garbage out of a 6th floor window across the street and it landed on the sidewalk with a loud splat. We both looked at it for a while, saying nothing. Amy had stopped laughing. After many minutes, she asked if I was ok.

"Things are starting to come together." I looked her full on for maybe the first time that night. "Dimensions are beginning to align."

August 1st

ONE YEAR LATER – PART TWO

WEIRD SKIES THESE DAYS. Sunshine magnified through clouds so low they double as fog, bathing the shoppers out front in white humid swirls. Late in the afternoons when the sun begins to sink it gets brighter on its way down, hitting the clouds at an angle that pierces right through the window, the glare blotting out many soccer matches and teenage gauntlet runs. Mariska had made a rare visit earlier in the week or possibly the week previous, I have lost track of days, snapping gum at me and bearing a note from The Pash. His name at the bottom is the only thing I can definitively decipher, although the word "Molako" appears scrawled within the third of four sentences and I can recall from Clockwork Orange that this is a term for milk. Mariska had placed her hand against the side of my face, feeling the stubble that had been rapidly accumulating, and made a gesture with her hands as if she were shaving. Then she was gone. The Pash has not been through here in quite a while. Rent money continues to accumulate in the envelope under the Yosemite Sam doormat, though the thought of waking up on the wrong end of an axe or lead pipe when he finally emerges from his vodka haze diminishes any pleasure at the availability of extra cash. Searching for recognizable words within the slang-

ONE YEAR LATER – PART TWO

drenched letter remains fruitless, which is frustrating since any word such as "Jail" or "Hiding" or "Holiday" would explain the entire letter and put my still-intact head at ease. My *Learn Russian in 90 Days!* book remains useless. Sometimes I attempt to signal Mariska from the window, though she is always caught up playing with her hair and the sill is painted shut so I cannot call out to her.

The *militsiya* often stop by the store for their two-bottle-weekly protection payoff, so I must be careful.

On my television the team with the red uniforms, who I have dubbed the 'Half-Crescents', seems to have made some sort of tournament and their fans have become even rowdier, some of them wearing red contact lenses and others bizarre-looking clown wigs and ski masks. When the camera sweeps out to get a wide angle of the stands during the inevitable fights on the pitch, the crackly reception makes them look like a shifting mass of red-eyed, psychedelic-haired phantoms, pushing and writhing all as one fluid whole. I can never tell the white static from the after-effects of a smoke bomb, though time has taught me one thing about the Half-Crescents: It is ALWAYS a smoke bomb. In the late afternoons, after the screams of the homeless tweaker children cease, the station has taken to playing pop ballad videos from Eastern European countries, flooding my vision with images of doves soaring over mountain ranges and my eardrums with Casio keyboard flourishes. Sometimes I will turn the volume all the way down, muted ballad imagery, Polish pop singers with hair of waxen gold spilling over milk white shoulders, vaguely medieval dresses and flower headbands, their cheekbones carved from diamonds, the fields in which they sing all lit up all green and breathing.

Following the video show is a talk program where some guy with a beard yells at some other guy without a beard as he wrings his hands dramatically and looks pained. This goes on for hours.

Sometimes I will turn the television off to concentrate on the shadows that spread further and further toward the ceiling

Travels and Travails of Small Minds by Daniel Falatko

as the day goes on, the final several inches often taking hours. There are 619 panels of tiling which make up the floor. There are 1,083 tiny holes within the terracotta-painted ceiling.

As the nights get cooler, beginning the inevitable slide toward the mini-ice age that is the Russian winter, people on the streets of the neighborhood grow meaner, their faces taking on blank scowls as if practicing walking on black ice, for it will be black ice that they tread upon in only a couple of months' time. Unlike the beginning of the summer, when people wander in a stunned drunken state, eyes to the night skies, not really seeing you as you pass, on my night walks recently they have begun to look in my direction once again. People are drunker, stumbling on the sidewalks, alone with bottles in hand. I've noticed more beer bottles this season, taking the place of cherished vodka, a frothy brand with a bright red label and two muskets forming an X below the lettering. People snarl at me, asking for a cigarette by making smoking motions with their hands, a universally recognized sign language, raising their fists at me, ready to bash my face for a generic-brand smoke. Sometimes they just snatch the lit smoke from my hand as they pass, not looking back, not laughing. Kiosk worker girls smile at me from their lighted, locked pods of alcohol and candy and eggs, though to stop and talk to them would risk confrontation with the roving teenage gangs from the block estate courtyards who seem to hop from one kiosk to the next, begging for freebies and shadowboxing one another, attempting to get the girls' attention.

The teen packs seem to be moving farther from the estate borders than they had before, out into the neighborhoods, and their normal glares have turned vocal with taunts and catcalls. One of them tossed a bottle in my general direction several nights before. I've seen them gathered on a destitute strip bordered by two garages, one abandoned and sporting a huge spray-painted fist and the other acting as the center of what appears to be a thriving street-level heroin market. Skinny men with pinpoint pupils have been lining up around the block all

ONE YEAR LATER – PART TWO

summer, scratching at their skin so hard that multiple red streaks are visible on their pale flesh.

Once when I had a bad cold, The Pash had given me a ride to the house of a doctor he knew even further out into the provinces, the Lada spitting dark smoke the whole way. He had pressed his foot to the gas and gunned it straight at the line of fidgeting junkies, causing them to dive out of the way with skeletal arms and legs flailing. I swear he ran over the foot of one. The Pash spit out the window and laughed. My hands shook for hours afterwards, until the doctor The Pash had taken me to, on the 19th floor of a monstrous high rise overlooking a vast forest, pressed a pill to my tongue that left me in a trance for several days, hours spent outside my own body, watching myself sit in a chair with dead eyes. The cold was completely gone when I snapped out of it, Russian medicine at its finest. The packs of teens have taken to canvassing the junkie block, randomly knocking over the weakest of the customers, bones cracking on the concrete, surrounding the few women, obvious prostitutes, for a quick group grope before the men in the garage emerge to chase the teens away. I prefer the colder months when the teen packs stick to the courtyards of their respective block estates, drinking and shoving one another, and hopefully the oncoming winter will place them right back onto those concrete slabs and the frozen communal fountains around which they congregate.

It is difficult to figure out if I would go crazy without the night walks or if the night walks themselves are making me crazy. On the several nights that I have skipped them the hours have been particularly hellish, just the moaning of drunks outside and occasional headlights, dogs howling, the television fading in and out and eventually switching to full static sometime in the AM hours. The boys of Gorky Park taunt me in the light generated by the television snow, teased-out hair and confident grins, some of them in spandex, one licking a guitar suggestively, their mascara-ringed eyes surprisingly bright and all-knowing: "We are ghosts. We are permanence. We exist in this moment forever." This is

Travels and Travails of Small Minds by Daniel Falatko

generally the time, once the Gorky Park boys begin speaking to me, that I turn off the television and let the flat sink into darkness, only the wind and voices from the store and the smashing of bottles outside.

Aside from the taunting of the teen packs, there are other things that have begun to bother me about the night walks. The air gets thinner as the winter approaches, crisper and stinging, less all-engulfing than the humid bliss of the July nights when all was covered with a sheen of wetness and every window in the block estates was lit up, shimmering towers against light skies. These days the horizon hangs low, swirling and dark, giving the already bleak outer ring scenery a claustrophobic, stooping feel. Many of the windows have gone dark, only several panes aglow with cheap yellow lighting, pinpoints on an otherwise blank grid, the balconies emptied and no more bottles tossed off the rooftops. People appear to be fleeing the ring for the provinces, where the minimal cost of living allows for one to drink all day and not have to even consider the thought of work. The abandoned feeling of these block estates, towers I had marveled at upon first reaching the neighborhood, seems to have permeated my footsteps, slowing my pace, no longer looking skyward.

The stray dogs have started taking closer notice of me, some loners and others rolling in packs like the teens, sniffing in my direction as I pass. The poplars thin out. The trash accumulates in the alleys. The junkie line spills out onto yet another block. I had enjoyed the desolation upon first reaching the neighborhood, a distinctly foreign despair unlike that of, say, Camden, New Jersey. There was a longing behind it, a history that stretched for dozens of centuries, a certain degree of strength in the survivors who staggered the streets. But all that has worn off now. No longer an observer, I am now a part of this. This scenery is my scenery. This place is my home. The hostile eyes, the dog fangs, the syringes, the rumbling skies, the empty towers, the burned and bombed *aptekas*. It's all mine.

I'm up to a pack-and-a-half a day.

ONE YEAR LATER – PART TWO

One night, stepping over an old drunk blocking a sidewalk almost completely overtaken by thick brown grass, a horrific odor fills my nostrils. Glancing down, I realize the man isn't passed out. He is dead. And he has obviously been there for days, his arms swollen up blue and purple and his face caving in, his skull striving to break free. Several blocks later, the reflection I catch in the window of an empty storefront reveals cheeks so pale they look powdered, eyes ringed red, scraggly beard, shoulders coiled and tense. Hyperventilation overtakes me while speedwalking home, lungs failing, and I duck into the tall dead grass of a vacant lot to vomit repeatedly, on my knees, some sort of animal brushing past me in the dark. It takes an incredibly long amount of time to be able to stand up, possibly an hour, maybe two.

Two blocks from home and The Pash's store lights come into focus. I'm delirious, almost laughing. The taste in my mouth is awful. Even my ears are sweating. Two of the teen pack boys are attempting to chat up Mariska behind the bulletproof glass. She files her nails, yawns. Even her headband is leopard- print. She waves to me. My body feels like it is made of aluminum, hollow on the inside. I try to smile at her but it hurts and saliva begins pouring from my lips in long strings. The teen pack boys watch me closely. Not wanting them to know where I live, I walk to the front of the building, its foundation soggy and rotting, then circle back and slip in the door while their attention is focused on the joint they are sharing under the blinding neon outside the store

Coming through the hallway, feet dragging, legs made of lead, I notice something has been placed outside my door. Cautious, I move forward, advancing slowly as my eyes adjust to the near pitch blackness of the hall. The objects come into view and I can't help but smile, though my jaw is so sore from vomiting and clenched teeth that it feels like a punch to the face.

A can of shaving cream and a Gillett Mach 3 razor in a sloppily-tied red bow.

The Girl in Apartment 3E Discovers Nathan in Her Stuff
"Were you just in my mailbox?"

AUGUST 2nd

SAME PANTS AS THE DAY BEFORE, a nice pair but crumpled beyond recognition, tucked-in, button-down, rolled at the sleeves, hair sculpted into something resembling normalcy with the aid of a fistful of glistening green LA Looks Ultra Hold Gel from Amy's medicine cabinet. Checked my face for zits, several drops to conceal any redness of the eyes, clean-shaven and overall looking much better than I deserved to considering that week's acute lack of sleep. Hands shaking, I popped two of the anti-anxiety pills from the bottle Amy had told me contained them, swallowing them with warm water from the faucet.

Later on I would be amused to remember that, as the sun rose over the pigeon-infested rooftops of Harlem, I had hoped that morning for a less weird day.

BY TEN O'CLOCK THAT MORNING I had reorganized not only my desk but the entire front half of the office. The paper sediment which had once lined the floor was now neatly piled into towering stacks next to the filing cabinets. If Edward had not forbade

Travels and Travails of Small Minds by Daniel Falatko

me, I would have gone through the cabinets as well with the intention of discarding any deeds or bill copies from before 1990. "Don't you see?" Edward had pulled me to the side so that Behr couldn't hear. "To eliminate outdated deeds and old bills would be to eliminate the entire filing cabinet! Plus all those stacks! Plus everything else! Are you getting the picture now?" He knocked lightly on my head. "If the clutter goes, then Behr might actually realize that he doesn't need us. We'll both be out of jobs."

I had also officially declared war on the dust. Chinatown Dollar General had provided a dusting contraption which resembled what would happen if a rattlesnake mated with a long caterpillar, plus a quart of heavy duty surface cleaner of a nameless brand. The surface of my work area gleamed in a way one would never have thought possible the day previous. The precious blue special assignment folder acted as centerpiece, with all my pencils and pens color-and-size coded in the drawers. Edward had chased me away from his desk when I tried to tidy it up, recoiling in horror from the dusting contraption. "Get away from me with that thing, you pervert!" He threatened me with a magic marker. "Why are you grinding your teeth?"

I didn't hear his last question due to the fact that I was on my knees cleaning up the black ropes of dust which had fallen from the paper sediment when I built the six-foot high stacks. Dr. Behr came to the doorway of his office twice during the early hours, once to check on the noise I was making when attempting to fix the molding along the far wall, the other time to scold me for failing to answer the phone while lost in a trance organizing my desk drawers. The first time he just shook his head and turned back to his lair. The second visit proved more formal, grunting at the now-silent phone in disapproval. When I started babbling at him about how the fall of Rome was caused by lack of organization, he headed for his lair once again without saying a word, moving quicker than I had ever seen him move before.

It wasn't until returning from a record-time Solid Ground run, all the way to Midtown and back in a mere 18 minutes, the coffee actually still hot in my hands as I passed it to a satisfied-looking Dr. Behr, that I finally noticed how much I was sweating. One drop landed upon the blue folder, staining it, followed by another. Then the faucets opened, an unstoppable deluge raining down off the tip of my nose and earlobes in a stream that wasn't going to let up any time soon. This arrival of the soaking sweats marked the exit of what had seemed to be a supernatural energy, my arms going limp and pangs shooting through my lower back, last night's wee-hour haze catching up to me on the 20-yard-line and taking me out with a sickening, bone-bruising tackle. Every cell in my body felt shredded. Every pour wheezed for help. I planted both hands on the desk, palms down for balance, feeling jagged and exposed to the elements.

"It looks like someone's... ahem... vitamins are wearing off." Edward beamed from ear-to-ear. My eyeballs felt as if they were made of sand at that moment. I fixed him with a glare that let him know I wasn't messing around. He just laughed. "And thank God for it. You've been bounding about like a chipmunk on PCP all morning. You do realize that your lips are chewed raw, right? Do you remember when you tried to color-code the folders that were all one color, sorting them instead by the number of papers in each, only backwards counting up from five? Or when you almost electrocuted yourself fixing that light bulb because you forgot to turn off the switch? Do you remember, Nathan? You said the electric shock felt...I'm trying to think of the exact words you mentioned...oh yea, you said it felt 'heavenly'."

"Fuck. Off. Edward. Seriously." My stomach felt shriveled and my temples pounded so hard I expected blood to begin spurting from my head at any moment. "I'm not sure what happened. I popped a couple anti-anxiety meds, but they seemed to have the opposite effect."

"And I take it there's no way you may have accidentally, I don't know, taken a *different type of pill* by mistake, my dear Nathan?"

"Oh shit," I seethed through clenched teeth, my whole jaw aching like I'd slammed it on a sidewalk. "Damn it, Amy."

Travels and Travails of Small Minds by Daniel Falatko

"Let's see, what could your adorable little GF have given you accidentally." He leaned in close so Behr couldn't hear, still beaming that ridiculous, Cheshire cat grin. "Look, don't think I haven't been onto you from the second you burst in here this morning. The incessant babbling. The grinding of the teeth. The constant sniffling. The inability to complete a thought or sentence or action. The dozens of ideas that went nowhere. The illogical organization. Definitely Adderall."

He took my arm and used my sleeve to wipe off some drool that had formed at the corners of my mouth. My nose was running. I closed my eyes, counted to thirteen, and when I opened them, unfortunately, Edward was still hovering with a needy expression upon his fake-tan orange-tinged face.

"I don't have any more," I told him, my voice a pathetic, sad squeak. "There were only two, Edward. All gone."

The morning sun must have passed behind a cloud, for it was now nearly pitch black in the office. Edward had his arms crossed, tapping his foot. He looked incredulous.

"What is it with you straight people always holding out on your drugs?" He raised his arms to the heavens. "Share the wealth!"

I put my head down on the desk, relishing how cool the surface felt against my cheek, the only relief affordable to me at that moment.

"Jesus, kid. Don't cry." He placed his hand on my back, grimacing when he noticed how sweat-soaked my dress shirt was. "I'm just kiddin' ya'. Obviously, you don't have any more because if you did you'd be off in the bathroom crushing and snorting them up to keep from jonesing out like you are right now."

"Edward, I feel so horrible."

He took out a plastic pill case.

"Fortunately for you," he snapped open the case. "I have a little something here to help smooth out your landing."

I opened my mouth, pointed into it.

August 2nd

"Don't tease me like that, straight boy." He tossed three inside.

"Jesus, you get one little assignment and you go completely off the rails," he laughed, moving back to his work station. "The paranoia, the intrigue, the drugs, the messy hair. Some people just aren't cut out for the workplace."

BY NOON THE BRAKES had been fully stomped on. My hands could barely move to look through the papers in the blue folder, the wording of the documents blending together until it was all just one messy typeset blur. The sounds going on around me, Edward humming to himself, pigeons screeching on the street, Dr. Behr snoring in his office, took on an underwater tone, muffled and filtered like faraway bombs. My head felt heavy, weighted down, and I wasn't convinced my legs would still be operational if I needed them. Edward's pills were working. The landing strip had been cleared. I felt worlds better, relaxed to the point of trance-like bliss, a grateful smile plastered on my face.

It took me a good number of seconds to realize that the shadow blotting out a sunbeam which had been illuminating my desk belonged to Dr. Behr. Hovering over me with an impatient look on his craggy face, he was rapping his knuckles on the surface of the desk as if he were knocking on a screen door and had apparently been doing so for a good amount of time. I had thought the banging was just Edward bouncing a tennis ball off the wall again, only faster. I smiled bashfully. From the corner of my eye I could make out the horrified, embarrassed expression on Edward's face.

"Look at that, Dr. B.," he said mock-cheerfully. "The kid is so engrossed in his work he didn't even know you were there."

Behr shot him a glance as if to say, "I know this is somehow your doing." Edward sank down into his chair.

Travels and Travails of Small Minds by Daniel Falatko

"Have you yet to eat?" he inquired of me, his mass of grey eyebrow hair rising and falling with the words. I had not even thought about food that day, nor had I witnessed Dr. Behr consume anything other than black Solid Ground regular. He had never invited me to accompany him anywhere outside of the office. I could feel Edward's jealousy breathing, breeding, from the other end of the room.

"Grab your coat." He zipped the Columbia windbreaker up to his chin. It was so hot in the office the thought of a coat nearly caused me to vomit. "Let us have a quick lunch. There are things to be discussed."

Too dazed to react to the situation with the proper amount of fear, I simply rose from the desk, trapped in a dream, and drifted after Dr. Behr into the hall. Catching a glimpse of Edward as I passed, his astonished expression, I tried to signal to him but my arm was paralyzed. He blew me a kiss.

THE SUNSHINE OUTSIDE was blinding, hallucinatory, watching with glee as the sunspots hovered and vanished before my eyes. I had to concentrate a little too hard just to place one foot in front of the other, moving at what seemed to be a glacial pace, though it was still too fast for Dr. Behr. He was almost a quarter-block behind me when I finally gathered the stamina to take a look at my surroundings, wheezing and straining to keep up with me. I stopped to wait for him to catch up, causing two Chinese men behind me to stop dead in their tracks, the huge carpet they were hauling rolling out of their hands. In no shape to jump, I could only watch as the roll came toward me at a fast clip, knocking into my lower legs with a force I had not anticipated. I was sent sprawling on my ass, the two Chinese men jabbering obscenities at me as they ran to fetch the carpet. For the second

August 2nd

time in less than five minutes, the hovering shadow of Dr. Behr blotted out the sun.

"You need to react more quickly." He offered his hand, calloused and spotted. Grimacing, I took it. Indeed it felt like splinters. "There are many obstacles to dodge in this life."

With a surprising show of strength, he managed to pull my essentially dead-weighted body to my feet. He beckoned for me to follow and I fell in place behind him. Together, we shuffled along the sidewalk, people behind us trying to pass on the narrow walkway, becoming frustrated, cursing. I concentrated on my feet, trying not to trip over anything, the whole time making sure not to lose sight of Dr. Behr's windbreaker ahead. He stopped in front of a corner eatery with large windows on each side set in oak panel frames, the tables inside covered with white tablecloths and occupied by people in perfectly creased slacks, the sleeves of their button downs rolled at the cuffs. They were smiling, relaxed, talking a little business. The lighting was dimmed and there were tasteful flower arrangements placed in the middle of most of the tables.

The hostess looked Dr. Behr up and down, her face scrunched up as if to ask, "Are you serious?" She looked to me for help when she realized I was with him, though when she noticed my dead, bloodshot eyes, she frowned.

Recovering from a coughing fit, during which the hostess had pressed herself against the wall in an effort to escape the airborne phlegm, Dr. Behr clasped his hands behind his back in a respectable manner. He cleared his throat loudly, reverberations echoing off the bricks of the building. The hostess flinched.

"My dear, I do like what Constance has done with the interior." He was inspecting the open column I had been using to prop myself up, his nose hairs flailing. "Not the direction that I would have chosen, but very welcoming. Very pristine."

The hostess had snapped to attention at the mention of "Constance," yanking the ringlet of hair she had been toying with so hard she grimaced in pain. Her eyes, pretty and dark, watched him warily, lips taut, waiting for his next move. Behr looked her dead on. He smiled.

"When I sold her the building…"

SEATED AT A WINDOW TABLE under a large, cheesy chandelier that filtered the light into rainbow-colored streaks across the restaurant walls, I was lulled into something approximating ease. Lounging gratefully in the air conditioning, Edward's pills had evened-out, like sitting on a comfortable and mossy plateau. Dr. Behr had ordered an orange juice and an unsweetened iced tea. I watched in astonishment as he took the tea and carefully poured it into the O.J., which he had already downed half of, mixing determinedly with the end of a spoon. The liquid took on the muddy orange color of vomit or wet foam. I placed the bread I was nibbling back onto the table. The waiter circled back around to take our orders. Dr. Behr nodded at him, slapped himself in the face, hard, where a fly had landed. "What is it that you're drinking?" the waiter asked, grimacing. "Did I bring you that?"

"Yes, you did," I slurred at him. "Yes, you did."

IT WASN'T UNTIL HALFWAY through our silent yet ultimately pleasant meal that Dr. Behr took a break from choking on his veal and addressed me with the loudest grunt I had ever heard him muster, much louder than the one which had nearly given Edward a heart attack the previous afternoon, causing every patron head in the establishment to turn our way. Our waiter appeared nervous, whispering something into the hostess's ear as she continued to play with the ringlet of hair.

August 2nd

"Have you ever heard of Thomas James Salanack?" he barked at me, phrasing the question more like an order, a challenge.

Salanack. Yes, James Salanack. Amy had been correct. *The trail of worms is open and the slasher boys are free.* Salanack novels, apparently. Closer to cracking the code. But what did any of this have to do with the grizzled tandem of Dr. Behr and the Oxford Man?

"I went to college with many hippie heroin addicts," I assured him.

"I see." He scowled at me. "And this means that you have sampled the works of this man?"

I pretended to cough, buying some time. Why was I being interrogated about some dead beatnik?

"I'll be honest with you, Dr. Behr," I motioned for him to lean in close to me. He didn't. "I got through about 15 pages of that *Rape World* book, probably about a decade ago. Couldn't stand it. Had to put it down. Never picked it up again."

I couldn't be sure, but it seemed as if Dr. Behr was smiling at me, or at least attempting to.

"You are acting a bit strangely today." He didn't sound angry or agitated, just curious. "Do you feel alright?"

I nodded, swallowed hard.

"Perhaps you should rest more in the nighttime hours." His voice had taken on a wistful, caring tone I was not aware he was capable of, though in a flash it was gone, snapped back to business. "But I am glad you have admitted to not particularly caring for this man, this Salanack." Now he leaned in, just as I had earlier, as if not enjoying the prose of this particular author was illegal or morally wrong, as if the patrons surrounding us would rise up and stone us to death for not being able to comprehend the genius of *Rape World*. "Perhaps I had heard of him, over the years, though as I'm sure you know, my specialty is in the Masters..."

How would I have known that? I was thinking. "How would I have known that when we have never, not once, spoken like

Travels and Travails of Small Minds by Daniel Falatko

we were now? I had assumed that, of course. I had received your Mark Twain gift, seen the Hemingway poster, the Fitzgerald volume on your desk with the back cover ripped off. Edward had mentioned you used to teach an entire course on one Faulkner short story, though I forget which one it was. How would you assume that I had pieced these clues together? Do you know of the things Edward and I say about you behind your back? Do you know of the things we think about you and don't even speak out loud?"

"...mind you, though a selective reader, I am perfectly willing to give anything a chance with no prior prejudice clouding the critical eye, so to speak." His voice kept going hoarse, rebounding, going hoarse again, like the treble level of a cheap stereo. "In the past weeks, due to a currently developing situation and an, ahem, opportunity which has presented itself concerning this, how shall I put it, *established literary monolith*, I have dutifully begun to explore the man's catalogue."

Long pause while choking again on another piece of veal. His face went entirely red and it looked as if the concerned waiter and hostess were about to intervene with some CPR actions. He regained his breath long enough to sputter a question. "May I ask," prolonged gasp, "why exactly," pounds on his chest, "you didn't find *Rape World* all that appetizing?" He finally seemed to clear the obstruction in his windpipe, sucking in air and stretching his arms with a symphony of cracking joints. He placed one hand under his chin, waiting for my answer.

"To me," I waved off the waiter and hostess, smiling to reassure them all was fine, "It seemed to be decadence for the sake of decadence. Not that I need a lot of depth in what I read, but something about that book, at least what I got through, was all surface level, just roaches and vomit and needles and buggery. It had an interesting structure to it, very forward-thinking stylistically, but flash and evil aren't enough to carry a whole book."

Dr. Behr was looking at me with something close to admiration in his eyes, perhaps realizing that I wasn't just some

August 2nd

dumb temp, that I could, in fact, read and even be able to form my own opinions.

"Plus," I let him know, basking in the attention. "I'm just really not into the whole wizened old junkie loser trip. I mean, yea, the world is a vampire. It sucks our blood. It rapes us. We all rape each other. It's a rape world. Blah, blah, blah. Get over it."

He nodded, lost in thought.

"That's why I'm going to have to stop reading Bret Easton Ellis in a couple years."

After a sip of his obscenely-colored concoction, inhaling the liquid like a vacuum, he let out a single cough from the depths of his throat at ear-shredding intensity. I thought he was going to begin choking again and was about to motion for the waiter and hostess, but he seemed to recover.

"My views are not much different." He blew his nose in what looked like an oil rag pulled from one of the many pockets within the windbreaker. "There is a certain level of pompousness to his works, a sense of being evolved beyond everyone else, especially those that do not share in his vices. Though I agree with you on the man's forward thinking, arguably visionary prose style which was certainly far ahead of its time, in the end I have come away from his catalogue with a very sour taste in my mouth. The endless paragraphs about insects in his veins. The midget sex. The, um," he glanced at the group of corporate types who were staring at us from the next table, didn't lower his voice. "…inside-out vaginas."

One of the men at the table sighed and placed his fork down on his plate.

"He seems like he'd have been a major dick," I added. "The kind of person who shouts at grocery clerks and beats his lovers. Kerouac and Burroughs and all those other dudes didn't really like him that much. He kind of rode on their coattails."

"Yes." Dr. Behr grimaced as if the mere thought of the man were causing him quite severe pain. "Though in Mr. Salanack's defense, my research has shown that the pedophilia charges were later cleared. The boys were under the influence of an advanced psychedelic. They had no clue what touched them. In the end he was only charged with administering the psychedelics to the children. Nevertheless, in a brief scan of the biographical materials available, I would have to concur that he did seem to be a bit of a....well...a dick as you had said."

Pleased that we were both on the same page, though still thoroughly confused as to why this topic was even on the table, I leaned back in my chair, waited for him to make the next move.

"I will need you to venture to the United Kingdom." Looking over my shoulder as he spoke, squinting at something on the wall behind me, he seemed afraid to make eye contact. "You do have a passport, I take it? We'll book you for a Sunday flight."

The words "United Kingdom" had a mysterious ring to them, tyrannical and mighty, a cold superpower. But alas he meant England, a place I only knew from early 90s Oasis videos, full of pubs and trippy light swirls and shag haircuts. England? Why was I being sent to England? What business did he have there? And what did any of this have to do with minor players in the Beat Movement?

"How long will I be gone?" I asked the most inane question I could think of, hoping the answer would branch into a full-frontal explanation involving the exact motives and details of the journey. "Where in the UK will I be going?"

For a second I thought that Dr. Behr was asleep. His eyes were closed and the grey nose hairs were all a flutter from heavy breathing. Just when I was about to snap my fingers in front of his face he jolted to life as if shocked, the thin tether keeping him in human orbit yanked back into place.

"Your confusion on the matter is noted." I could not tell if he was being understanding or was scolding me in some way, annoyed that I would be so bold as to ask questions. "The full details of the situation are still working themselves out. Various dimensions are still in the alignment process. But I can tell you that you will be gone for two weeks, that your expenses will be

August 2nd

fully covered, that you will be meeting a contact in Wolfton who will take you to the needed destination. I can tell you that you will be carrying deed papers on your person, originals which will need to be kept on you at all times until the deal is made. I can also tell you that this is very important to me and that, although not the most difficult of missions, I will be very appreciative of a job well done."

Drained from what had to be the most coherent conversation he had participated in for the past five years, Behr hunched his shoulders and rocked forward, his eyes glassy and exhausted, magnified by the lenses.

"I am not fit for travel," he admitted, staring once again at the point on the wall behind me, his voice weak and pleading. "Will you do it?"

"Why not send Edward?"

Dr. Behr winced as if I had just stepped on his foot. He clasped his hands, pained, choosing his wording very carefully.

"Edward has his strengths," he started, then stopped, lost in thought for a full minute. The narcotic haze I was under kept me patient, waiting for him to continue. Behr took a sip of the concoction, dribbled most of it on the windbreaker. "And those strengths are better suited to man the office frontlines while you are gone. I need him in position."

Behr placed his hand on the table as if to signify Edward remaining still, on guard, mired in his current role. "Edward's outer personality is too vivid, too confrontational. For this trip I need someone who will simply do as he is told, who will get the task done and not complain or concoct conspiracy theories and the like."

It was now clear. I was a better foot soldier than Edward, someone who could navigate a the thorny path of direct orders, no matter how vague those orders may be, without outwardly questioning the purpose of the mission, never driven to distraction by mental revolt. Dr. Behr had me all wrong, it seemed.

Travels and Travails of Small Minds by Daniel Falatko

"Will it be Oxford Man that I am meeting?" I squinted at him in the suddenly blinding sunlight flooding the table. "Is Dr. *Snail* the contact?"

Behr scrunched his brow in the way that he did every time I handed him a cup of cold coffee.

"Dr. Sneil," he corrected me, waving me off like a gnat. "The name is Dr. Sneil and he is a great, great friend of mine. You will be meeting him, yes. Perhaps not in Wolfton, but you will be meeting him indeed."

I nodded, relieved, like a drunk guy who woke up in a holding cell finally reaching court to hear the judge list his charges. I closed my eyes, waiting for more, but there was no sound from Dr. Behr.

Opening my eyes, I found that he had somehow fallen asleep while sitting upright. All that disclosure had apparently worn him right on out. It was tempting to just let him sleep, to get up from the table and head back to the office, spill the details about the UK trip to Edward, maybe leave a little early, surprise Amy as she left work, but I could see the waiter getting nervous as he waited to clear the table. I finished off a glass of water and shook the ice close to Dr. Behr's ear, the clanking bringing him back to life with a sudden start.

"Your day-to-day expenses will be funded," he started talking as if in mid- conversation. Was he perhaps dreaming these details in such vivid light that when snapped back to the conscious realm he could just pick up where the dream left off? "Though I do expect receipts. This is not a vacation, young man. This is not some youth hostel expedition. There will be no wine or music. There will simply be the task of following orders."

"Sounds like a blast, sir." My legs were beginning to fidget, wanting desperately to get out of the restaurant. "I take it these orders you speak of will be coming from Dr. Sneil?"

He furrowed his brow, grimaced.

"As I said before, the exact details will be forthcoming before you depart."

August 2nd

I thought about quitting. What would happen if I did? Right there on the spot. Just tell him I am done, that I don't like the sounds of this mystery trip. Get up and walk out. There was nothing back at the office that I needed. I could walk right past that enclave of dust and paralysis and head for home. No man is shackled to any one job, after all. We are voluntary servants who can walk out at any time. There was an uncoiling within, a tingling in the base of the spine when I realized the infinite possibilities even within my admittedly limited grasp. But at the same time a parallel line of fear snaked out to strangle those possibilities before they had a chance. Thoughts of rent dates, eviction notices, the eating of other people's leftovers, the selling of possessions, the end of a relationship, the lack of possibility for new ones, temp agencies, job searches online at public libraries while homeless people surf porn around you.

"Not all dimensions are aligned." Behr was looking to me as if he understood exactly what I was pondering, as if he had forgiven me for thinking of deserting and felt for his torn soldier a strange sort of pity. "You just have to find the right one and inhabit it at all costs."

Exiting the restaurant I couldn't help but notice the hostess shake her head as she gazed at us, a complete sense of disbelief in her big brown eyes. I was drawing up the rear, barely even moving as Dr. Behr plodded out the door before me. His windbreaker was dotted with fresh stains from the sips of his drink which did not quite reach his mouth. Once he was safely out the door, I turned and looked back before following and witnessed our waiter whispering conspiratorially to the hostess before breaking out into uncontrolled laughter.

Not a word was uttered on the walk back to the office. Edward's tranquilizers were edging down, the harsh realities of the day once again making their presence known on the periphery. The sun was an intensive, blinding thing that rendered my vision blurred and my steps labored. Even at my zombified pace, I looked back at one point and realized I had left Dr. Behr far behind. The old man was barely visible, nearly two blocks back. *Fuck it* I thought to myself and kept walking.

"EDWARD, YOU WILL NOT BELIEVE what I am about to tell you." My hands were flailing, blinking hard to clear my vision upon entering the dim room from the shiny realm outside. Edward was spooning a salad into his mouth, his lips greasy with some sort of yellowish dressing. "You may want to hold your breath for this. You may want to be careful not to choke on that fucking salad."

His mouth was full, eyes bulging, trying to swallow quickly so he could ask me what I had to tell him.

"I am fairly certain, my dear friend, that the business trip in question will be taking me to the land where rock music is still popular and where dollar stores are called Pound World."

He finally got his bite down. Head tilted slightly to the side, he asked me to slow down and be more specific about what I had just stated.

"I will repeat," I closed my eyes, enunciating each syllable, relishing greatly the breaking of this news. "Behr Properties is paying for this brother to go to England. Unless he's just spiraled off into a world of dueling delusions, that is." I pointed toward Dr. Behr's office. "Don't worry. The old man's asleep."

My eyes were having trouble adjusting to the dark, giving the room a ghostly, dusk-like feel. I blinked hard, shook my head trying to clear it. Edward came slowly into focus, smirking at me from across a watery divide. He was still smirking at me in a way that made me nervous.

"Being strung-out often makes boys sexy," he purred. "But it certainly doesn't work for you. You look like Miley after a night out with Wayne Coyne."

August 2nd

I attempted to fall back into my seat but ended up sprawling across the chair sideways, my legs tangled in the armrest on one end and my head lolling off the other. Struggling to assume an upright posture, the swiveling of the chair making it impossible, I sighed, stayed put.

"You're a fucking spectacle!" Edward was howling. "Just call it a day, my friend. Write this one off as lost. Get back at em' tomorrow, tiger. Jesus."

I managed to spin around to the point where I was facing him. Edward cackled.

"I think I'll leave you there for a little," he gushed. "Helpless boys are the best kind." He grinned at me. I attempted to kick him but was unsuccessful, only causing the chair to spin uncontrollably toward the far wall. I was on the verge of vomiting when Edward mercifully halted the spinning chair with his foot. I had managed to untangle my legs, planting my feet on the ground and angling for position. Edward smirked, planted a sneaker on the back of my chair and sent me hurtling toward the wall. I held out my feet to break the impact, pushing off the wall back toward him, but I was weak and the chair didn't rocket back as fast as I had envisioned, petering out before it reached Edward, who was cackling wildly. I managed to get one of his legs into a scissor hold and, using my last bit of reserved strength, sent him sprawling into a mountain of manila folders against the far wall.

"I may be a bit strung out," I smiled as the folders spilled their contents over him. "But I can still kick your ass."

He tossed a folder at me, papers flying everywhere, and rose to his feet. "I just cannot believe he's sending you to England. I mean... England? What the fuck for? To administer a sponge bath to the Oxford Man?"

His eyes were bulging, peeping his head into Dr. Behr's chambers to make sure he was still asleep. He began pacing, kicking over stacks of papers as he passed them.

"It all has something to do with that dead junkie Thomas Salanack," I said softly. "That is the key. The trail of worms is open and the slasher boys are free. Those are Thomas Salanack novels. *The Trail of Worms* and *Slasher Boys.* I wouldn't suggest reading them."

He kicked over another stack of papers, turned to me.

"What would that stale-ass Mark Twain fan in there have to do with the *Rape World* guy? That is like a Kenny G. fan attending a black metal concert, a union just not meant to take place."

"Don't make fun of Kenney G.," I warned him. "Behr mentioned that some sort of opportunity has presented itself concerning Tommy Salanack. I'm supposed to have a deed on me, a deed for what I can only guess would be my favorite building on Avenue B. The Oxford Man is involved. But apparently I'll be meeting someone else first in a place called Wolfton. How it all connects I have no idea."

We heard a short, sharp squeak from the chambers, a noise we both knew to be the groaning of Dr. Behr's wooden chair under the burden of movement. Edward rolled his eyes, whispered, "It moves." He tore off a sheet of notebook paper and, using my desk, scrawled a collection of words around the edges of the paper, forming a circle. The words were: T. Salanack, Oxford Man, Alphabet City, Wolfton, *Trail of Worms*, *Slasher Boys*, and Dr. Behr.

"I'm going to figure this out for you," he whispered. "I can already make one connection."

He drew a line connecting Dr. Behr with Oxford Man.

"Now we just need to connect the rest."

We had not heard the usual shuffling of Dr. Behr's feet on the tile since he was not wearing his padded slippers, just a harrowing pair of green and purple argyles sagging at the ankles. He had snuck up on us, his arms crossed, eyes sleep-ravaged and magnified by the glasses. Edward folded the sheet of paper and slipped it into my top desk drawer.

"I need you to do something for me." Behr nodded at me.

I tried not to roll my eyes. Was I not now above coffee runs? The thought of riding all that way on the train just to deal with

August 2nd

the coffee snob clerks at Solid Ground, who would scowl at my plain order of black regular which for some reason took a full ten minutes longer than a double-mocha iced espresso, was not an appealing proposition considering the state I was in. Edward smirked at me, mouthed "Have fun, bitch."

"Edward," Dr. Behr said in a dignified voice. "Can you please purchase a large black coffee from Solid Ground and bring it back to me. I am feeling quite lethargic after lunch."

The look on Edward's face at that moment, an unflattering combination of outward-shock and inner-pain, seemed to instantly age him five years.

"Here is ten dollars," Behr said. "I will want the change."

On the verge of hyperventilating, his cheeks flushed, Edward held the ten-dollar bill out before him as if holding a dead rat by the tail. Dr. Behr placed his hands on Edward's shoulders, turned him around, and steered him toward the door. "Make sure not to let it get cold," he warned. Edward took a final glance in my direction while being pushed out into the hallway. "Have fun, bitch," I mouthed to him, blowing a kiss.

Dr. Behr turned back to me. I slowly wheeled my chair in from the corner. He had his hands in his pockets and seemed to be in a chipper, fairly lucid mood.

"I need you to venture to a property just ten blocks from here," he grunted toward the blue folder on my desk. "You should be familiar with it from your research. I will give you the mail key. I had placed a correspondence in the mailbox of a tenant in apartment 3E. I have not heard back from this tenant, even though the correspondence was quite urgent."

My face felt paralyzed. Checking to make sure I wasn't drooling, I looked up to find Dr. Behr hovering dangerously close, handing me a small key.

"All that I ask," he said. "Is that you open the 3E mailbox and check to see if a letter addressed from me is within it. If so, this simply means the tenant has not yet read the correspondence. If it is not there, then this means the tenant does not understand

Travels and Travails of Small Minds by Daniel Falatko

the urgency of the correspondence and I will be forced to take further action. Please do not disturb any of the tenant's mail. Just check for the envelope and return to the office to let me know if it was there."

I held the tiny key in my hand, relishing the glint from a lone sunbeam. This indeed sounded like an easy assignment, and the thought of a stroll through the East Village was far more appealing than spending the afternoon spinning in a dust cloud. Perhaps Dr. Behr knew that I had already staked out the apartment building. Perhaps this is what he meant by mentioning my "research." Either way, this was a far more simple assignment than the one I would be embarking on that coming Sunday. It could not be denied, however, that the usually cautious Dr. Behr was now entering into some truly paranoid and borderline illegal activity.

"Isn't this a federal offense?" I asked him with my eyes closed, twirling the key in the tips of my fingers. "Can't you just call the tenant and see if he has received the letter?"

Silence. Opening my eyes, I was confronted with the vision of Dr. Behr deep in thought, tugging on one of the tufts of hair sprouting over his ears.

"If I were to call," he explained softly, "Then the urgency of the situation may be perceived as harassment."

I bobbed my head like a boxer, asked, "But isn't sending someone to snoop around through tenant mailboxes crossing the harassment border just a little bit more than a simple phone call?"

Dr. Behr was staring at me, nostrils flaring. He had stepped into the path of the sunbeam, a seemingly-holy glow behind his grey-fringed head.

"Can you please just complete the assignment?"

There was a seething tone to his voice, a mark of slipping patience, that lifted me to my feet and sent me for the door, sighing deeply.

"It is always best to keep a layer of distance between myself and the tenants," he spoke to my back. "If something can be

August 2nd

completed without involving the tenant in question, then this is always the best route to take."

I continued out the door into the hallway.

"It is hard to explain," he was still mumbling. Before exiting I looked back, watched him shuffling into his chambers.

"You're so weird," I said to him, not without affection. He turned his head slightly and smiled.

OUT ON THE STREET the sun had toned it down a level in harshness. Sweat no longer poured from my forehead as I crossed Houston and began strolling once again the streets of Alphabet City. I purchased an ice cream sandwich from a corner bodega and walked along Avenue C. The red brick building looked the same as it had the previous day. Most of the windows were open. An air conditioner propped haphazardly in a 4th floor window was humming loudly and spitting black water streaks down the side of the building. My stomach felt raw. Why was I doing this? Was it a trap? Was there danger involved about which I had not been forewarned?"

The outside door was open, the lock broken, and I could vaguely recall seeing an invoice cross my desk from a locksmith several weeks back. Either the work had been billed and not completed or the lock was simply broken once again. Your typical row of metal mailboxes along the wall, the apartment numbers marked clearly on each one. I located 3E, took a look in both directions, and slid the key home.

A *Nylon Magazine* fell to my feet, Chan Marshall's stoned-out eyes staring back at me. A Verizon Fios bill, a Sovereign Bank statement, and a postcard announcing the opening of a gallery named "Nothing Room" occupied the small metal box. There was no correspondence from Dr. Behr. I ran my hand around the

Travels and Travails of Small Minds by Daniel Falatko

inside, making sure there were no cracks an envelope could slip through. I had placed the bundle of mail back inside and was in the process of closing the box when I detected movement behind me. Playing it cool, I locked up the box and turned to leave.

"Um, hi." A voice hit the back of my head with the force of a fully-swung aluminum bat. I turned and did a slight wave, playing as if I were a fellow tenant, and was surprised to see the girl I had observed leaving the building the other day, the very same girl who had committed the heartbreaking sin of selling off her ex-boyfriend's vinyl collection. I nodded to her, kept moving, my hand already on the door.

"Excuse me," I was halfway outside, pretending to be in a hurry.

She was in the hallway, smiling wickedly, her head cocked to one side and observing me strangely. "Were you just in my mailbox?"

I found myself hypnotized by her hair, a vaguely 70s style, parted in the middle and spilling over her slight shoulders. My knees and thighs ached. It had been a long day.

"Sorry." I was busted and I knew it, didn't really care anymore, not willing to be dragged to the basement of a post office by men in blue hats and shorts to be interrogated and tortured until I gave up Dr. Behr's name as the man who ordered the mail tampering. "I was sent here by my boss, your landlord, to check if there was a package in your mailbox. I'm just doing my job. I didn't mess with any of your other mail, and believe me I desperately wanted to read the Cat Power article to see what types of yoga she's been practicing since going sober."

She squinted at me, extending her thin, long arms in a questioning pose.

"So this is what you do for a living? Snoop through people's mail?"

The word "living" struck me as odd for what I did at my job. Her attention was focused on me in an unrelenting way, no sense

August 2nd

of rage in the furrows of her forehead, yet it was apparent she was not going to let me off the hook, to just let the incident fade into the background of her memory.

"This is the first time I've been ordered to violate any federal laws," I assured her. "Usually we just do violations of local housing codes, zoning ordinances, that type of thing. Oh, and coffee too. I fetch a lot of coffee."

I was shuffling nervously as I spoke. She let out a sudden laugh. My hopes shot up, though she managed to stifle the giggle and return to her vestibule interrogation.

"So I take it you're a lackey for this Behr person, whom I have never met." She folded her arms, staring me down. "As a matter of fact, none of us have ever met him even though he's the one we send our rent checks to. Not that this is a bad thing. The more distant the landlord, the better. And the maintenance people he uses are fairly efficient. But when I receive a form from him letting me know to evacuate my apartment within three months for no listed reason, thus violating the lease agreement I had signed when the nice gay guy showed me the apartment last year, I suddenly start longing to see his face so that I can spit directly into it."

I backed away from her instinctively.

"I'm not going to spit in your face," she smiled, holding up her hands, three tasteful silver rings lining her fingers. "If you brought me your boss, I would spit in his face. You seem like an okay dude. Maybe you should get another job?"

"Maybe you're the ninth person to say that to me today."

She snorted, "Ninth time's a charm. Listen…"

She stepped forward, her upper lip curled slightly to reveal a straight row of healthy-looking teeth, and placed a hand on my shoulder. I was too spent to become excited by the contact.

"Nobody else in the building has received a 'Get the fuck out in three months' letter. Why me? I've paid the rent on time. I haven't altered or destroyed that shithole of an apartment. It

Travels and Travails of Small Minds by Daniel Falatko

isn't even a proper form. Just some personal letter letting me know to leave. Of course I haven't responded to it. The only thing I've done is read it once and sent it directly to the NYC Tenants Association. They should be in touch with your boss more sooner than later."

She removed her hand. I nodded and backed away.

"Well, I guess my work is done here." I bowed to her for some reason, causing her to laugh at me once again. "Just another hard day at the office. Enjoy your magazine."

I was halfway down the steps, panting, when she called after me.

"According to last month's issue," she held the glass door with the broken lock open, her long shirt billowing in the hot breeze. "Cat Power practices hot yoga and mixes this with elements of Wiccan theology."

I thanked her genuinely for letting me know. "Now I won't have to follow her Twitter feed," I told her.

She stepped back into the vestibule.

"Tell your boss to fuck off," she ordered just before the door clicked shut.

IT WASN'T UNTIL MUCH LATER in the afternoon, closing in on four, that the reality of the business trip truly set in. I had been halfway passed out at my desk for nearly two hours, my head resting on my hand, ready to spring into action and look busy if Behr were to emerge from his chambers. Edward, still angry that I had drifted off in the middle of his complaints about his humiliating coffee run, would occasionally pelt me in the head with a crumpled up deed paper or maintenance invoice. At some point Dr. Behr had appeared and asked how the mission had gone. I had let him know that no letter addressed from his person was present in the tenant's mailbox. He nodded wickedly and shuffled back to his quarters. It all came down to this:

I was being offered an all-expense paid trip to England and all I would have to do was dick around with some old people and unravel some mystery concerning a dead beatnik. There are worse things that could happen to a person.

"WELL, HELLO." Amy sounded pissed off and mean. "No coffee runs today?"

It took three clearings of the throat to be able to speak.

"Those weren't anti-anxiety meds you gave me."

"Shit," she muttered. "I'm sorry."

"It's ok, easy mistake. I mean they're both blue, right?"

"No, I meant I'm sorry I'm now out two Addies. I love those little blue angels."

There was a pause.

"Slow day at L.O.L., baby?" My voice sounded disturbingly like the Oxford Man's at that moment. "Did you guys just discover that Heath Ledger can't die every day?"

"Fuck off," she said, a real edge to her voice.

"I'm going to England," I announced proudly as Edward rolled his eyes on the other end of the room. "Some place called Wolfton and then to visit Oxford Man, but I don't think he lives in Oxford anymore."

Laughter, starting out as a small giggle but building quickly into barely controlled hysterics, from Amy's end.

"A business trip to England?" Her voice was full of bewildered scorn. "For Dr. Behr? For that hole-in-the-wall you call an office? For that thing you call a job? Do you realize they wouldn't even front me a train ticket to Boston when Ben Affleck was supposedly holed up in his garage with his favorite indoor palm tree and a four-month supply of freebase?"

Travels and Travails of Small Minds by Daniel Falatko

A movement behind me, Edward eavesdropping. I waved him away without looking at him. He muttered thoughtfully, "Affleck freebases? I would have thought him more of a ready-rock man."

She ignored this, asked me why specifically I was being deployed to England for an entire week.

"I can't figure it out," I sighed, trying to bleed some of the exhaustion I felt into my voice, to make her understand. "It has something to do with Thomas Salanack. You were right, darling. Those were his novels. And it has something else to do with this building Behr owns over in Alphabet City, more specifically with Apartment 3E in that building. That's where the key lies, just like in those strange codes they used to type into the pyramids or whatever."

I thought for a second that she had hung up on me, but her voice cut back onto the line like a supposedly drowned killer's hand emerging from the water in a horror flick.

"Mystery Englishmen? Ever-evolving eccentric casts of characters? Intricate layers of plot involving absolutely nothing? Two unaware and wayward employees leading the story? Nathan, you are living in a Wes Anderson film. And I'm not sure if I like it. You're definitely more *Life Aquatic* than *Rushmore* at this point."

"You want me to go back to eating your leftover Seamless orders?" I sighed, jabbing at a pain in one of my temples with a trembling finger. "To living in Ridgewood with four roommates in a two bedroom apartment and a Hassidic sex offender for a landlord?"

Silence on her end.

"Don't freeze me out on this." The desk's cool surface felt good against my head, shielding me temporarily from the horrors of my day. "You're my only neutral confidant. I don't know if I can take it."

"What about your neighbor?" She yawned audibly. "Terry the data-analyst meth freak?"

"Yea, him too." I thought for a second. Anyway, am I still coming over tonight?"

She sighed, distracted and distant. "I think I need some me time tonight."

Edward was arching his eyebrows at him from across the room, clearly entertained by this turn in the conversation.

"I feel like I'm stuck in a mystery novel written by an unhinged individual, Amy."

"Perhaps that's where you belong right now," she said before hanging up.

IT WAS A LONG TIME before I could remove the folder and pick my head up from the desk. At one point I felt the presence of Dr. Behr hovering over me but I didn't care anymore and let him stand there until he finally went away with a confused grunt. When I finally emerged, it was a changed world. The room spun. My eyes felt charred. It seemed to be getting dark far too early in the afternoon. There was a half-dead wasp atop the pile of folders I had arranged that morning, its stinger striking half-heartedly against their surface.

"You're a very unaware narrator," Edward told me.

WITH ONE PERFECTLY-EXECUTED SWOOP, straw-in-nose and using no hands, Terry snorted up a thick rail of glistening crystals, uncovering Rod Stewart's swarthy, drunken face. He had spilled the powder out onto the Faces CD shortly after I'd knocked on his door, chopping out five huge lines, each one blotting out another member of the band's snickering mugs. "Wanna' free up Ronnie Wood?" He offered me the pile.

I waved him away. "No thanks."

"No?" he asked with not much disappointment. More rails for Terry. "Aren't you feeling well?"

Travels and Travails of Small Minds by Daniel Falatko

Reclining in a ratty office swivel chair, I tried to get comfortable. It would have been better at Amy's, watching a movie and having sleepy-time tea or else just turning off the lights and sitting there in the dark not speaking as we often did, listening to bottles smashing in the street in front of the liquor store and cats wailing on the high winds.

I waved him away, grabbed a book off the shelf next to me without looking to see what it was. *The Ginger Man*. On the inside cover someone had written, "Just in case you can read. Love, G." Many minutes later I was still wondering who "G." was to Terry. An ex flame? An old roommate? Someone in his family? A teacher? One of his fellow data freaks? Loud snorting sounds emanated from the other end of the room. Short blasts followed by gasps, then more snorting. Ronnie Wood and Ronnie Lane's faces were now visible. "Terry, take it easy." I said to him.

He looked up at me, the straw still sticking out of his nose. Little puffs of white powder blew out the other end when he exhaled.

"Sorry, Nate." There was true concern in his raspy voice. "I didn't know you were reading."

"I'm not. Can't concentrate. It's been a jangly day."

"It could be what you're reading. That's a very minor work right there."

Realizing something, I looked to Terry with new interest. Shirtless, he wore a paper Burger King crown. A powder-caked straw protruded from his nostril.

"Hey, Terry," I realized something. "As an idealist, drug-addicted, bohemian-leaning, ever-searching young man, have you ever delved into the vast works of Thomas Salanack?"

At this he fell to his knees and bowed in a vaguely worshipful gesture. He was beginning to develop love handles despite the heavy stimulant regimen.

"That man was a genius." He jabbed a finger in the air, the straw falling from his nose followed by a thin trickle of blood. "A true breaker of boundaries. A progressive soul who never once sold out or compromised. Everything he touched was sheer decadent gold!"

I watched him warily, hoping he wouldn't fall into the coffee table. Of course he would be a Salanack fanatic. His aura just screamed it.

"I take it you have read this genius's works? And not just *Rape World*? You've sampled the obscure stuff too?"

Terry placed a hand over his surely rapidly pounding heart.

"I have read every word the man ever published, with the exception of that book of letters he wrote to Ginsburg. Those were just sick."

I slung a leg over the side of the chair, the most drastic movement I could make at that moment, and eyed Terry with renewed interest. He was up from his knees and pacing, swaying, hands on his head, his armpit hair matted and long.

"So I take it you've read *The Trail of Worms* and *Slasher Boys*?"

He whirled to face me, eyes gleaming. "Of course. Each many times. I love how Burroughs' cut-up method was utilized in *Slasher* to create a sort of modernist twist on man's constant need to…"

"What do they have to do with one another?" I cut him off. "Were they published back-to-back? Are there recurring characters? Is there anything in there that has to do with England or real estate or apartment buildings on the Lower East Side?"

Terry was looking at me as if I had just broken a solemnly held oath.

"Do you mean to tell me you've never read these works, Nathan?" He sounded truly wounded, gnawing on his bottom lip, his body sagging as if recently punched.

"I've always meant to get around to them," I tried to explain myself. "But books with true literary merit always get in the way. But that's not the point. You never answered my question. Is there any connection between these two books other than the fact that they were both written by the same old junkie?"

"*The Trail of Worms* and *Slasher Boys*?" Terry thought for a moment, the strain apparently causing him to lose his balance.

Travels and Travails of Small Minds by Daniel Falatko

He would have crashed headfirst through the glass table if I hadn't held out my foot to prop him up. "Those two are actually quite different, vibe-wise. Granted, they both contain the same infectious genius the man injected into all of his works. Both are surreal, borderline nihilist in scope, and so far ahead of their time that that they most likely won't be fully understood for at least another couple of decades."

Speaking in strangely lucid and fluid sentence structures, as if speaking in a lecture hall in front of dozens of rapt students, Terry gestured to me as if he were opening up the floor for questions.

"Did you memorize all that off the latest reissue dust jacket?" I said. His rant sounded suspiciously like the pompous, definitive ramblings of a gushing critic. "Impressive. So that's all they have in common?"

Terry smirked at me, his scolding finger at the ready. I cut him off before he even opened his mouth.

"I know, I know. I should read them and found out for myself. Dude's a demented genius who found transcendence through decadence. Blah."

"Couldn't have said it better myself." Terry was kneeling again, sweating, the strain of remaining on two feet apparently too much for him to handle. I wondered when the last time was that he had taken a vitamin. "*Trail* was one of his earlier works, a full eight-or-so years before *Slasher*. The structure is far more linear than his later output, though it was still incredibly surreal and groundbreaking at the time. It was borderline science fiction, dealing with space-age paranoia at an angle that Mr. Philip K. Dick himself never quite captured. I mean, Dick had never imagined robotic alien rape machines that ejaculated worms, super intelligent worms that could burrow into a woman's brain and take over her body, eventually leading the newly formed woman army to overthrow their oppressors, did he? The book can be seen as a precursor to the feminist movement of the 60s."

I told him he had lost me at the words, "ejaculated worms."

August 2nd

"*Slasher Boys* came out when he was already famous and acclaimed, greatly leaning on the cut-up method to chop things up and make it sing." He closed his eyes and pretended to write on the air. "It reflected the late 60s, an apocalyptic and incendiary vision of guerilla warfare with deep roots in the Nam conflict and pop culture nightmares. The scene where the Slasher Boys cut out the heart of the prostitute and repeatedly have sex with the bloody chest cavity can be read in so many ways, can relate to so many perplexities within the human dilemma it is utterly breathtaking."

I wiped some of Terry's spittle off the side of my face.

"So the books were published eight years apart and bore little similarities?"

Terry was counting on his hand, his eyes closed, eventually giving up.

"Probably around eight years. Or twelve. But the germs for all of his works were always incubating. There are drafts for all his stuff dating back to the 50s, late 40s. It is rumored that, early in his career, he would write only in his own blood. Eventually, he started to, you know, faint and stuff from lack of blood. So he started writing in ink after that."

I thought this over. Perhaps these two specific works didn't have the significance I had envisioned. They seemed to have come at different stages of his career and bore little relation to one another. Perhaps their titles were simply used to make a cool-sounding secret code, most likely thought up by the wily Oxford Man. *The Trail of Worms is open and the Slasher Boys are free.*

"Thank you very much for this information, Terry. Now I'm beginning to understand why he took the anti-freeze antidote."

He looked down on me, gently swaying on his feet.

"Don't joke about the anti-freeze, dude."

Terry's laptop rested on the floor between us, its lid opened partially. As the room got progressively darker with the setting of the sun, the screen began to glow, casting the reflection of a spreadsheet across the hardwood. Terry slumped onto his side on the floor, head propped up by a hand, his legs wired with nervous energy and teeth grinding away. He looked at me with glistening pupils.

"Why are you asking all this, Nathan?" He scratched at his chest hair. "Why those two books? I guess it's never too late to go through your Beat period."

He was studying the shadows on the ceiling with an intensity I found disturbing.

"Actually, it's for work," I sighed. "I've been given an important assignment. That sick junkie freak ties in with it somehow. I just need to figure out how. Preferably before taking off to England on Sunday."

"Dude, no way? I want to work where you work! Salanack? England? Sign me up!"

"It isn't fun at all," I assured him. "There is nothing rewarding or creative about it. Even the mystery is boring and tedious. I swear, after this mission I am OUT."

"Sure you don't want any?" Only one of the Faces was still obscured, Ian Maclagan. I waved it away. "Maybe I can help." He placed a reassuring hand on my knee. "As you can most likely tell, I'm a huge fan of Mr. Salanack. I'm truly scary good at cross-analyzing data. Tell me what you know so far."

Terry worked from home, compiling data for some frightening, shadowy tech company. Tracking clicks. He listened intently as I talked, losing only once in order to bump the last line, finally freeing Ian's young rocker mod haircut. I told him of the day the blue folder was placed before me, continued on through the weeks of staring at those deed papers, the scouting missions to Avenue B, the Oxford Man and his place in the whole conspiracy, a brief background sweep and explanation of the ways of Dr. Behr, how the Salanack angle tied in with things, the secret message, lingering for a long time on how Edward had been seemingly demoted for no particular reason as my star began to rise.

August 2nd

"Where did you say was the first destination?" Terry's head popped up as if yanked back by a rope. I repeated the name of the English town of which I had never heard.

"Wolfton," he repeated, drawing out the "f" in a creepy-sounding purr. "That's easy. You should have just told me that to begin with. We didn't even need to do this fucking spread."

I forced myself to sit up, fighting against great strain. He flicked the laptop shut rather roughly, slid the thing across the floor. I motioned for him to proceed.

"I'm desperate for an Advil," he replied.

Had I been stronger I would have punched him. He was up and racing for the bathroom, and I heard him fishing around in the medicine cabinet. The running water in the sink let me know that he had found what he was looking for and was presently gulping it down. I hoped he didn't overdose before letting me know what he knew. Just as I was about to scream his name, the bathroom light clicked off and he stood in the hallway gagging, smacking himself in the chest, throwing his body lightly into the wall. I didn't know CPR and started to get nervous, but he recovered rapidly and, leaning against the living room doorframe with a jittery grin, let me know that an "Ad-Villain" had gone down the wrong pipe. I begged of him to tell me what he knew of a connection between Tommy Salanack and Wolfton, UK.

"The place is a shithole," he let me know. "An industrial wasteland worse than Cleveland. Cold and grey and unforgiving. But it also happens to be home to the founder of the Thomas J. Salanack Society, some rich-as-fuck factory and warehouse owner whose name escapes me right now. To tell the truth, he seems like a straight-up prick, but he has the pounds to pay the bills if you know what I mean."

"How do you know all this?"

His story sounded made up, like something you would come up with off the top of your head when trying to impress some girl with your vast knowledge on some subject she was only vaguely interested in.

Travels and Travails of Small Minds by Daniel Falatko

"I've always wanted to own a *Rape World* first edition. That's how I know about the Thomas J. Salanack Society. He owns the first editions of all of his books but doesn't sell them. Some say he purchased up the first edition copies of *Rape World* for literally hundreds of thousands and keeps them in a vault in his house. The dude is definitely a freak. A Salanack fascist. I read an article on him. Dropped out of school. Poor background. Worked as a ditch-digger, a construction man, an ice cream vendor. A total hippie in the early 70s, following Hawkwind around and dropping tons of DMT. Getting into the Beatnik shit. Only he *really* got into Salanack. Like an obsession. Apparently, he met him once when Salanack was living in England and hanging around with the Pretty Things. Totally staked out his basement flat, and Salanack threatened to lower him headfirst into a vat of jellyfish if he didn't get the fuck out of his face!"

"Sounds like quite a chap."

"Quite a chap indeed. He was horribly injured on a jobsite, nailed in the knee with a wrecking ball when the crane operator had a few too many pints over lunch. Hobbled for life. Got a huge settlement and used it to buy a warehouse, made tons of money, bought other stuff, factories and whatnot. Very typical. Hippies always turn into total capitalist punks at the first scent of money."

"But he never lost the Salanack obsession, did he?"

"Nope. He started the Thomas J. Salanack Society, even though he had absolutely nothing to do with the man and was essentially just a non-educated working class geezer out of Wolfton. True Salanack fans, as well as the Salanack estate, are very critical of his methods. That is what the article was about. The guy buys up everything and refuses to display it or let people see it. First editions. Letters. Various memorabilia. Clothes. Syringes. Drivers Licenses. Raw manuscripts. Unpublished works. He will stop at nothing. It would be different if he were simply a private collector. But he calls himself the Thomas J. Salanack Society and throws his money around to acquire everything. He doesn't even have an office, just stashes the stuff in his house. If you happen to end up there on your little trip, make sure to nab a *Rape World* first edition for me *por favor*."

"Interesting. So what do you think this guy has to do with my demented old boss?"

Terry moved into the room, threw himself down on the sofa. After only seconds he sprang back up and began pacing. He was making me dizzy.

"My guess," he stooped to look out the window, his back to me. "Is that the property in question has something to do with Mr. Salanack, may he rest in peace. Maybe there is something in that building of value to the Thomas J. Salanack Society. And believe me, if there's anything in there that he wants, he's probably throwing a lot of money around. Hence your boss's interest. Hence your trip to Wolfton."

"Hence the eviction notice for that girl." I was excited, feeling blood rush through my head in a mighty sweep. "Whatever it is, it has to be in that girl's apartment."

"Indeed." Terry walked to where I was sitting and kneeled before me, making me very uncomfortable. "Here is what we will do. Obviously there is something very valuable to the Thomas J. Salanack Society in that girl's apartment. It could be anything, an original manuscript within the walls, the mummified head of a male hustler he murdered, who knows? Or maybe the girl has something. Maybe the girl is a Salanack freak too. Maybe she's managed to obtain something valuable, something the Salanack freak in Wolfton doesn't possess. The bowler hat he wore in the 50s? A stray first-edition copy? It could be anything. Remember, this guy is a freak and would pay like thousands for anything connected with him."

"Perhaps she has the empty jug of anti-freeze?" I knew where this was going and already wanted absolutely nothing to do with it. Terry was far more gone than I had even realized, drifting into the nadir of harebrained criminal schemes and get-rich-quick grasps. "And what is your point?"

Travels and Travails of Small Minds by Daniel Falatko

"Don't you see?" He tapped his fingers against the side of my head to check if anyone was home. "You can get a key from your comatose old boss, right? We stake out the building, see what her routines are, and slip in there when she isn't home. We scour the place, find whatever she has that relates to Salanack, and take it straight to the Society ourselves! Whatever it is, it's obviously very valuable to the Salanack freak in Wolfton. If there's enough money on the table to send you over there, then we have to be talking at least six figures with today's pound-to-dollar conversion rates. We'll split it down the middle. You can quit that lame-ass job and I'll buy an Air Force base and finally wage war, my man."

"Absolutely not," I scolded him. "It isn't worth going to jail over some dog-eared first edition. Plus, I happen to like that girl and will not advocate for her place being burglarized by some data-fried, coked-out maniac."

"But we have to!" he whined, curling into a fetal position at my feet. "What? You think the old man is going to send this item with you on your trip? Hell no, he won't. You're just going over there to discuss the deal."

"Exactly," I lightly pushed him across the hardwood, away from me. "And that is precisely what I will do. I'm a good soldier, my friend. I play it by the book."

Terry sighed heavily and rose to his feet.

"You are absolutely no fun," he said. "Like, none at all, actually."

I nodded.

"Not to be a bad host," he swept a lock of greasy hair behind his left ear in a deft movement, his interest rapidly deflating as the promise of cash and adventure waned. "But I really need to go get some food to feed the boys."

He offered the now-clean Faces CD for inspection.

I nodded, rising from the chair. "Thank you for the information on the Thomas J. Salanack Society," I told him genuinely as he paced the room, mumbling about how strange he felt. "This really does make the details shine a whole lot brighter."

August 2nd

"I wish you the absolute best," he said. "Hit me up from England. Let me know if you need me."

Moving for the door, he followed me, counting out some crumpled cash he had pulled from his jean's pocket. "You're going out like that?" I asked him.

He wiped one hand on his bare chest while adjusting the Burger King crown with the other, his bare feet leaving streaks on the floor.

"Yea, why?"

THOUGH AS EXHAUSTED as I had ever been, sleep still eluded me that night. The covers on my bed felt dirty and mangled, entirely too hot, so I threw them off and tried to get comfortable. I found myself longing for Amy's soft, sponge-like mattress which seemed to suck your body into a comforting pod. Every bump could be felt digging into my back as I writhed about. With the window open it was too loud, the traffic a deafening roar and car alarms ringing through every realm of the East Williamsburg night. With the window closed it was a heat-zone, sweat gathering in pools over my collarbones and stale warm air tingling in my nostrils.

The Thomas J. Salanack Society. This pretty much solved it. There was something in that girl's apartment that was valuable to this crazy-rich Salanack obsessive in Wolfton. I was heading over to talk to him about it. Even my toes hummed with excitement. A trip to England plus a date with a certified, beatnik-obsessed maverick. I wanted to call someone, share this information, though I realized with a sudden sadness that I really had no one to call. Edward had told me he and Michael were having dinner and that he "might give it to him tonight but he has to get on that scale first." I certainly didn't want to interrupt. Amy apparently needed space for reasons both tangible and existential. She had cast me out to dwell in my own rapidly declining personal space.

Travels and Travails of Small Minds by Daniel Falatko

All of this could be forgotten if I just made it to Sunday. Take off for overseas and put some distance between myself and these hassles. Images of what I thought to be Wolfton, of black soot and grey mist and row-homes stretching identically for miles, comforted me as I writhed in my tangled, sweaty sheets.

The dimensions were nearly aligned.

On COPS four officers ambush a man as he shouts,
"Ya'll mess with this snake, ya'll get the motherfuckin' venom!"
My neighbor, Terry, appeared deep in thought (and coke).
"Sometimes when I'm real wired. It feels like my veins are snakes."

AUGUST 3rd

THE FACT THAT IT WAS FRIDAY was nearly enough to compensate for the horrific pounding in my skull, painful reverberations echoing through the mush, the vine of ease severed far too easily by realities of the day. Seven Advil Liqui-Gels perfectly spaced over a two-hour period worked to dull the throbbing to a manageable level. The jug of water purchased for only a dollar at the Chinese convenience store around the corner worked to feed moisture into a body which had felt so shriveled at dawn I feared there was no coming back. Amy's calls clicked straight to voicemail. Behr was in-and-out, mostly holed up in his chambers, blowing his nose with an impassioned, honking fury. I decided not to ask him about the Thomas J. Salanack Society, reveling in the fact that I knew about something he didn't realize I knew.

    I had ducked out around noon to wander Delancey Street, pausing for a long time to stare at the rows of bottles lined up in the top window of the Bowery Ballroom, slurping down noodles and broth from a basement eatery whose counter girl wore a snakeskin bandana. When I returned, there was an envelope on my desk containing two plane tickets in a Jet Blue pouch, what

Travels and Travails of Small Minds by Daniel Falatko

looked to be a full trip itinerary sloppily written in block letters on a piece of notebook paper, and a check for seven hundred dollars. I slipped the check and tickets into my shoulder bag and tossed the itinerary onto Edward's desk. "Tell me what it says," I ordered, awakening him from a peaceful-looking post-lunch nap.

After taking some time to rip apart Dr. Behr's handwriting ("It looks like what would happen if you asked one of the zombies from *Night of the Living Dead* for a short story."), Edward informed me that I would be leaving very early Sunday morning and landing in an airport outside Wolfton in the afternoon. I would be picked up by a car service ("Oh, give me a fucking break.") and ushered to a private residence for a meeting ("Plus dinner!"). That night I would be staying at the residence in question ("Cheap bastard!") and in the morning would be driven to a train station bound for a stop in a small village called Stiltonfordshire. My Stiltonfordshire contact ("And I believe we both know who that will be!") would meet me at the station and, at this point Edward whispered the words mysteriously, "You will be questioned on the outcome of the meeting and given further orders."

He passed the paper back to me, a gleam in his eye.

"That's it?" I fumed, what felt like cold blood pulsing through my head. "That only takes me to Monday night. I'm supposed to be there two weeks!"

Edward laughed and threw up his hands.

"More concerning is the fact that I'm being sent directly into the clutches of the Thomas J. Salanack Society, some lunatic geezer with mass riches hungry to acquire everything even relatively associated with this particular beatnik in a fit of completionist glee."

"Um, what?"

Making sure that Dr. Behr, who was buried in his chambers, didn't hear me, I whispered to Edward the details relayed by Terry concerning the demented warehouseman. He looked it up on his iPhone and, though there was no website for the Society, there were many Google hits for beatnik literature forums, mostly threads in which the members of these forums complained that the TJSS, as they referred to it, had eaten up all of the first editions.

"Perhaps Dr. Behr and the Oxford Man are convinced you have a secret microchip implanted inside your skin containing the text to an unpublished Tommy Salanack manuscript. You will be taken immediately into custody by the warehouseman and taken to the Oxford Man to be dissected."

"You wish," I headed for my desk to grab my bag. "You goddamn snuff pervert. Working here is sort of like being dissected alive, when you think about it. Tell Behr I was sick. I'll meet him on Sunday as scheduled. Have a good weekend. See you when I get back, if I get back."

Edward called out after me but I couldn't make out what was said, heading outside into a nearly-blinding sun.

STARTING OUT walking toward the financial district, I changed my mind and doubled back through the heart of Chinatown, worked my way across the end of Little Italy, heading toward the East Village and Alphabet City beyond. Stopping in McSorley's, I ordered two cold ales and downed the first one quickly, instant comfort from the heat which had been nagging at me all that day. While nursing the second, I overheard a man next to me tell his friend, "When it all comes down to it, the only thing I truly care about is the dog. Jill, I could leave or take." I left before finishing the ale.

The building on Avenue B looked the same as it had the day before, no halos floating atop the flat roof or sinister red glares in the windows as were present in the dream which came to me during my one hour of sleep that morning. The same red bricks

Travels and Travails of Small Minds by Daniel Falatko

and rusty fire escapes. Not wanting to loiter out front, I walked by without even glancing up, took a left past a Spanish grocery, moved around the block, and walked past again. What was I doing there? What answers could I possibly get from stalking out this structure? Deciding my time would be better spent at the cool record shop I believed to be up the block, I headed toward Avenue A suddenly feeling crisp, sharper than I had in weeks, the messenger bag swinging merrily at my side. I was tempted to begin whistling. It wasn't until I'd made it half-a-block past a coffee shop that I stopped dead in my tracks in front of two Haitian men carrying large bags filled with crushed cans. They nearly collided with me, the cans clanging together in a horrific racket. One of the Haitian men had wild, menacing eyes, his mouth scrunched in anger, cursing me in his foreign tongue. I apologized and pushed through them back toward the coffee shop.

From outside the window she looked tiny, easily the most compact person in line and also the only one bobbing up and down on her feet. Not impatient or anticipatory, it just seemed like she needed something to do while in line. Her fringe of bangs swung lazily with each hop. Her face appeared placid, happy, until she noticed me staring at her through the window, the joy instantly draining from her cheeks. I held up a hand as if to communicate, "Oh, no. It isn't what it looks like. I'm not stalking you!" but it came off like I was ordering her to stay where she was. Her eyes were pure murder and I wondered if I should remain standing there. This seemed less threatening and weird than going inside to confront her, though just turning heels and walking away was also a tasty option. In the midst of deciding, I was interrupted by her voice coming through the door of the establishment.

"Well, if it isn't the mail thief," she greeted me in a not entirely hostile tone, arms folded as if to shield her midsection from projectiles. "Now he's following me around my neighborhood. You aren't armed with any hydrochloride needles, are you?"

August 3rd

"Aren't you going to get your coffee?" I backed away from her, feeling as if I were floating. "Hydrochloride needles?"

She let out a relieved breath, regarded me.

"Well, I guess it's fairly redeeming that you don't know what that is." A crowd of people on the sidewalk, most of them dressed in red boxing robes for whatever reason, forced her closer to me. "I didn't want coffee anyway. Not even sure why I was in there. So tell me, scary stalker guy, what is your name?"

In going through an interior list of fake first names I could have given her, none of them sounded as fake and masking as my own.

"My name is Nathan."

My voice squeaked. This seemed to please her.

"So tell me, Nathan," a hint of a smile on her lips, bangs swaying in the warm breeze. "Are you still stalking me for business or is it now for pleasure?"

This was a tough question to answer. A little bit of both, perhaps. But was I really stalking this poor girl with the perfect bangs that hugged the tops of her eyes with symmetrical ease? Is this the reason I ditched work that afternoon? She was certainly a passageway within the maze I had found myself lost in work-wise, although for whatever reason I had not been able to shake her image since she caught me rifling through her mail the previous day. Business or pleasure? This one seemed to stand firmly on both sides of the fence.

"I'm really not sure," I waved away some sort of insect that had been hovering over my head. "Probably business. I mean, why would I seek you out looking like I do today? All sweaty and blotchy. At least I could have spruced myself up a little."

She looked me over.

"You wouldn't be the first psycho-stalker dude to appear 'sweaty and blotchy'." She used her fingers to enunciate the quotes. "As a matter of fact, I believe that would be pretty much par for the course."

She made a move as if to begin walking away. I made sure to stand very still, letting her know with my body language that she was free to leave and that I would not chase her. A mellow stalker, respectful and sweet.

"Can you just tell me your first name?"

She laughed, not vicious or condescending, more of a sudden unexpected intake of air.

"You don't already know that? Don't you work for The Man? With proper access to all files, contracts, leases, background checks, security deposit information, credit checks, criminal background scans, face recognition, phone and utility records, internet usage reports, fingerprint records, DNA swipes... what else? Blood-type and dating history? My name is Cally, by the way."

Cally. The name fit her, folded into her features nicely. The warm green eyes, the thin lips, the way her cheeks creased when she smiled or grimaced. Cally. This I could work with.

"My boss," I informed her. "The Man, in this case, does not keep the most organized of filing systems. We don't even have computers, let alone face recognition technology, and if we did, the files would be lost amongst a sea of dust."

"You don't have computers?" She held her head to the side, teasing me. "How completely retro! And this sea of dust you mention, is that the substance that is all over your feet and pants?"

Glancing down, I noticed that my shoes and lower pant legs were indeed covered in clumps of stringy dust.

"Or is that just from your apartment?"

More people on the sidewalk, Puerto Rican kids talking about Morrissey, this time forcing her to take several steps away from me, separating us.

"Well, I really do need to get going," she shouted over the children's pompadoured heads. "But seriously, thanks for stopping through. I'm very relieved now."

"Relieved?" Did this mean she was grateful to see me again? Perhaps she couldn't shake my image from her head just as I couldn't shake hers. Perhaps she felt she would never see me again after catching me going through her mail. Perhaps my presence that day was a benefit to her.

"Yea, I'm relieved to find out that my enemy landlord doesn't even know how to use a fucking computer." She started to walk away. "I'm relieved to find out that his office is not the sophisticated tower of evil I had imagined and is instead a highly disorganized dust cloud. I'm relieved that this will be the easiest eviction opposition in history just for the fact that he has violated federal laws in having my mail ransacked. And I'm relieved to find out that his trusted lackey can't even keep his head in an assignment without developing a stalker crush on the very person they are supposed to be evicting."

She doubled back suddenly, walked right up to me and kissed me on the cheek. I would have been less stunned if she had punched me in the face. She mussed my hair and backed away with a smile.

"So thank you, Nathan. You have very much made my day."

With that she turned and walked away toward Avenue B, her white Chuck Taylors skipping over cracks in the sidewalk.

SITTING ON THE GRASS at Tompkins Square, I watched two shirtless men aggressively shadow box, swinging wildly at one another and knocking into a passerby until the walkway was completely cleared. A last slurp of the iced coffee I had purchased from Cally's coffee shop left a bad taste in my mouth. I bummed a piece of Trident from a passing teen with "Hot Sex" stitched on the seat of her jeans. The heat was stifling, my clothes clinging to my skin in an exceedingly uncomfortable way. The hour I had spent wandering around the air-conditioned Wiccan book store failed to provide any sense of long-term relief. One of the shadow boxers unleashed a vicious-looking roundhouse kick that caught the other man accidentally on the top of his head and sent him sprawling. He leapt straight to his feet, a thin trickle of blood visible on his forehead, and suddenly the shadow fight became a real one. Police whistles approached and I moved away from the scene.

Heading to my apartment did not seem like a very appetizing option at that moment, but I had already walked for miles that day and my feet ached within my Coles dress shoes. There were far too many NYU girls in belly shirts spilling onto the sidewalks for the warm weekend, shades of pink and pastel green, making it impossible to navigate the walkways. It all made me long for Amy's apartment, the cool air and the still lifes and Amy in a large t-shirt and panties, Netflix cued up on the television. Perhaps I could work my way back in there, blow off the England trip and show up on that Harlem Street with a boom box hoisted at her window, fingerless gloves and rolled jeans, mouth set in determination, my love like steel.

She still wasn't answering her fucking phone.

I slumped north toward the L Train, the numbers on the large clock calculating world debt whirring out of control over the low-slung buildings under Union Square. Nothing is more depressing than when the only place you have to go is home.

"WILL YOU PICK A FUCKING CHANNEL and stay with it? You're going to give me a seizure."

I tossed a pillow at Terry, who was clicking away at the remote with a glazed, zombified expression, his lips moving. It bounced off his head and rolled off the couch, landing on a Kate Bush LP on the floor.

"There's no such thing as a seizure, my man. That's just God sending flashes of illumination your way. Hey look, *Cops!*"

August 3rd

He dropped the remote as if it were burning his hand. Leaning forward, he held up a small red packet to the light from the flatscreen, squinting as he inspected it.

"You call choking on your own tongue illumination?"

He had pressed a straw into the packet and was snorting loudly. He then broke open the packet and licked it before stuffing it back into the pocket of his Gucci pajama bottoms.

"If God says it's illumination, then it is."

A man on the TV emerged from a smashed-up red pickup and made a run for it, appearing terrified as he hopped several fences with the spotlight from a helicopter on him the whole time. Just as he rounded a corner, four officers ambushed from all sides and tackled him hard into the side of an above-ground pool. As he was being led toward a line of police cars with wildly flashing lights, the man cried out, "Ya'll mess with this snake, ya'll get the motherfuckin' venom!"

My neighbor appeared deep in thought.

"Sometimes when I'm real wired," he said. "It feels like my veins are snakes."

I nodded.

"That sounds like something your boy Salanack would have written in junior high. Surely you can come up with some better cocaine psychosis nightmare imagery than that."

Terry giggled at this.

"Well, the snakes are *electric*," he said proudly.

ON OUR BUILDING'S ROOFTOP at midnight the shadows were running scared, driven crazy by a nearby Dunkin' Donuts neon sign. Points of light moved in nonsensical patterns across the tar roof, gaudy swirls, never quite repeating their trajectory. Voices in the hallway through the iron door sounded female and

Travels and Travails of Small Minds by Daniel Falatko

drunken. Before me lay the long, low skyline of East Williamsburg. Figures on the streets moved in packs. Lights glittered in some of the apartments, others dark, like burnt out strands of Christmas lights stretching all the way to the black waters of the East River. Kellogg's Diner glowed gaudy and green, directly under a low-hanging half-moon. The BQE sliced right through the center, its endless stream of traffic leaving headlight trails over the streets below, intertwining to form an impenetrable, complex code, slivers of light dancing over billboards and half-built condominiums like electric snakes.

August 3rd

Nathan and Amy Hit a Rocky Patch

AUGUST 4th

SOLID GROUND AT MID-MORNING. Always an opposing structure, something in the way the sun glinted off the immense steel and glass façade that day, nearly blinding me as I approached, bore the mark of a monolith. Edward had told me that at one point Solid Ground had been a "shit-hole Ma and Pappi operation with roaches in the grounds." Now, as with most of the establishments in that particular section of Midtown, it had been revamped as a clean, towering business with chilly central air and John Mayer piped in at a low volume from invisible speakers. Owing to the fact that it was Saturday and that very few people actually lived in that section of town, the place was nearly empty. A bag woman was being ushered out by two teenagers in Solid Ground Tradition visors as she complained about the flies in her brain. A pair of lost-looking tourists shouted at one another in German, cameras clanking off their chests. It had been a challenging subway trip in from Brooklyn, with the train coming to a dead stop several times due to door malfunctions and backed-up train traffic ahead. Not having anything to read, I stared for a long time at an MTA sign which read, "A crowded train is no excuse for an inappropriate touch."

Travels and Travails of Small Minds by Daniel Falatko

Dr. Behr was already seated at a table against the far wall, under a mirror which reflected him at an angle that made the brittle old man seem a giant. "Nice and hot," he grumbled, gesturing to his coffee as I slunk into a seat. Well-rested for the first time in days, it felt good to have my wits about me, my thoughts crisp and concise, completely ready to deal with whatever this final briefing held in store. I didn't even flinch when Dr. Behr, after staring into the murky vortex of his coffee for a good three minutes, suddenly jolted upright and exclaimed, "I will be so glad to get this over with!"

I had placed a folder between us on the table, opened to reveal the hand-scrawled trip itinerary, the tickets, and the deed document to the building on Avenue B I had grown so familiar with over the past several weeks. Dr. Behr looked upon the folder with disapproval. It was apparent to him that I meant business.

"I am going to state the facts as I know them," I gestured to the paperwork. "Just to make sure I have everything correct. But there are some holes I'm going to need you to fill in along the way."

He choked on a sip of coffee, the bags under his eyes more pronounced that morning than usual. Perhaps, he seemed to be pondering, I was not the correct person for this job after all.

"I am to fly out before dawn tomorrow morning. Coach class with meal served. Upon landing I will be picked up by car and taken to a 'private residence' for a meeting. I will also, apparently, be spending the night at the 'private residence' in question. This is fine by me, although obviously this leaves two questions I would appreciate you clearing up for me."

His glasses dug into the top of his nose, broken blood vessels snaking out like red spider legs across the skin. "Was I not the one who arranged this meeting?" I noted.

He sighed so hard that spittle flew from the back of his throat, reluctantly gestured for me to go on. "If you must."

August 4th

"If you could please let me know what this 'private residence' is, who I will be meeting with at said 'private residence', and what this all has to do with the building on Avenue B, more specifically Apartment 3E, I would very much appreciate it."

Dr. Behr appeared to be laughing at me, though it was hard to tell since his guffaws often came off like grimaces.

"This is why I have called you here today, for a briefing of sorts. I did not want to send you off on this trip in a confused and blinded state of mind."

"Confused, yes. Blinded, no."

"Don't think I haven't heard you and Edward conversing in whispers," his voice an all-knowing, borderline-evil tinge. "It seems the two of you have already sorted out the details. Quite impressive, really, in a bumbling sort of fashion."

I glared in his direction. Bumbling? This coming from a man who regularly tipped over his own office chair and had to be rescued from beneath the stacks of papers that enveloped him when he fell?

"It is true," Behr continued, "that I have gained a new client. Certainly an interesting individual, though not the maverick he is made out to be. And it is true that the apartment you mentioned, within the building I own which you also mentioned, holds a very special interest to this individual. The exact details are unimportant and, to be honest, rather baffling. But the fact remains that a very good deal is on the table. You will be meeting with this individual at the headquarters of the Society he represents, where you will present to him this paper."

Dr. Behr handed me a document so yellowed, so completely ancient, it resembled the *Declaration of Independence*. I didn't study it for too long before sliding it in with the other papers on the table, but from a glance it looked like a lease agreement for Apartment 3E, only, instead of "Lease," it said "Ownership."

"What about Ca..." I caught myself, not wanting the old geezer to know I had interacted with Cally. "What about the current resident of Apartment 3E?"

Travels and Travails of Small Minds by Daniel Falatko

He stared at his hands for what seemed an eternity, nose hairs bristling with every breath.

"The Resident in question has nothing to do with your mission." A blunt warning, his voice so guttural it sounded as if his vocal chords were shredded. "Thank you for checking the mailbox. I will handle the Resident from here."

I longed to ask him how he planned on evicting a legal, rent-controlled tenant from her apartment for absolutely no reason, but held back when I noticed the darkness breeding in his scowl. The old man was demented. There was no denying this. No matter how flippant I had managed to be with him over the past couple days, still he scared me.

"Next on the itinerary I will be traveling to Stiltonfordshire to meet with another individual. I take it this will be your friend, Dr. Sneil? Also, the trip is scheduled for a full fifteen days. The itinerary only covers three days. What happens over the remaining days? Is this down time? Time to hit the pub?"

Behind the lenses his eyes appeared made of glass, calm and still and grey, staring me down with insect-like precision.

"Once again I must let you know that I am aware of all whisperings amongst my staff. It seems that the two of you have figured out the identity of my true friend and colleague, the esteemed Dr. Sneil, formerly of Oxford University. Good work, though I am perplexed as to why this was such a revelation. Dr. Sneil's identity was never a secret. You could have simply asked me."

He patted my hand which was shaking on the table, his skin so rough I nearly cried out in pain.

"Whatever the case, you will be meeting the mysterious Dr. Sneil at Stiltonfordshire to hand to him the payment you have received from the Society. As I said, Dr. Sneil is a trusted friend who will see to it that the money finds its way to the proper account in the proper increments."

"Why can't I bring the payment back on my own?"

August 4th

"Why can't you?" he smiled at me, his gums red and black. "I am not very familiar with air travel, though I would assume certain suspicions would be aroused if an individual were to attempt to board a flight carrying $300,000 in cash. This is why you will be meeting with Dr. Sneil. Besides, it was Dr. Sneil himself who made this particular contact and sparked this deal into motion. He will, of course, be receiving a cut of the proceeds which he can conveniently take right off the top."

"Why does it have to be in cash?"

Dr. Behr flinched as if someone had swung a hammer at his face, missing by inches.

"There are certain obstacles." He viciously cleared his throat. "Certain obstacles that make the exchange of cash much more convenient in this instance. If this were not a cash transaction, you would not be needed."

"Fair enough. What about the unfilled days on the itinerary? No pub time?"

The German tourists had excited Solid Ground and were having a loud argument in the blazing sunshine outside, their voices garbled through the heavy glass window.

"Those days are a window, Nathan. A window during which you will oversee that the money is taken care of properly. You will see to it that Dr. Sneil takes his cut, thirty thousand dollars, which unfortunately for him the exchange rate will not favor. You will see to it that the rest is wire-transferred, over the course of twelve days, into my account by Dr. Sneil from his personal bank. The transfers must be spaced out over twelve days at $22,500 each."

I had been taking notes, an action that seemed to agitate Dr. Behr tremendously.

"One last thing." I looked up from the notebook. "If Dr. Sneil is such a good friend and outstanding individual, then why don't you trust him to complete these transfers without me looking over his shoulder?"

Travels and Travails of Small Minds by Daniel Falatko

He exhaled loudly, obviously relieved that this was the last of my questions.

"Dr. Sneil is indeed a trust-worthy and upstanding individual, as well as one of my dearest friends. He is, like me, getting on in years. As a matter of fact, Dr. Sneil may be older than I am. At this age one begins to tune out the finer details. This is why I will soon need someone looking over my own shoulder." Thankfully, he did not gesture in my direction. "You will simply be there to oversee that the handoff of his payment and my series of deposits run smoothly. There is nothing specific that you will need to do. Your presence alone will be enough. There is very little thought or action required. I'm sure you will do a fine job. And I thank you for it."

A slap in the face if I'd ever heard one; nonetheless, it didn't sting that badly, my brain preoccupied by an array of intricate suspicions.

"A better question would be: Why do I trust you?" Dr. Behr made a grand, sweeping gesture in my direction, in the process knocking his coffee clear off the table, dark steaming liquid streaking across the floor. Immediately, a very loud voice came over an overhead loudspeaker, "Jerome to the front!" A sullen man in sweatpants, carrying a mop, appeared. For some reason I nodded to him and he just scowled. Dr. Behr ignored the situation completely.

"Why do you trust me?" I replied but couldn't help yawning.

Already on his feet, Dr. Behr was zipping up his trademark windbreaker. He fastened two Velcro overlaps and made sure his fanny pack was in place. Bewildered, I remained seated. Dr. Behr began shuffling for the door. With a sigh, I rose to follow.

"Get some rest tonight," he said without turning around, somehow sensing that I had moved behind him. "Have a safe flight. Maneuver through the proper dimensions. I will certainly be in touch along the way."

"But how do you know you can trust me, Dr. Behr?"

August 4th

Out on the street now. Intense traffic but nobody on the sidewalks. Another hot morning, steam already rising from the pavement, the street signs appearing twisted, melted, from the heat of the previous days.

"Please call me Ronald," he bowed to me before moving away at what was for him a fast pace, leaving me standing in the doorway of the Solid Ground.

PHONING EDWARD while heading toward the subway, passing the German tourists now engaged in a full-on brawl in the middle of the street, the woman hitting him about the head and neck with her fists, swinging wildly while he tried to push her away, their cameras clanging off one another, I realized by the second ring that it was a little early to be calling Edward on a Saturday. He picked up just as I was about to click the phone shut, gruff voice announcing himself with a "What the fuck? Who the fuck?"

"Sorry to call so early but I wanted you to know that I am now officially on first name terms with our boss."

Long pause, the sounds of sheets brushing over the receiver and a clanking noise that could have been an empty bottle of wine knocked off a nightstand. Michael's voice in the background, equally gruff, whining, "That better not be some little trick, Edward. I'll track down that guy from Staples in a heartbeat."

"I'm going to go back to sleep and pretend what you just said was nothing more than a nightmare."

Which was just as well since I was entering the underground. A respectable-looking woman was shouting "Don't fuck with me!" at the attendant, who was imploring her not to use cuss words in his presence. Safely on the 6 Train, I remained standing even though every seat in the car was open. The air conditioning was blasting and, being all alone, I thanked the cool air out

Travels and Travails of Small Minds by Daniel Falatko

loud. Cautiously, I checked the text message I had received that morning once again, finally a communication from Planet Amy. UNION SQUARE AT NOON.

AN HOUR-AND-A-HALF EARLY, there was nothing to do but sit. The change-begging acoustic guitar pickers and saxophone men had not emerged as of yet into the morning heat. Scattered homeless folks passed the time listening to radios or rocking back-and-forth alone on the benches or in the grass under trees. People running, shirtless men in short shorts and gelled hair. Women in spandex swinging small blue dumbbells. A low haze hung over the park, just above the tree line, giving the acres a boxed-in, stifling feel. I had no reading material. No headphones. No coffee. No thoughts.

It was clear that things were over with Amy the very second she entered my line of vision that morning, Express boots and hair askew, hugging herself as she stepped over debris from a trash can, Starbucks cups and mini-Martel bottles, that had fallen or been pushed over the night before. She looked guilty, the lines under her eyes that she usually covered with makeup left exposed.

"God, it's hot as a bitch out here." She patted the top of her head, not sitting down, staring longingly toward the GNC on Madison. "You look horrible, darling. And not in a cool French way."

I told her that she looked horrible as well. She shrugged this off, still refusing to look at me. A man in an orange jumpsuit rolled by on a golf cart, stopped and picked up two dead pigeons, placing them in a heavy black bag before rolling on.

"I may as well have slept on this bench," I laughed, not wanting to sound bitter. "My apartment is now psychedelic due to a rogue Dunkin Donuts sign. Plus my neighbor hasn't slept in nine days and thinks his veins have turned into snakes."

Amy finally sat down, laughing, a rim of dirt along the bottom of her white skirt.

"I'm sorry to laugh at your plight, Nate, but if you're trying to pick a fight here, if you're trying to make me feel guilty for leaving you alone in your time of need and blah blah, then please don't. Remember that we all create our own realities. You've created your wacky reality and it doesn't have to mesh with mine."

The temptation to just get up and walk away was nearly overwhelming, but it was just too hot. My mind was off in England, cold rainy England, where men wear plaid scarves in July.

"I would much rather be amongst the still lifes."

Heavy sigh from Amy. Pained. Annoyed. Not buying it for a second. Her knee, which usually bumped against mine from time-to-time whenever we would sit next to one another, remained still.

"Not to be nit-picky, kid, but I'm just not willing to deal with it. Not just you, but all of it. All of humanity. I like when people are focused and know where they're going and what steps it will take them to get there. So why have I never, and I mean ever, come across a single member of this species who is doing anything other than drifting, getting by, taking up space? And the eyes! Yes, the eyes. Always roving. Always wandering. Always scoping out the surrounding nooks and crannies for something more promising. They never settle. They never just resign. Nathan, you are no different. And don't try to give me any bullshit about trying to find your place or being confused. This lovable wayward act you inhabit so well. You're just one in a long line."

I found myself nodding at most of the things she said. Her tirade sounded rehearsed, as if she had written it out and spent hours pacing around her apartment memorizing the lines, practicing in front of a mirror, making notes and taking out dialogue. But it did sound sincere. There was truly no way to respond. She had cut off all of my verbal escape routes, already sliced into any excuse I could think of.

"Wow, you really have a lot to say," she taunted me. "So convincing in your counter-debate. Perhaps I had you all wrong. There really *is* a lot of substance there." She sat upright on the bench, tapping a finger against her thigh impatiently. I was watching a 300-pound jogger struggle past, oozing large squirts of sweat onto the paved trail.

"Last night was great without you," she quipped.

Ok, now she was just being mean.

"Is all this about that 'walls wet with tears' girl?" I spoke to the side of her head, trying to engage her to look at me. "I totally wasn't checking her out. You're going to ditch me over some Molly-fried Bushwick artist commune girl?"

She laughed, a low-volume giggle before rapidly blossoming into full-on hysterics. I joined her, both of us laughing until we were red in the face, disturbing the sleep of a woman with sweatpants wrapped around her head as a makeshift turban on the next bench over.

There was a hand on my wrist, moving up my arm, stroking my shoulder compassionately.

"I really do hope you have a good time in England, Nathan. I felt real bad for kind of raining on your parade there. But you really do need to quit that wacky-ass job sooner than later, regardless of this new international perk. Seriously, when you get back, you really should work on getting your head together. Nothing major, just keep it steady. You dart all over the place."

I tried to take her hand in mine but was rejected with a smile and a shake of the head.

"You've been the best one so far," she said, examining my face. "That isn't saying much, of course, but it's true."

For a second it seemed like she was going to lean in and kiss me, potentially on the lips, which seemed more exciting now that we were broken up than it would have if we weren't.

August 4th

Instead, she just pushed her Apple headphones onto her ears and rose from the bench, not looking back as she walked purposefully north.

I SAT FOR AWHILE in the rapidly increasing heat. I felt empty, though not in any type of desolate or forlorn way. Just a vague sense of defeat and a restlessness. I started walking but got distracted by a stand hawking tiny turtles in large glass domes, the turtles trying their best to leap out of the domes and onto the street. "Only about seven of the little fuckers a day" the guy let me know when I asked him if the turtles ever succeeded in escaping. The thought crossed my mind to ride in the air-conditioned subway trains all day long, up-and-down the island, though this plan seemed to mesh a little too closely with the daily routine of a common derelict. The promise of pizza lured me into a parlor just off the park on 14th, the plain slice's nutrients and the air conditioning of the establishment restoring most of my energy, which had been thoroughly sapped by the twin-sensory assaults of the Dr. Behr meeting and the surprise Amy breakup. Suddenly, the day stretched out before me in a promising fashion. There were no obligations and nobody to answer to. I was footloose and fancy free and set loose on the streets.

The East Village, which was well within walking distance, seemed a natural place to gravitate to that early afternoon. By the time I reached 1st Avenue I was thinking of Cally, the way her cheeks creased when she smiled in the manner of a much older individual. Those creases suggested experience, nights fraught with worry and battles won the hard way. Moving onto Avenue A, a man with waist-length hair tied back behind a yellow bandanna and heavy black eyeliner asked me what day it was. "Oh man!" he exclaimed when I let him know that it was Saturday. He jumped

Travels and Travails of Small Minds by Daniel Falatko

onto a rickety old Vespa parked on the sidewalk at A and 9th and roared off onto the traffic-less street.

Tompkins Square. Bright sunshine and gymnastics majors doing incredible splits and human formations on the grass. Teen squatters drank beer from 44 oz. cans, some allowing their dogs with chain mail collars to have a sip as well. Some sort of jazz festival was taking place to the East, annoying sax scales carrying like the far-off honking of car horns. I paused for a moment and listened as a man in a green camouflage shirt passionately strummed a ukulele. "Send in the pink drones!" he kept screeching. "Send in the pink droooooooones!" Exiting the park by the huge Joe Strummer mural on the side of Niagara, I found myself pulled, as if by radar, in the direction of Avenue B.

I started off down 7th, determined to figure out just what it was about this building that would rouse the attention and deep pockets of the Thomas J. Salanack Society. Cutting onto Avenue B, I noticed a figure exiting the building and almost broke my ankles coming to a dead stop. Squinting, the figure appeared far too slow, too stooped, to be just your average individual. Cautiously, I picked up the pace while keeping a close eye on the figure as it headed in the other direction. The shuffling gait and abject lack of speed, combined with the posture and overall decrepit vibe cast by this figure could only mean one thing: Dr. Behr.

Ducking into a Spanish convenience store, I purchased a red, white, and blue popsicle, taking my time unwrapping the treat and loitering in the doorway until a small man carrying a garden hoe threatened to whack me in the legs with it if I didn't move out of his way. Dr. Behr had barely made it half-a-block. For what seemed like hours, I watched from my hiding place next to a conspicuously empty trash can until he finally vanished around the corner.

The outer façade of the structure had taken on a majestic reputation in my mind, this normal run-down tenement building elevated to the status of a Temple. Great mysteries lurked behind those chipped red bricks. Valuable artifacts. I was looking for side door, a cellar grate, anywhere that would provide alternate access to the hallways of the building. There seemed to be no way to penetrate the walls of the fortress other than the front door, which was far too dangerous. Content to stare at the side of the building, trying to pinpoint which apartment was 3E, I shielded my eyes from the sun. Someone was blasting an old Lemonheads album from inside. Most of the blinds were closed. An air conditioner spit black water from above.

"Are you serious?" a voice asked me, half irate, half playful, from somewhere up above. "Is this the point where I will need to call in the cops? You tell me. I've never been stalked before."

Leaning out a window, her long hair falling out before her, Cally was wearing what appeared to be tank top, her shoulders slim, a cell phone in her hand. I was overjoyed to see her.

"It isn't what it looks like." I held my hands in the air as if she had a gun on me. "I was just taking a walk."

She shut the window with a chintzy sound that nonetheless managed to rattle up and down the street. Not quite sure what to do, I started walking east toward the project high rises along the waterfront. Best to clear the scene before the coppers arrived. The projects seemed the easiest place to vanish for several hours. I hadn't even made it across the street before Cally was calling out to me.

"Nathan!" The sound of her voice, the way it stretched my name into two distinct syllables, was quite appealing. "Hey, come back. I was joking about the cops. At least don't run *that* way. They'll shoot you over there."

I was so eager to cross back that I was nearly hit by a white van in the process.

"Jesus, take it easy." She was holding her hand over her mouth as I approached. "Didn't yo' momma' ever tell you to look both ways when crossin' da' damn street, fool?"

"You look nice today," I told her. "Your hair is doing that thing."

Travels and Travails of Small Minds by Daniel Falatko

Looking herself over, she shot me a bemused look. "You mean the 'not showered and sweaty' look? Yea, real sexy. Although you seem to pull it off rather well. So tell me, what's the secret for developing the type of nerve it takes to blatantly hit on the person you and your dickbag boss are trying to have evicted from her apartment for no reason at all?"

"I want you to know that I had no part in today's operation." I placed my hand on an imaginary bible as if under oath. "I swear. We did meet earlier, although that was in Midtown at this horrible place that makes Starbucks seem like a Ma and Pa store, and there was absolutely no discussion about visiting here. I met a friend in Union Square and decided to take a walk. That's when I saw him coming out of here. And yes, I was scoping out the building. You caught me. But I'm just curious what it is about this place, about your apartment, that has everyone so riled up."

"Believe me. There is absolutely no reason for anyone to get riled up about my apartment. It's cramped, dirty, hot, and crumbling. There isn't even a closet. It *is* a fucking closet. And it just seems strange that you would show up here literally two minutes after Dr. Death departed. It feels like a harassment campaign. A blitz."

I was watching her face, her mouth, the way she looked in both directions before swearing.

"I was as surprised as you to see him. As a matter of fact, I'm afraid he's still around. What if he's watching? If he sees me talking to you, I would lose my job or at least have my England privileges revoked."

The thought of Dr. Behr watching us from behind some corner or tree proved so horrifying that I moved my hands up to shield my face, then pulled the neck of my t-shirt over my mouth so my lips couldn't be read. She watched me the entire time with a bemused look which had softened since I'd last seen her outside the coffee shop the previous day, a warmth to her cheeks as she gave me an exacerbated shake of the head.

"Come on up," she sighed, shaking her head. "God, you are such a trip."

August 4th

The stairway was so narrow it was impossible to imagine a bed frame, let alone a couch, fitting through the corridor, as dusty and streaked as the floors in Dr. Behr's office, so steep that I had to flex my toes just to stay on the individual stairs. Though I was struggling, ahead of me Cally ascended fluidly and with little difficulty. I cried out in fear when I lost sight of her. She came back down to take me by the wrist and literally pull me onto the top landing.

"Try doing this drunk," she said. "Word amongst the old school residents is that the place is haunted by the ghosts of tenement dwellers of the past who lost their footing in the dark."

As the apartment door opened, I half expected to behold a glass case with the original manuscript for some classic Salanack novel on display, backlit by halogen lamps, behind shatterproof glass. Or perhaps she had the mummified body of the old writer laid out in her living room, in a cryogenic chamber, his bloated hands and still growing fingernails folded solemnly over his body. Instead, I was greeted with a sparse and fairly shabby one-bedroom with an ancient paint job and scuffed hardwood with visible splinters that creaked with every shift of the foot. There was a cool-looking old radio, a re-upholstered couch, and a vase of flowers on a coffee table.

"Has my boss been in here?"

Cally had vanished for a second, came back in offering a glass of water. There wasn't a single point in the apartment where you couldn't reach out and place each hand upon the opposite walls.

"You really think he could get up those stairs?" Her eyes bugged out in a cute way, full of life and venom. "We spoke in the hall. He basically told me that I'm evicted as of two weeks from now. I couldn't really understand why. Dude mumbles quite a bit."

"Did he give you any papers? Did you sign anything?"

She asked me why I didn't know any of this already, being an employee of the man and all. "He tried to hand me something, but I refused it."

Travels and Travails of Small Minds by Daniel Falatko

"So what are you going to do?" I noticed that the ceiling was waterlogged in the corner of the room, wet streaks causing cracks to spread out like busted windshield. "You do realize that the ceiling is going to come down soon, right?"

"You try getting that asshole to fix something." She took my shoulders and playfully spun me to face the offending corner, pushing me gently toward it. "Finally I have someone from the landlord's here. Now fix it! Why do you think I brought you up here?"

"I'm not a handyman. I'm a personal assistant. Second in command, to be exact."

"Out of how many? Two?" She spun me back around to face her like a life-size doll. "I'm not going anywhere. That's what I'm going to do. I'll file a complaint with the tenants association and just kick back and watch you guys take a hit. I have a rent control agreement and lease on this apartment. I've done nothing to violate the terms of this lease. I'm golden."

From Cally's lone living room window could be seen, if you squinted real hard and focused on the point between a new Sovereign Bank and a white building with a huge naked Jesus mural painted on the side, the very edge of Tompkins Square Park.

"Have a seat," I said. "You're making me nervous. Don't stand by the window. He'll see you."

She motioned to the strangely upholstered couch, what looked like the patterns in those old silk rocker shirts you see on Mick Jagger or Jimmy Page in images from the 60s, dragons and Japanese flowers. She sat down as well, our knees almost touching.

"Why does the old man want me out of this apartment so bad? You have to at least have an idea. He hasn't been bothering anyone else in the building."

A framed black and white print of Anna Karina hung a little too high on the opposite wall, lips glossy and face aglow, her

August 4th

eyes fixed on the waterlogged part of the ceiling. I kept looking back to this print, using it to keep my bearings, as I told her the entire story. I told her of the blue folder, the looming trip to England, and the Thomas J. Salanack Society. I told her what I knew of Dr. Behr's history, of the Oxford Man, of the apparent large sum of money on the table for them both. Cally mostly remained silent, every now and again attempting to interject or offer an aside, though these efforts were plowed over by my onslaught of strange facts and suspicions. She gasped at appropriate moments and her green eyes grew wide, covering her mouth in horror whenever any particularly sinister point was touched upon.

"You managed to keep a straight face while relating all of that," she said as she studied my forehead, my eyes, with what I hoped to be compassion but seemed far too clinical. Her knees touched mine once again, lingering for a moment, quizzical. "And nobody would even bother making that up, much less try to pass it off as a true story. So I guess it must be true. Jesus."

I nodded, studying the way her shoulders slouched in her sitting posture. She was looking around the nearly empty room with a vague sense of panic.

"What is it about this apartment that could be so valuable to the crazy beatnik fanatic?" I questioned, more to myself than her.

She gazed around the apartment, shrugging her shoulders. "I've never even read anything by that dude." She bit her lower lip and blew a puff of air that made her bangs jump up. "Perhaps they want the apartment itself."

For a second, it seemed as if she was going to place her head on my shoulder or perhaps hook her arm around mine. Instead, she kicked off her sandals and stepped into the pair of Converse she had been wearing the previous day, which had been resting on the floor next to the couch. She walked toward the door, motioning for me to follow.

"Let's go to the park," she said.

Travels and Travails of Small Minds by Daniel Falatko

"**I'VE BEEN PARK-HOPPING TODAY,**" I told her as we sat in a sliver of shade by Avenue A. "Did Union Square earlier. Got dumped."

She nodded, lost in what seemed to be a lively interior monologue. "NYC parks suck these days. You can't even get raped or killed anymore."

"True dat'."

"Sorry you got dumped," she smiled. "And I'm very sorry you only have the person you're stalking to turn to in this tough time."

I shrugged.

"I've lived here for five years," her voice sounded sad. "The apartment was my uncle's. Uncle Jeffrey was killed in San Francisco trying to cross the street. He was there for some conference. Uncle Jeffrey was in medical publishing. It was a moped that hit him. One of the only known cases of a pedestrian being killed by a moped. We could never understand it. Uncle Jeffrey was big and built. He left the apartment lease to my parents, who gave it to me since I'd always wanted to live here. Best present I've ever received. Thanks, Uncle Jeff!" She raised a hand to the sky. "Two hundred dollars rent. That's what I pay for that fucker. Your average one bedroom in this hood now goes for twenty five hundred. Next year mine shoots to two twenty."

"If I were Dr. Behr, I'd want you out for that reason alone. Not some beatnik wild goose chase."

"Things were real good for a real long time." She was looking off to the point where Avenue B intersected with 7th Street. "Jonathan was living with me, playing in this band that kept getting mentioned on *Brooklyn Vegan* and even the *Times* even though I can't seem to remember them playing all that often. Big In Belgium? Ever heard of them? That name was ironic since they never had a record out there. Anyway, I was working at Penguin and loved it. Things were definitely good."

"Then you sold his record collection."

She slapped me very hard on the shoulder, causing me to roll onto the grass.

"That was YOU! Jesus, you really are a little stalker. Why am I even sitting here with you? You and your whole operation are really sick!"

"I've told you before, it's my job. I didn't even know you then. But I really like you and I'm on your side now. Even though I'm getting paid by the other side, I'm working for you too. A double agent."

She pulled me back into a sitting position.

"Hey man, you would sell his record collection too if he left you for some 22-year-old Greenpoint girl with great legs and a loft. Turns out he was banging her the whole time, too. Along with others, I'm sure. Besides, I needed the money. Penguin laid off all their in-house copy editors. I'm still living off that money. What will I do when it runs out? Who the fuck knows? None of the publishing companies need copy editors anymore. They either outsource to compositors in India or use freelancers who work for chump change and no benefits. It's the only thing I'm qualified to do. It sucks."

"You could always come work for Dr. Behr. I could probably get you in. He's already impressed with you. I can tell."

She glared at me, not amused. A laser beam of sunshine broke through the tree above us, streaking across her face, making her appear slightly evil.

"I'm genuinely sorry to hear that the copy editing dried up." I shielded my eyes from the sun. "That must have been some vinyl collection for you to be living off of it for so long."

"It was magnificent." She sounded very far away, as if shouting from a different room in an old, empty house. "You know, in all those years running spell checks on horrible mystery novellas about Jackie O imposters, I tried to tell myself that I should be miserable, that this was soulless work on soulless product, but the truth is I loved it. I never woke up with a feeling

Travels and Travails of Small Minds by Daniel Falatko

of dread about going to work. So when the carpet was pulled out from under my feet, it just hit me really hard. There's nothing to do. Apply for jobs all day. Get coffee. I'm one of those people you see on the street mid-day and wonder why they aren't at work. I'm sensing a line on the horizon and I don't want to cross it."

A large mutt chased two low-flying pigeons past the place we were sitting. "Lucifer, get back here!" a voice was calling.

"I can't lose that apartment," she told me, stone-faced. "It's the only thing I have. There'd be nowhere to go."

I nodded, thinking hard.

"It worries me. Even though my paperwork is in order and there is no legal way he can kick me out," she gulped. "I get the feeling he's prepared to resort to illegal means. It seems like there's enough money involved here that it would be worth it to him. He's already had you raid my mailbox. He's stopping by here in person. That apartment certainly isn't anything special, but I'll dig in my nails and cling to it for dear life."

She exhaled, blowing a strand of hair off the side of her face. Catching me looking at her, she held my gaze and I didn't look away, the two of us locked in an uncomfortable test of wills.

"Even sadder is the fact that the only person I can talk about this is the person working for those attempting to have me evicted. How do I know that everything I'm saying to you won't be related back to him verbatim?"

She sprung at me with a surprising agility for her frail frame, catching me completely off guard, and started patting down my chest and sides. I managed to get a hold of both of her hands and hold them still. "What the hell are you doing, Cally?"

"Making sure you aren't wearing a wire." She was dead serious, her eyes slits. "Nice pecs, by the way."

People were staring. I released my grip. She stood, massaging her wrists.

"Well, as always, it's been strange. Look, this whole thing just has me far too bugged-out and paranoid. I need to go lie down. Sorry to assault you." I propped myself up on my elbows, looking up at her. She appeared quite fragile standing there in the shade of the tree, biting her upper lip in worry. She was slump-shouldered, staring at the ground. The bottoms of her jeans were frayed in a natural way, shoes kicking at the grass.

"You will not be evicted from Apartment 3E," I assured her. "I'm the one on this assignment. And I can mess up an assignment like no other."

She regarded me, unhooking her lip from her teeth.

"This isn't going to come out like much of a compliment," she smiled. "But messing up an assignment seems like something you'd be extremely good at."

"Everyone has to be good at something," I told her.

Two pigeons, the same ones that Lucifer had chased earlier, came waddling by on their stick legs, this time being chased by a woman in a neon sweatshirt weighed down by two enormous plastic bags filled with empty cans.

"Thank you." She sat back down and patted my knee, her face flushed. "I'm not sure why you're doing it, but I'd like to think it comes from a place of at least semi-genuine compassion. And just how, may I ask, do you plan on messing up this whole thing?"

Before I could answer or even begin to ponder the question, she leaned in and planted a kiss on the side of my lips. I turned to her, trying to hold her lips on mine, parting them slightly and breathing in her breath. She put the tip of her nose against mine and looked straight into my rapidly blinking eyes.

"I'll figure something out."

She rose to her feet, the joints in her knees cracking audibly, and offered a hand to pull me up with her.

"So we're really on the same side now?"

My feet and lower legs were asleep, tingling as if pulsed with electric current.

"I've never been on any other."

Travels and Travails of Small Minds by Daniel Falatko

NIGHT TIME IN THE CHELSEA DISTRICT. I was slightly late and very tired, concerned about the early hour of the next day's journey. Everything seemed to be at loose ends. Nothing was organized. I had no focus or plan. Pausing outside the floor-to-ceiling windows of the too-brightly-lit restaurant where Edward had ordered me to meet him at eight, I closed my eyes and planted both feet on the ground in hopes of losing the spinning feeling which had permeated my senses since leaving Cally's in search of a cab uptown. It was a curious form of nausea, a feeling of being kicked around through a series of events and conspiracies like a hacky sack at a drum circle. A distinct lack of control.

Edward was beckoning to me from a table by the window, waving a long piece of bread to get my attention.

"You look horrible," he informed me after I had maneuvered my way past a variety of obstacles, including a woman at one of the tables with peacock feathers jutting from her hair which almost poked my eyeballs out when she threw her head back to laugh. A completely stoned waitress approached our table bearing a pitcher of water so clear it seemed to magnify her black dress.

I was thinking of the owl. A large brass bust in the corner of Cally's room over which she had draped several silk scarves ala Steven Tyler, with large eyes made out of blue glass buttons. Something seemed a bit off with the Owl's stare, borderline unhinged, and I had asked her how she could sleep knowing it was staring at her in the dark. "His name is Freddie the Owl," she had explained, stooping to pat the brown head of the bust. "He watches over me in the night."

Edward was asking me what I had done that day. "Other than awakening me from a blissful Saturday morning sleep to brag about being some old fuck's number one sidekick." Menus had been placed before us but we had not bothered to touch them.

"I had a briefing with the old fuck in question at Solid Ground. He looked like he had spent the night in a blender or a particularly savage wind tunnel. He gave me the rundown on the assignment. Shady shit. I'm meeting with the Salanack Society wacko first and then staying in one of his guest rooms. He'll be sliding me a huge amount of cash for the borderline-illegal ownership of Apartment 3E. Then I have to run it to Sneil, who naturally gets a cut of the money, then have to hold his hand while he puts it in an account for the Behr Man. Oh, and I think they are going to kidnap or kill the current resident of the apartment, who I happen to sort of be in love with, or at least get real scary with her. Behr even visited her in person today. She has an airtight rent controlled lease. You filed for it five years ago. You even showed her around the place when she inherited it."

Smirking and shaking his head, Edward slumped in his seat.

He let out a slow-rolling demented cackle which didn't faze the waitress who was trying to get our order. "What ever happened to just pushing paper?" he asked her, her flawless face remaining placid, neutral. "Just collecting a paycheck and going home? All this intrigue! All this drama! Where will it end?"

Beaming, the waitress started reading off the specials.

WE HAD DONE SOME RESEARCH that afternoon. Cally's laptop was ancient and very large. Dust flew from the keypad as she typed, looking up Tommy Salanack. We learned many things that we would rather not have known, anal heroin suppositories and sex with co-joined twins, jars of vomit and fisting circles, though nowhere on any of the sites was there listed anything about Cally's building. From what we could determine, the man had lived in various apartments throughout the city during his several New York periods, all on the Lower East Side. The addresses did not match Cally's. We scoured the apartment, knocking on walls, unscrewing electrical outlets, reaching behind sinks and toilets, crawling on our knees the entire 350 square feet looking for hidden Salanack mementos. At one point Cally had thought she found a false bottom in one of the cabinets in the tiny kitchen. We knocked out the bottom of the cabinet with a hammer but only found the skull of a mouse.

"DID THE TWO OF YOU KISS AND HUG when you parted?" Edward was referring to Dr. Behr and I, munching distractedly on a piece of bread. "Did the old perv at least cop a feel? But then again, why be into you when there's much more obvious beauty close at hand?" He gestured to himself.

"My dearest Amy dumped me cold today," I informed him. "I'm not sure how I feel about it yet."

He smiled and nodded, as if this was something he had been expecting.

"Well, if you need someone to talk to," he said in an assuring tone. "I'll give you Michael's number. He's very good at sympathy and advice. I, however, am not."

I placed a hand over my heart.

"I appreciate that you're always there for me."

He raised his glass.

"I had a close call this afternoon." I downed half a Heineken in one fast gulp. "I went to snoop around the Salanack building and, lo and behold, there was a grey rat shuffling about. I had to hide in a corner store for half-an-hour listening to some guy rattle off 138 lottery number combinations in Spanish."

Edward stroked his chin, nodding.

August 4th

"So you caught him stalking while you were also stalking?"

"Basically."

His eyes gleamed with wicked, pure mischief. "And what, may I ask, were you doing down there in Alphabet Town this morning? That's a little bit out of your way, isn't it? The L line runs along 14th Street, does it not? You must have been taking the long way home, a leisurely stroll through the historic East Village. And I'm sure it had absolutely nothing to do with a certain soon-to-be-evicted tenant with way cool bangs and a great ass, even by my strict standards."

"I was working. It was for work. Investigating the building."

"Uh huh," he finished his drink, started waving his glass in the air for another. "I'm sure your mind was on work, having just been savagely dumped for no clear reason. The fact that the one you pursue in this instance happens to be the person you are actively working to evict from her beloved, rent controlled flat speaks volumes for your current mental state."

A plate of food had been placed before me at some point. I was pretty sure they had mixed up our orders, that Edward was currently digging into my plate, but decided not to say anything.

"We scoured the apartment for clues. We left no rotten wood beam unturned. We were doing research."

"I'm sure you researched her thoroughly." Edward was slopping his food like usual.

"I completely adore her, Edward."

He choked on a sip of the drink the waitress had hesitantly re-filled.

"Her name is Cally."

With a dismissive wave of the hand, Edward indicated that he was growing bored with this line of conversation.

"Just don't forget that your relationship will be short lived once you successfully play a role in having her kicked out onto the street. See how much you adore visiting her in a homeless shelter."

Travels and Travails of Small Minds by Daniel Falatko

THE LIGHT IN ALPHABET CITY is a different kind of illumination, grainy and thin even on the brightest of days. Lingering air particles left over from years of abject poverty and junkies, no matter how much they attempt to clean up the neighborhood, settle over every surface, shielding the light. From Cally's windows the buildings looked grey, the streets laid out in nonsensical grids, the people on the sidewalks directionless and sad. Cally's lips felt tentative, undecided, on the verge of drawing away. I held her face to mine, our eyes locked, our breath mixed, running my lips over her cheeks, her jaw line, down onto her neck, her collarbones, coming up to find her head thrown back and her cheeks flushed. With a sigh she fell back and pulled me on top of her, her fingers crumpling up the back of my shirt. The owl watched us from the corner, its blazing blue eyes seeming alarmed, and I tried to put it out of my mind.

"CALLY WILL NOT BE EVICTED." I finished my Heineken, didn't signal for another. "I'm going to blow the mission. We're on the same side."

Edward rubbed his hands together as if relishing a plot twist in *Nip/Tuck*.

"Ok, now this is getting good. Please enlighten me as to how you're going to mess up this most simple of missions? Even you may not be able to blow this one. Everything appears to be set and in place. You're just babysitting."

"I'll think of something. I really will."

He nodded, smirking.

"And to think the old man trusts you." He shook his head. "To think he chose you over me for this mission. I wouldn't have started double-dealing with some girl with great bangs. He made the wrong choice. I knew it."

"What he did," I pushed the plate aside, not hungry in the least. "Was underestimate me."

"I'm just worried."

"I'll be fine."

"I know you." He smiled and placed his hand on my shoulder, ignoring the buzzing of his phone on the surface of the table. "You won't be fine."

NAKED, CALLY APPEARED TO GLOW in the hazy light, her body a lot smaller than it had seemed in her baggy tank top. We kissed hard, sucking on each other's tongues, side-by-side and running our hands over each other's thighs and shoulders. It took me a deliberately long time to work my hands down her body, running fingers down her spine, the small of her back, over her stomach. She exhaled sharply at almost the exact moment I finally slid my hand between her legs and I knew she had just come. I needed to taste her, worked my way down her torso with my mouth and tongue, lingering over her nipples, down across her stomach, looking up to make sure it was ok. Her legs started squirming and I had to hold them steady in order to stay in place. It seemed like hours, her moisture on my lips, dripping down onto my chin before drying, savoring the taste, her hands massaging the top of my head. I was waiting for that same sharp exhale to signal again, chasing it, thinking it was almost there several times but losing it. Like always, it finally came when I least expected.

Exhausted, my jaw aching, she pulled me to her and held me against her until we both stopped shaking.

Travels and Travails of Small Minds by Daniel Falatko

"HOW ARE WE DOING HERE, BOYS?" The stoned waitress's voice resonated in a lobotomized monotone. "Will you be wanting to see the dessert menu?"

"I don't know about him, but I'm doing very well." Edward beamed at her, extending his arms into a "Ta Da!" pose. "Because I am fucking out of here, baby!"

Expressionless, the waitress turned to me for help. I told her that everything was indeed ok and that we would not need to be seeing the dessert menu. Check please and she was gone.

"What are you talking about, you crazy fuck?"

He was still grinning like a mental patient, his teeth bleached so white they momentarily blinded me.

"I'm fucking out! Gone! History! I got another job! At Michael's office. The boy finally came through on something. It only took him six years, of course, but still I've never felt more free!"

His bliss was infectious, the excitement cascading into me as well.

"No way! You sneaky fuck! Have you told the Crypt Keeper yet? He may be forced to show some emotion on this one. You're the only one whose name he remembers at all times, and that's including his mother."

He extended his glass and I clicked my empty one against it.

"He knew he was driving me away the second he gave you that assignment." He shook his head sadly, as if he still couldn't get his head around it. "I've been pushing papers for that demented old kook for years and years and years, the only one he can truly trust, slaving away in the dust while all my friends rose in their careers with their corner offices and company car services and Christmas bonuses. So when the time finally comes to hand out an important assignment involving overseas travel, he chooses instead some young whippersnapper who goes off and sleeps with the evictee like a true idiot? No offense."

"None taken."

"So alas, the time has come for me and my beloved Ronald Behr to part. I'll probably let him know next week." Edward's eyes began to tear. "I'd be lying if I said I wouldn't miss the decrepit old dude just a little."

I got up from the table and offered a hug.

"Well, congratulations on getting out while you're still relatively young." I had to bat his hand away as he playfully reached for my ass. "I'll miss you around the office if I still have a job at Behr Properties."

He bowed to me for some reason, perfect in form like an old silent film.

"My spirit will coast forever upon the dust particles of that office." He looked like he was about to cry. I gave his shoulder a reassuring slap.

"I'm really worried about this trip, about you. Don't lose it out there. I'd like to see you again. The whole thing doesn't feel right."

"It doesn't feel right at all." I agreed with him. "But even if it all goes sideways, I'll still be just fine in the long run."

This seemed to satisfy him.

"Great, kid. Then you can get the check."

THERE IS SOMETHING INHERENTLY SAD about sex in the afternoon. Stripped of the darkness and the tantalizing option to roll over and fall asleep for six-to-eight hours once it is done, the act is laid bare in the sequence of the day. There are clothes to be put back on, conversations to partake in, chores that need accomplishing. It is a strange thing to talk about various ways to thwart your employer from collecting a large sum of money after engaging in some seriously intimate activities with a woman you are just realizing you have only known for a combined total of less than two hours.

"The fact remains," she had nuzzled her head in the crook of my shoulder, sipping the cinnamon tea she had made. "He has no legal right to kick me out of here. I shouldn't even be worried about it."

"He will." The tea made me cringe and I placed it back on the side table next to a beat-up copy of *Bright Lights, Big City*. "I do believe he's prepared to go all-the-way-illegal with this one. Whatever money that beatnik obsessive is offering must be enough to take the risk. He'll find some loophole to evict you. Or he'll just have you thrown out for no reason and take his chances with the housing committee. Maybe pay them off. Hell, Cally, he may even get ugly. The guy has some serious old age dementia going on. And I don't think he was that cool an individual back in the day when he was lucid either."

I shifted on the bed to try to elude the eyes of the owl. There was nowhere in that apartment where the owl didn't watch you.

"You don't like the tea?" She pointed accusingly at the still-full, rapidly cooling cup. "I still don't understand how you're going to mess up this mission. What is the exact plan?"

Headlight beams snaked their way across the ceiling, intersecting at odd angles with one of the light trails off from the others, forming a sharp point like a long sword.

"I have absolutely no idea what the plan is. There is no plan. I'll just blow the mission somehow and you can keep your apartment. It's as simple as that."

"I have faith in you. I'm not sure why. Dr. Behr seems to have faith in you as well. And yet here you are cavorting with the enemy."

"Exciting, isn't it?"

I forced myself to take a sip of the tea, her green eyes watching me carefully, and managed with some difficulty to force it down my throat.

"Then we'll stay here.... Just don't you dare touch that owl."

Travels and Travails of Small Minds by Daniel Falatko

"I don't feel safe here. You shouldn't either. Where do you live, Nathan?"

I bit lightly at the bottom of her earlobe.

"East WillyBurgh. My neighbor has electric snakes for veins."

Cally nodded as if this were not the least bit strange.

"Then we'll stay here." She reached for her jeans lying crumpled against the wall. "Just don't you dare touch that owl."

Saturday night on the A Train. The text from Cally read: *All clear. No Behr. Sushi?* Two girls in their 20s, both wearing leggings under black skirts and sporting horrifically angular hair patterns, were speaking loudly about the distinct lack of both "quality pills" and "quality boys" in Brooklyn and the Lower East Side. "It's getting ridiculous," one of them yawned. She nodded her head in my direction and asked of the other, "Quality?" Looking me up-and-down, her friend replied, "For a boy or a pill?"

There were hundreds of people in the street, moving in packs as I pushed past them away from Union Square, their young faces sweaty and their hair perfect as they conversed loudly or shouted across the street to other groups. The moon hung low over Stuyvesant Town, casting halos of light over each building. The flashing lights of NYPD vehicles indicated they were shutting down Tompkins Square for the night, bullhorn voices shouting orders to clear the bushes and basketball courts. A girl in a metal-studded vest, swigging from a bottle of Mad Dog 20/20, emerged from the bushes shouting, "I was built to last centuries!"

I nodded, walking fast toward Cally's.

August 4th

ONE YEAR LATER – PART THREE

THERE IS NO NEED to keep track of time when you have absolutely no obligations, no need to structure your days when all you have to do is make it through them to the next.

    The Half-Crescents are eliminated from the tournament during a match in which at least six of its members are kicked out for fighting or raking their cleats down the opposition's legs, drawing blood. During the final seconds, which take place late in one of the rapidly chilling nights, I hear a collective howl rising up in the neighborhood which at first I presume to be the wind. Then comes the sounds of things breaking, glass being shattered, masses of trampling feet. The howling turns to chanting, random banshee shrieks. The sound of metal scraping on pavement finally draws me to the window in time to witness a pack of skin-headed men in striped windbreakers dragging a small overturned car on its roof out into the middle of the street. It takes them almost 20 minutes to light the car on fire, fumbling with various lighters and kerosene concoctions, their brows furrowed in business-like concentration. The surrounding crowd, who had been chanting and cheering in a ring around the soon-to-be-crisped vehicle, eventually starts booing before moving on to other interests. By the time the car finally catches fire there

ONE YEAR LATER – PART THREE

are other cars on their backs, open fighting in the streets, bricks and rocks and bottles hitting the side of my building with dull thuds. In America this scene would inevitably be soundtracked by the ringing of dozens of car alarms. The absence of this chorus makes me feel very much alone. One of the bald arsonists is running, his leg on fire, toward The Pash's store. Within seconds his lower half is swallowed in flames, streaking out behind him as he reaches the booth and, as I can decipher from my post at the window, asks in a surprisingly calm fashion for a bottle of water. I watch as Mariska holds out her hand, demanding money, and the man points to his flaming lower body. Rolling her eyes, she hands him one of the smaller bottles, looks on passively as he rolls on the floor and douses the flames. A severely thin teenager kicks in the door and tosses a brick at the counter, bouncing off the glass right next to Mariska's head. She doesn't flinch, sticks her tongue out at the youth and flips him off.

Knocking on the store's window until it nearly shatters, I manage to get her attention and motion for her to come and hide out in my apartment. The first thing she does upon us entering is run her hand down the fresh-shaven side of my face and purrs. We watch TV until the riot dies down at dawn. When the station fades to snow, we continue watching. At one point I try to ask her where The Pash has been, puffing out my chest and pantomiming swigging on a bottle. She laughs and shrugs. The station kicks back on, the pop video show, a swarthy Romanian dude dancing and singing in an alley in the pouring rain. He falls to his knees in a puddle, emoting wildly, his shirt open and a tuft of soaked black hair spilling over his face. The song is awful, but it must be one of Mariska's favorites. She immediately springs from the chair and begins dancing, perfectly synchronized with the swarthy singer, mouthing the lyrics, her eyes shining. Smiling, she reaches for my hand to pull me up into her dance. This is the first time another person's skin has made contact with mine in a very long time. We whirl around the room for what seems like hours, under the watchful, judging eyes of the Gorky Park

Travels and Travails of Small Minds by Daniel Falatko

boys. Once the sun is up and streaming through the window and the shouting outside had subsided, she wraps the leopard-print jacket around her shoulders and, after mussing up my hair, walks out the door with a smirk on her pale face.

Mariska. I enjoy the way this rolls off the tongue, repeating it while attempting to sleep on the coldest morning thus far this fall. Over a cold Pop Tart breakfast, making sure to break off any edges nibbled on by my rodent roommates, I watch the early morning foot traffic at the store, a boy I don't recognize with large dark circles under his eyes working the booth. The torched car frame has been pushed onto the grass at the side of the road. Rubble from the riot, mostly broken bottles and crisped Denmark flags, seems to blend perfectly into the usual scenery. People going about their mornings like nothing had happened. Babushkas purchase milk and baking soda plus bottles of vodka or spirits for their spouses. Early morning drunks, just getting back to the outer rings from their night out rioting, stop by for a beer to ease their shaking hands. I even see one of the thugs who set fire to the car walking by on the opposite side of the road, his shaved head hung low and breath streaming from his nostrils.

Then comes a sight that causes me to fall to my knees. A *militsiya* car, even more battered than the usual police vehicle, sagging to one side on nearly bald tires, rolls to a slow halt in front of the store. I keep my head down, mumbling "oh fuck, oh fuck, oh fuck" as the rumpled-looking officers hop out and enter the store, barking at the kiosk boy, holding papers against the glass. They must be looking for The Pash. One of the officers stares at my building from the side of the kiosk, seemingly right at me, my heart pumping so hard I can feel it in my throat. This is it. The time has come. Within hours I will be beaten against the wall of a holding cell by raving packs of Krokodil addicts while the guards laugh and film it on their phones. I rock back and forth on the floor, waiting for the steps in the hallway, the splintering of the door, the bellowing voices, the kicks to the head and

ONE YEAR LATER – PART THREE

body. Several panicked minutes inch past, but all is silent. Picking myself up off the floor, my legs aching and my back cramped up with spasms, I allow myself a peek out the window. The officers are laughing. The Kiosk boy is laughing too as he slips them two bottles through the slit. He and one of the officers fist bump through the glass. Each cracking open a bottle, they saunter back in the car and, after each lights a smoke and takes a swig, tear off into the oncoming lane, one of them spitting out the window at the charred vehicle carcass.

I remain on my knees below the window until both legs go numb. Then I fall to the floor.

Where the fuck is The Pash?

Billionaire Eccentric and Salanack-Freak Milton Perth races Nathan to his mansion in his "rocket-powered" cart

AUGUST 5th

THERE IS NOTHING MORE BORING than miles-and-miles of sea. From my window seat in the very last row of the plane, this had been what I was staring at for the first twenty minutes of the flight, after the shimmering buildings of Manhattan and predictably grim Jersey sprawl gave way to an endless, soul-destroying blue. Still it was better than attempting to read the Salanack novel I had purchased for three dollars in a thrift store that Cally and I had visited the night previous. I found her lingering in the paperback section. She turned to me with a book in her hands and, smiling, blew off the dust to reveal the craggy face of Mr. Salanack on the back cover. The very first line of the novel, a boast about robbing blind men in order to fund his junk addiction, proved to be an obstacle. Wasn't he from a rich Connecticut family? Why would he be robbing blind people in the street? It was back to staring at the endless blue as the plane kept rising, until an equally boring cloud cover enveloped the scenery and rendered the window seat useless.

The hollow tube interior of the plane was mostly dark, people either sleeping or staring at their electronic devices or at the aisle or the seats ahead. Most people had drawn the shades on their windows. Yellow shirts seemed to be in fashion on this

Travels and Travails of Small Minds by Daniel Falatko

flight, giving the captive colony an Easter pastel vibe that I quite enjoyed. As my seat was immediately next to the bathrooms, I ended up watching the flow of people visiting the cramped space once the plane hit cruising altitude, each one for some reason flashing me an apologetic grin as they passed. Stewardesses that looked fine from a distance, but faltered up close, wandered the aisles meekly asking sleeping, zombified people if they wanted any coffee or orange juice. I requested both, and the smile the stewardess flashed me from her weathered face revealed teeth that appeared to be filed flat. Every half-hour the pilot would pipe in over the loudspeaker and gruffly let us know that we were still over the ocean and would be for some time. "Yea, no shit," the middle-aged guy in front of me said, whirling around and, in an accent that sounded almost musical, asked if it was at all inconvenient for me that his seat was pushed back. I let him know that this was fine. He asked me where I was headed, mentioning something about the north of England being a wasteland, and I had to think for a second before telling him.

"Wolfton?" His eyes nearly bugged out of his head. "What the bloody hell business do you have in Wolf Town?" At this he let out a low, warbling wolf howl that thoroughly unnerved the people around us.

"You wouldn't believe me, even if I told you, dear sir." I smiled at him before he turned back around. "But it sure beats knocking the canes out of blind folk's hands for smack money."

Against great odds, I somehow managed to slip into a black, dreamless sleep sometime toward the end of the flight. Something was tapping on my shoulder, at first a calm series of nudges decorating the outer layers of the dream, growing more insistent until a particularly harsh *thwack* brought me spiraling back into the recycled air reality of the plane. A steward with fairly creepy, gleaming eyes and a buzz cut was hovering over me, his fingers poised to rap me on the collarbone once again had I not regained consciousness.

AUGUST 5th

"Buckle that seatbelt, partner," he ordered in a mocking southern American accent. "We're a' headin' into Bustlington International... dude."

THERE WAS SOMETHING so obscenely bright about the airport that I found it nearly impossible to navigate. Not only was the cavernous space lit up by what seemed to be hundreds of high-powered generator lights lining the tops of the high walls, but the ceiling was just one enormous skylight with non-functioning beams intersecting at odd angles, causing the space to feel weighed-down by a post-apocalyptic industrial sky. Sparse crowds on the floor, the blemishes on their faces exposed under the unforgiving light, rosacea and broken blood vessels and lines under their eyes. I kept my head down while making my way toward the ground transportation section that yellow signs with bold block letters pointed out just beyond the baggage claim. An ancient woman with yellow-tinted glasses, moving at a slow pace with the aid of a walker, was shouting, "Where is my Gerald? Bring me my Gerald! I demand that you bring me my Gerald right this second!" I purchased a pack of Benson & Hedges that set me back nearly twenty dollars on my debit card.

True to what was outlined in Dr. Behr's itinerary, there was an extremely short man, bordering on a midget, standing on the outside pavement holding a piece of cardboard with my name scrawled on it. He appeared very much out of place, the only individual standing in the designated area waiting for someone "important," and was drawing mocking catcalls and scoffs from people filing out to their cars or trains. Embarrassed, I attempted to motion to him from several feet away, but he just scowled and shook his head. "It's me," I hissed at him. "You are here for me." The little man rolled his eyes and barked "Let me see some ID, sir!" in a startlingly loud voice that turned every head on the sidewalk, including those of two neon-vested Bobbies who began to make their way over. Offering my driver's license, the man studied my face, checking it against the license photo for an uncomfortably long time. He smiled up at me. "Nice shot. They let you do glamour photos for your licenses in America, Oi!" Wasting no time, he grabbed the bag from my hand and began walking away. "Well, come on!" His voice sounded amplified as he barked orders, causing the two cops to break up laughing.

The general sense amongst those loitering outside the airport, workers on their smoke breaks or passengers just off flights waiting for their rides, seemed to be that I felt I was some sort of big shot. "Have a look at im'," an extremely round man told his wife as we passed. "Probably has someone to hold his dick when he pisses. Three shakes, sir?"

The car idling at the curb was standard-issue car service, much to my relief, as a Rolls or Bentley would not have gone over too well with those particular onlookers. "Let's get the fook outta' here." The little man tossed my bag into the trunk, even though it was small enough for me to carry in the car. "I hate bleedin' airports." Without checking for oncoming vehicles, the little man hit the gas and the black car peeled from the curb accompanied by the high-pitched squeak of burnt rubber.

Under a late afternoon sun that was surprisingly bright, the car shot out onto a freeway and began weaving through traffic. My stomach, already unsettled by a plane landing which had been decidedly less than smooth, agitated with each stomp of the brake or rapid lane sweep. The little man could barely see over the dash, and I noticed he was aided by sitting atop a stack of newspapers. England looked nothing like I had expected. In place of the low-hanging, moisture-soaked skies I had envisioned was instead bright sun and endless blue with white tufts of clouds like you would see in any American suburb. The freeway looked suspiciously like the Garden State Parkway, only with the cars traveling on opposite sides of the road. A city peeking up from beyond the miles of developments appeared downright

AUGUST 5th

gritty, huge smokestacks belching pure black into the air and a minimal skyline of maybe ten unimpressive structures. At first we appeared to be approaching this city, the developments giving way to an industrial zone not unlike those seen from windows of the New Jersey Transit trains approaching NYC, before the lanes swept to the left, away from the ominous-looking city, shooting a straight line through miles of fields dotted with further developments.

"Well, are ya' just gonna' play around with those or are you gonna' offer me one?" The man was gesturing at the Benson & Hedges pack I had been fidgeting with. I offered him one, which he immediately lit with his own lighter, exhaling in great satisfaction. When I moved to light one myself, he barked, "No smokin' in the car, sir!" His smile in the rearview indicated he was joking. "So what brings you to these parts?" His peaked driver's cap bounced jauntily as he spoke.

"Business."

The man nodded profusely, though I wished he'd been keeping his eyes on the roadway. During our exchange he had already almost run a blue Toyota off the road and was encroaching dangerously into the space of a very angry-looking motorcyclist in a black helmet. "Business? Let's get a look at the address." He consulted an iPad, flicking ashes over the smudged screen. "Ah! You're headed to the Wolf Town!" Before I could stop him he threw his head back and broke into a series of high-pitched howls. The highway had thinned down to two lanes, with some of the towns we were passing beginning to resemble the quant villages with ancient church steeples surrounded by green hills that I had originally envisioned.

"Do you know anything about the address?" I asked him. "Have you ever heard of the Thomas J. Salanack Society?"

The man was in the midst of throwing the biker a two-finger salute, the British version of the middle finger, to which the cyclist responded by spitting onto the windshield. "You better

Travels and Travails of Small Minds by Daniel Falatko

be careful, you fuck! I could take you out with one sweep of this wheel!" At first it genuinely seemed like he was going to do it. I felt the car drifting into the next lane, but he came to his senses and straightened out. "The wot?" He yelled over the seat. "Never heard of it. Look, I don't make judgments on how people live their lives. Just keep that gay shit to yourself, you know?" Baffled, I tossed the butt out the window and let the car sink into a thoroughly uncomfortable silence before the driver finally, mercifully, switched on the radio.

Thin Lizzy piped in over the stereo system as we pulled off an exit, maneuvering under several on-ramps before finding ourselves within a town whose outskirts matched the slate-grey grittiness of the city we had passed. Several high rise projects could be seen, fish n' chips joints and Indian takeaways, an alarming number of old people in the streets. The driver wasn't particularly fond of these old folk, cursing them as they took their time crossing the narrow streets, at one point even gunning the car at an old man in a trilby hat who hadn't finished crossing when the light turned green.

We entered a better section of town which boasted several gleaming monster malls and better-dressed, younger people with shopping bags, swigging bottled water. Almost every building lining the street had the prefix "Wolf" adorning it....the Wolf Centre, the Wolf Market, the Wolf Thrift, the Randy Wolf Pub... and when I attempted to ask the driver about this, he let out another howl, this time with the window rolled down, shouting "You're all a bunch of Wolfies!" at people on the street, some of whom began barking or howling back at the car as it passed. We seemed to have passed through the town and were coming out on the other end, the masses of old people returning, their high rise apartments towering into the already dimming skies. The driver informed me that we were headed to an address outside of the town's limits. "I wouldn't worry, mate," he smiled before demanding another smoke. "You don't want to spend time with the Wolfies."

AUGUST 5th

HEADED THROUGH THE SUBURBS, developments and gas stations and 24-hour convenience stores, we turned onto a road and found ourselves surrounded by lush overgrowth. There were no houses along the road, nothing but dense forest and knotty bushes strangling one another under the last of the day's sun. The road seemed to be situated on a hill, and we climbed for several minutes before dead-ending at an ominous-looking white gate.

"Geez," the car man shook his head. "What in the bloody hell have you gotten yourself into?"

He re-checked the address, found it to be correct. In a flash he was out of the car and at the window with my bag, saying "Well? Go on!"

"You can't just leave me here." I exited to inspect the white gate, finding it heavily chipped and dented. "How do I get inside?"

He crossed his arms and scowled at the gate.

"I wouldn't worry." He nodded at a motion camera set high atop the white brick column at the side of the gate. "They know you're here."

I handed him another smoke, not wanting to be left alone on the dense hilltop. It would have taken nearly an hour to walk back to civilization should nobody from within the white gate come to my rescue. The little man took the smoke, checked his watch, said "Ten minutes and not a fookin' second longer."

WE WERE SITTING ON THE HOOD of the car when the golf cart approached. Coming from around a bend just behind the gate, it appeared to be turbo-charged, moving at a disturbing speed for a mere golf cart. The man in control of the cart was very tall, towering over the wheel as he bore down the path, dressed in black with long white hair cascading majestically behind him. There was something about the white of the gate, the white and orange of the golf cart, and the white of the man's mane that clashed in an obscene fashion with the yellow and green plant life.

"Yer Majesty awaits." The driver hopped down and bowed in the direction of the approaching cart. "Best of luck to ya'."

Debris from his screeching tires barely had a chance to settle before the rocket-propelled cart reached the gate. The man stood, a towering figure in a black turtleneck and matching jacket, and aimed a remote control device at the gate, causing it to swing open with enough force to kill anything unlucky enough to be standing in its way. The gate came to a stop with an alarming clang, white chips of paint scattering across the bushes. He motioned for me to approach.

Inside the gates the dense shrubs gave way to less cluttered woodland, with a wide road snaking back into the forest and out of sight.

The man with the black turtleneck and long white hair, though obviously in his 50s, had a face as smooth and wrinkle-free as a man 25-years younger. His hair, not necessarily grey but instead simply stripped of color, along with his light-colored pupils, made for an albino vibe until you noticed he also sported a deep tan.

"I see you are making friends." He swept his arm in a grand gesture toward the settling dirt from the car's peel-out. "Although I would advise your friends not to drive recklessly upon that road." Producing a moleskin notebook from the pockets of his tapered black pants, pants that would have looked rock n' roll on anyone but this man, he flipped through the pages until he found what he was looking for. "The car service will be hearing from me on this one. Tyla, the owner, is a friend of mine." He ominously circled something with an expensive-looking pen, flipped the notebook closed and regarded me with a resigned sigh.

"Well, I suppose you will do."

Firing up the cart, he flipped his hair to indicate for me to jump on the back. To feel the boards vibrating under my feet was to confirm this was indeed no ordinary golf cart, the frame masking what must have been a rocket-fueled engine sparking and revving under the decks. The last thing I wanted was to put my arms around the Salanack freak's waist, bracing myself as the cart took off at full speed and nearly threw me full off the back. The man obviously knew the road quite well, had every turn and bump and potential hazard memorized, though this didn't stop me from screeching when he took a near-90 degree turn at a high rate of speed without breaking and it felt, for a heart racing second, as if the cart were about to go up on two wheels and send us hurtling into the landscaped rocks lining the side of the path. The split ends of the man's white mane kept flicking me in the face and it was difficult to concentrate on ducking the flying locks while nearly being thrown overboard on the winding dirt driveway. Finally, after he hopped a mud hole, achieving considerable hang-time, crashing down on the other side with teeth clashing fury, I resigned myself to place my hands around his waist, which to my abject horror I found surprisingly sculpted.

My eyes closed after a cloud of dirt overtook us when rounding a sharp bend, not opening them until I felt us rolling to a halt. We were in the grass in front of a large wooden house, three stories high, with stained glass windows on the bottom floor that gave it the feel of a modern, tasteful church. The outside appeared fully lacquered, gleaming in what was left of the day's light. The roof was flat, giving the structure a boxy feel despite its massive size. A white fence identical to the front gate could be seen along the edges of the yard, video cameras roving from strategic positions atop the bars. The man could tell I was impressed, examining his quarters as if he too were seeing it for the first time.

"Milton Perth," the man finally extended his hand. "And I take it you are Edward."

Travels and Travails of Small Minds by Daniel Falatko

"Nathan, actually," I corrected him, his hand cold and clamping mine like a vice, the tendons on his thin wrist like rubber bands sticking through the skin.

"Ah, he sent the other one," Perth sniffed, seemingly not at all happy with this change in plans. "Well, as I said before, I suppose you will do."

Flashing back to Dr. Behr letting me know that I was the right person for this mission, that Edward was far too flakey to risk sending, that the assignment was mine from the very start.

"I'm happy to be of service."

ONCE THROUGH THE THICK OAK DOOR which creaked and groaned and required considerable effort in opening, Perth straining even harder to pull it shut behind us, I was confronted with a similarly tasteful interior. Wood columns everywhere, floors soaked with the same gleaming lacquer as the outside walls, high ceilings and an open layout that made no effort to conceal the massive amount of square footage contained within this house atop the gnarled hill. There was a piano in the entrance, dozens of black coats flung over a rack, and two framed photos of Thomas J. Salanack. One was a shot of a grizzled, shrunken old man sitting on a porch holding a rifle, his eyes free of emotion, mouth agape like a black hole. The other picture was a high school portrait, the face gaunt but smooth, dapper in a private school uniform. The only way I knew this was the same person was by comparing the calculating voids of the man's eyes, unchanged from childhood through old age. Perth seemed suspicious that I was studying the photos so closely. He demanded that I remove my shoes and ushered me past the entrance area, limping dramatically but not a cane in sight. The main living quarters and kitchen beyond were visions of comfort, an overstuffed couch and flat screen so huge it more resembled a theatre screen, all

AUGUST 5th

modern appliances and tract lighting, the stained glass windows casting red, gold, and green streaks across the floors. The walls were lined with silver-framed, vaguely abstract photographs of warehouses and factories. Mid-day grey skies hovered over the rooftops in every picture, giving them the feel of a sequenced series. An ancient, battered typewriter was centered on a small table near the kitchen, an equally worn sheet of paper in the device that, as I saw when I stooped to check it out as we passed, bore the title *Rape World* at the top. The body of the text was covered with X marks and seemed to have no paragraph structure. A rough draft.

Perth began to inquire if I cared for any brandy and I answered with an emphatic "Yes!" before he could complete the question. "I never use hired hands," he told me, his tone indicating that I should be very impressed with this stance, making a big show of exposing the bottle's label while pouring the brandy into predictably stylish tumblers. "Where I originally come from, we pour our own booze."

"Me too." I accepted the glass, ignored his cocksure glare. "You're a photographer?"

It took him a second to realize what I was referring to, the factory and warehouse photos lining the living room.

"Not at all. Those are my buildings, photographed by Wilson Frampshire. The man was not easy to commission, but in the end he turned in a fantastic series, as you can see. Several publications have approached me to run those on their pages. I've turned them all down."

Again his tone indicated that I should be extremely impressed by this. His gaze, already a bit chilly, turned noticeably colder when my face remained impassive.

"I have only one passion," he sighed, not sounding all that passionate about his one true passion at that moment. "And it is for an art which is not my own."

A predictable sweep of the arm, leading me into a room beyond the kitchen. The room's layout was similar to that of

Travels and Travails of Small Minds by Daniel Falatko

the living room, with glowing wooden floors and incredibly high ceilings held in place by oak columns, only this room was even more expansive.

"In New York this room alone would run you 22 grand a month," I let him know.

He seemed highly disappointed at this comment, at my flippant attitude toward the items which filled the room. A large red banner reading "THE THOMAS J. SALANACK SOCIETY" hung from a strategically placed point on the ceiling, hovering over a scene that resembled the interior of a museum. Eight glass-encased manuscripts, some so yellow they resembled the deeds and notices scattered through Dr. Behr's filing cabinets, formed a row on a table along the far wall. Tables throughout the rest of the room displayed typewriters, guns, a dubious-looking box with tubes and wires that Perth later explained to be a heroin-kicking device, clothes hanging from elaborate-looking pulley systems… vests, little black hats, creased trousers… bookshelves with thousands of hardbound and paperback editions, each-shelf dedicated to a single book's various printings, magazine articles and newspaper clippings arranged into an enormous scrapbook mural. The walls were lined with hundreds of framed photos, that same gaunt face and insect eyes aging as the photo timeline went on, posing with other writers and celebrities, posing with guns, always wearing vests, until he becomes so completely shriveled, near the end of the montage, all that was left was the cold eyes set inside a shrunken head. There were even several syringes, carefully placed in small plastic Ziploc-style pouches, proudly on display. I wondered if perhaps one of these syringes had been filled with the anti-freeze he used to do himself in, though I realized this particular syringe would no doubt be placed high above all the others, in its own glass case for sure. He had apparently not acquired this important piece of history as of yet. The shelf closest to where we were standing was marked, "RW 1sts."

"Have you ever read any of Salanack's stuff?" I asked him, slightly freaked out by the man's dedication.

AUGUST 5th

"I'm married to the man's works," he sniffed, refusing to acknowledge the joke. "Many a spectacular woman has exited these premises due to my dedication to this particular subject."

This statement, though tinged with a practiced melancholy, to me seemed like just a way of proving that he did, in fact, get laid despite spending his days pissing away his fortune on used syringes and old man diapers.

"I picked up my first work on a whim, a 99 cent paperback at the local drug store. That paperback was the beginning of my collection and holds its special, dog-eared place amongst that shelf." He pointed to one of the bookshelves which was filled with paperback editions. "I've read every word the man ever wrote. I can quote entire passages by heart. I've typed out his books from beginning to end only to feel that rhythm. He was abstract yet structured, surreal yet mired in gritty reality. He was a drug-addled sex fiend and a classic New England gentleman, a counter-culture figure who nonetheless celebrated the rules. The man was an incredible mass of glorious contradictions, and I will stop at nothing to acquire every item he ever owned and every dwelling he ever so much as sharpened a pencil in. The apartment he rented in Thailand, for example, is mine as of last week."

Unlike the accent of the Oxford Man, a voice genuinely ingrained with the type of intelligence and class that is passed down through the blood of generations, Mr. Perth was nothing more than a mimic, clearly appropriating his bombastic, pompous style from a thousand stereotypical upper crust English characters portrayed in film and literature. It was a good thing I would only be staying at this joint for the night.

"I don't suppose you would know how it feels to experience a genuine connection and passion for a modern day genius." He held his chin high, surveying his vast collection. "But I do understand that you have been sent to aid me in that passion, so we may as well get down to business."

Travels and Travails of Small Minds by Daniel Falatko

His hands held behind his back, he limped toward me in a vaguely aggressive manner, as if he were determining whether of not to slap me.

"I understand that you have some papers for me."

I rolled my eyes. This was all too much. "And I understand you have some money for me."

He laughed, shrill and condescending, stamping his foot against the floor.

"I'm not sure if your boss had told you," he smiled, his teeth straight but stained deep yellow and brown. "But this is not a standoff situation. You are a guest here for the evening. I will go over the papers, treat you to dinner and a bed, and send you off with the money in the morning. I can assure you," he led my gaze to the stained glass, the ceilings as high as a cathedral. "The money is not an issue."

My eyes felt tired, scorched, as I rummaged through my bag for the folder, handed him the apartment deed. He immediately began to inspect the document, turning his back on me to hold it to the light of the window, and I used this as an opportunity to grab one of the many *Rape World* first edition paperbacks and slip it quickly into my bag for the T Man.

"I take it your undying passion allows for you to take over apartments from people who legally own the lease?"

He whipped back around, not furious, a sense of reckless amusement creasing the sides of his mouth.

"It is referred to as collateral damage. Only in my quest, unlike those of conquerors and warlords, people do not pay with their lives. They pay with their leases. They pay with the property in their possession that I would like to own. And they are paid handsomely."

His eyes never blinked as they scanned the apartment deed.

"Not in this situation."

He finally tore his eyes from the papers, regarding me like a fly that had just dive-bombed into his soup.

"You might be paying the sum to my boss, but you're forgetting about the current tenant of the apartment. She is being illegally evicted without seeing any money."

With a withering roll of the eyes, the man slid the papers into a leather sheath.

"I am covering my end. The rightful owner of the apartment is being paid for said apartment. It is his business to clear up any remaining technicalities."

"And how do you suppose my boss plans on clearing up this remaining technicality, a technicality which happens to be a human being named Cally."

"That also is not my business." He turned his back to me and wiped away a fleck of dust from the surface of an old table that Salanack must have owned at some point in his life. "Though I would assume there are certain methods."

"You mean illegal methods? Things like harassment? Blackmail? Non-official evictions?"

He turned to me and nodded.

"Why yes, those sound like rather fine options," he advanced, standing entirely too close and looking me directly in the eye. "Pardon my asking, but do you feel Dr. Behr would be very happy with this line of questioning, with this aggressive stance toward what I assume would be an important client? Don't get me wrong, I am not going to phone the man with complaints. It is good to ask questions. It is good to wonder. I simply advise you to do so in a different tone, my boy."

I smiled, nodded, backed away from him a little.

"Also, upon ingesting your string of questions, it does not sound as if you are privy to the entire story." He stuffed his hands into the pockets of his baggy black slacks, his body language softening noticeably. He shook his head, pitying me. "Fair enough."

It was clear I had lost the standoff. Perth had pulled a trump card. Perhaps I didn't know the entire story. Perhaps I didn't care. But either way, he did know more than me.

Travels and Travails of Small Minds by Daniel Falatko

"Why do you want the apartment so badly?" I didn't want to let on that I had been inside the apartment, that I had seen its waterlogged, sagging state, that I had personally searched the entire apartment and found nothing related to the writer the man was obsessed with. "Is it stuffed full of valuable syringes and burnt spoons?"

At this he laughed.

"I must admit your ignorance is quite amusing." He had moved on to inspecting a *Life Magazine* from the 60s that no doubt contained a Salanack article. "If you were to read every biography written on the man, and there have been 63 of those, you will not see a single mention of the address in question. Nor will you find it on any of the various internet biographies and information sites. Even in pulling up the official records, the residence history, you would find that the man never officially had any connection to the apartment for which you are here this evening."

Perth seemed to be fond of dramatic pauses, during which he would flash a wicked, all-knowing grin.

"But one person you will find on the residence history is a certain Ruth Gunnings. And although this name may not mean anything to you, indeed may not mean anything at all in the scope of history, the fact remains that she was indeed an acquaintance of a man you may be familiar with: Mr. Jack Kerouac. It seems that Ms. Gunnings, a Columbia student from a relatively wealthy family, would travel in the summers and allow certain friends of hers to sublet her apartment in Alphabet City while she was gone. One of these was Mr. Kerouac, who was at that point still writing wooden, melancholic prose in hopes of mainstream approval. If one digs deep, he could find this in Kerouac's history, the summer of 1944. What nobody else knows, however, is that Mr. Kerouac fell into a bout of alcohol-related illness that summer, abandoning the apartment after two weeks to run home to Mommy. Guess who stepped unofficially into the sublet for a grand total of four weeks, only leaving when a temporarily sober Kerouac came back to reclaim the apartment?"

AUGUST 5th

"Oscar Wilde?"

"Thomas J. Salanack." He ignored me, plowing back into his story like a proud father recounting his son's little league grand slam. "The official record has him living with his first wife Mary, may God rest her soul, on 13th St. at that time. But I happen to know, in fact may be the only one who knows, that he moved out for four weeks to work on... are you ready for this? The first draft of a little ditty called *Rape World*. Not only do I presently own the typewritten first draft of this undisputed masterwork, but I now shall own the residence in which he composed it."

"Wow."

"My knowledge on the man runs deeper than any of his biographers. I am aware of places Mr. Salanack had resided that don't even show up on the radar. Pick any given day during his lifespan and chances are I can let you know precisely what he did on that day, what he wrote, his activities, his consumption. It has taken a lifetime to amass this information. But I won't write a biography myself. I won't divulge it. The information is mine only and will stay mine."

There was a faraway look in his eyes, bits of spittle on the sides of his mouth working to eradicate any sense of class and refinement he was attempting to project with his accent and surroundings.

"October 17th, 1973."

He snapped back from his stoic, thousand-yard-stare, white tufts of hair rising from his head on waves of static. "Pardon?"

"October 17th, 1973," I repeated. "What was Thomas J. Salanack up to on October 17th, 1973?"

He grinned, accepting the challenge.

"Let's see," he scratched his chin, staring once again at a point in the distance beyond my head, beyond the house walls, beyond everything. It was getting dark, the stained glass light shrinking closer to the windows and shadows setting in over the paraphernalia in the room. "In 1973 he would have been residing in London, living with an alchemy buff and chemistry student by

Travels and Travails of Small Minds by Daniel Falatko

the name of Charles Swelson. They shared a basement flat in the Soho District, a flat I presently own, and in the fall of '73 would have been going through some hard times. Swelson was not fond of Thomas bringing home young women to be tortured, quite willingly, in a chamber Salanack had fortified in the flat, though Salanack continued to do so anyway, ignoring the unenlightened complaints of his lover and working on a series of avant-garde pieces for small presses, including such works as *Fly Veins Necromancer* and *Semen Cocoon*. On that particular date in October, I can deduce that, since *Fly Veins Necromancer* was submitted to Little Minds Press on November 26th, he was most likely wrapping up the manuscript while Swelson was in class, perhaps taking breaks in order to whip a tied-up participant in the torture chamber, his special way of brainstorming ideas. His habit at the time was nearly a gram a day, so his London connection, Michael Whitnall, would stop by around noon with the goods. Swelson would come home late in the night to find him slumped over the manuscript with the needle often still in his arm, freeing that day's torture victim and calling it a night. I would stake thousands that this is what went down in the life of Thomas J. Salanack on October 17th, 1973."

He bowed to me, the white mane sweeping with him.

"Impressive."

Pleased by this, as if all he wanted to do over the course of our treacherously long conversation was impress me with his obsessively detailed knowledge on the subject, he finally seemed to relax.

"Indeed," he moved to kill the lights in the display room, motioning for me to follow him out into the main room toward the stairs, hugging the leather sheath containing the deed papers to his chest protectively. "Let me show you to your room so you can freshen up before dinner. Travel seems to have gotten the better of you, Nathan, as you do appear a bit greasy this evening."

Moving up the wide stairway behind him, watching as he took the steps one-at-a-time due to his hobbled gait, I wondered

AUGUST 5th

if he sometimes dreamt about moving his entire collection into a pile on the back of the manor and setting it all on fire, of setting himself free.

THERE WERE MANY THINGS I needed to tell Cally. I wanted her to know about the wolf whistles, about the tall thin man with pure white hair and rocket charged go carts who dished out thousands for used needles which may or may not have been utilized by his idol to inject opiates. I wanted her to know about the room in which I was ensconced, each of its four walls taken up by giant posters for independent films based on Salanack books as well as a bed with sheets softer than anything I had ever touched. I wanted to warn her about potential upgrades in Behr's harassment campaign, to let her know that he would stop at nothing. I wanted to tell her not to worry, that I was going to foil the passing of the money somehow, that she didn't have to bite her nails about being evicted as long as I was on the case. I wanted to tell her that I missed her.

After six rings I was kicked to her voicemail. Good thing I was calling from one of Perth's phones next to the bed and not my cell, as the international fee would not be cheap. I waited with great anticipation to hear her voice on the recording, disappointment setting in when confronted with a computerized voice instead. I hung up without leaving a message. She was most likely at the coffee shop.

THE LAST THING I WANTED TO DO was go back out there. Perth had let me know to join him in the main dining room in 20 minutes. I didn't bother unpacking anything as I would be leaving the next morning, hopefully very early, and didn't want the feeling of being settled into that borderline-creepy house upon a hill tangled in uncontrolled trees and vines. Pacing, I noticed my feet left prints on the ancient-looking throw rug. Other than the monstrous posters the room was sparse, with an oak dresser, a comfortable bed, and a night table being the only furnishings. On the windowsill there were several small glass figures which, upon closer inspection, turned out to be strategically-placed mini-Salanack dolls from each stage in his life, from a young boy to a rifle-toting old man. Jesus Christ. Dinnertime was fast approaching. The room had a small bathroom and I stared at myself in the mirror for five full minutes before reporting downstairs. The lighting was harsh. I did look greasy.

 I had envisioned servants, stone-faced and pouring drinks, along with well-dressed company seated in couples around a magnificent table, relaxed and cracking non-offensive jokes, their faces reflected in the silver of the serving trays. Instead there was just the table, even more gigantic and magnificently polished than I had imagined, absolutely gleaming under a massive chandelier that somehow, against great odds, managed to be tasteful. At one end, almost out of sight from the other, sat Mr. Perth. The enormity of the room and comical length of the table made the over-six-foot man appear short, a dwarf with windblown hair, perched over a salad with a salty look on his face. He tapped his wrist, indicating I was late, and let me know to sit down, dig in. There were no silver serving trays, no robotic-motioned servants with weary faces. The meal was some sort of meat, steamed vegetables, and salad. Simple, fresh fare. I was halfway to the far end of the table with my plate before he halted me.

 "You will not be able to hear me clearly from over there. I will be letting you know some important details."

 The urge to sit as far away from him as possible was nearly overpowering, though I didn't want to miss any details. Perhaps he was about to reveal the parts of the story I was not aware of.

AUGUST 5th

With a heavy sigh I couldn't mask, I moved to a nearer seat that still turned out to be very far away, needing to squint just to see him. He let me know to come in just a bit closer. I moved one seat down.

After five minutes he had not spoken a word. I had torn through my first course and was onto the second before he pointed at the fairly beat up piano in the corner and let me know that it had belonged to Salanack during his "Lower East Side, sad molester, clown faze." I recalled seeing a photo in the museum of Salanack in full clown costume, smoking a cigarette on a street corner, those insect eyes gleaming through the white paint. The mouth makeup was set in a frown and his pants, for whatever reason, were around his ankles. "It cost a fortune to have it shipped. Too bad Thomas never could play for shite," he told me. I shrugged and reached for more meat. He viewed me with great distaste, bordering on disgust. A pause so awkward it was nearly unbearable. It felt as if we were on a very unsuccessful first date. I asked him if he had prepared the food himself and he launched into the same speech he had given earlier about never using helping hands, about coming from stock that prepared their own meals. He asked me if I was, by any chance, hungry. Ignoring this verbal slap, I reached for another piece of bread.

"So," I thought of something to say nearly ten minutes later, after I had finished a second salad and another small portion of the mystery meat. "You own factories and warehouses?"

I was learning quickly. All the man needed to keep him occupied was something to espouse on bombastically for long periods of time, preferably something to do with himself and how amazing he was, or about Thomas J. Salanack and his mad drive to own every last molecule the junkie ever came into contact with on earth, and how amazing he indeed was because of this most noble and solitary of missions.

"I used to work in them." He took a sip of the wine I just noticed sitting near him on the table, a large bottle, causing me to get up and make the trek to retrieve a glass for myself.

165

Travels and Travails of Small Minds by Daniel Falatko

"Most people will say that working on assembly lines or loading product into lorries are essentially demeaning jobs which require very little thought."

"Let me guess, you beg to differ?" The wine was red and strong and I coughed a little on the first gulp.

"I most certainly do beg to differ. A man has lots of time to think while performing menial labor. There is a certain rhythm to the tasks, differing depending on what job you are working, which allows for your thoughts to flow in a guided cadence. It gives them structure, makes them strong. It makes one realize that thoughts are meant to lead to outcomes, just as an assembly line is created to build product or a lorry is loaded in order to reach a certain destination. Thoughts are not meant to drift or go to waste. They are meant to be acted on and turned into results."

"So, for example," I was balancing a hunk of juicy meat on top of a bread slice. "If you admire the works of, say, a certain author, then you should follow that thought and plunge all the way into obsession-mode, stopping at nothing to acquire every object the author ever touched and every residence the author ever set foot in?"

Heavy sigh. I thought for a second he was going to get up and walk from the table. Though my actions were following a general plan, to piss this guy off enough that he wouldn't hand over the money and the deal would go sour, I realized at that moment that this would never work. The man didn't care how much of a prick I was, or how shady Dr. Behr was in clearing out the apartment and demanding the money in cash. All he wanted was the apartment. No matter how badly I blew it with him the deal would still go down eventually. I could poke out my own eyes with a fork, right there in his dining room, and it would only serve to prolong the deal for a small period of time. Cally would still be evicted by the fall.

"So how did you go from working in the factories and warehouses to owning them?"

AUGUST 5th

Though I already knew the answer to this question, I just wanted to hear it come from his mouth. I wanted to hear him admit that all this came from a simple lawsuit as opposed to the culmination of all the deep, structured thoughts that came to him on the assembly line all those years ago.

"Fortune struck," he smiled. "In the form of a wrecking ball."

He extended his leg and rolled up the black slacks. I only pretended to look, instead focusing on the point where a shadow on the wall formed what looked like the outline of a very fat cat.

"Caught me right on the knee. Tore the damned cap right off." His voice was suddenly tinged with a working class inflection, as if boasting of a horrible injury to his mates on the assembly line. "A pissed-up wrecking ball operator. The nutter dozed off at the yoke. Years later we crossed paths at the Randy Wolf. I stood the gentleman a round and thanked him."

He rolled his pant leg back down, settled in over his wine.

"They didn't really do lawsuits then. All I know is I was laid up in hospital, my leg high in the air on a pulley system and doped up to the gills when a man came in and offered a cheque. And it was with that cheque that I purchased my first gutted warehouse, saving it from imminent demolition, and from that warehouse spawned lorry clients which spawned steady business which spawned more employees which spawned many more cheques which grew to spawn further warehouses which served to spawn several factories spewing out kitchen appliances and septic piping and spawning into many, many more cheques."

"That sure is a lot of spawning."

"It most certainly is."

He poured himself another glass of wine, his third in only a couple of minutes. I went in for my second.

"So now you get to chase your Salanack obsession with all those... ahem... cheques."

"Indeed, indeed." He surveyed his massive dining area in a self-congratulatory way. "The further one builds an empire, the further one gets from the hassles of running it. There are people

Travels and Travails of Small Minds by Daniel Falatko

now who do everything. I'm as removed as one can be from their own chain of success. But I do, I can assure you, venture into the warehouses and factories on a regular basis. Not to inspect them, but to work. I do it anonymously, sometimes disguising myself, working a long day on the line or loading boxes, against doctor's orders, if only to never lose the rhythm to my thoughts, the sense of impending victories."

A big gulp of wine, his eyes clouding over.

"And the only satisfactory outcome will be to fill this house with the master collection of the life of Thomas J. Salanack and to be able to stand and breathe freely in every dwelling in which he ever struck a key on one of his masterworks."

"Tell me," I asked him with genuine interest, the wine starting to loosen up the knots in my stomach. "It seems as if at this point you are more interested in snatching up everything the guy ever touched or owned than actually reading his works and delving into any of the cultural significance they hold. Why don't you write a book on him? It wouldn't have to be a biography. You wouldn't have to give up what you know. A book taking a critical look at his works and studying what he meant to you, what he meant to culture as a whole. A detailed analysis, perhaps?"

He was studying my face, not exactly disapproving of what I was saying. He seemed surprised that I was able to string sentences of more than a few words together into a coherent question.

"Something tells me you are the only member of this Thomas J. Salanack Society. Is that true, Mr. Perth? Why horde all this stuff? Why make it into such a war, complete with covert dealings and borderline illegal behavior? Don't you think there are others out there who love the guy too? Who love his works and are interested in his life? Don't you think they would like to see all this stuff? Why not share?"

He was nodding at me, unblinking and shaking slightly. I thought for a second he was going to have a seizure.

AUGUST 5th

"But just as a word of advice, if you do go the sharing route, I would get rid of the syringes before displaying all this to the public. Those might creep people out just a little."

He crumpled into his seat, looking fatigued, his cheeks flushed from the wine. His long white fingers tapped against the tabletop, before replying, "This collection is private and shall remain private."

A hard stare put me in my place. This was final. This was *The Word*.

"So I thought you would be letting me in on some details I was not privy to."

I thought about letting the wine sit for a second, not wanting to become drunk or sloppy in Perth's presence, let him slide into drunkenness so I could have some sort of advantage, but took a big gulp instead.

"Don't be a tease with the details, Mr. Perth."

He relaxed a little, his shoulders less tense, obviously happy to be onto a different subject.

"I am not sure what the politics of your workplace entail, but I must admit the organization does appear to be a bit on the dysfunctional side."

"Abso-fuckin-lutely."

"I see. My observations were spot on, though frankly it is none of my business to comment. I have no stake in your organization, nor do I want to. I was merely pointing out that, from what you were saying earlier when you appeared to be attacking my character, it seems you have a handle on only a portion of the true scope of things."

"Only a handle? Well, I'm glad I possess even that." The stained glass windows glowed ethereal in the faint light of the enormous room. "So tell me, which dimensions of the story do I not have a handle on?"

"Dimensions?"

"Yes, dimensions. Realms. I've learned about them from my boss."

Travels and Travails of Small Minds by Daniel Falatko

"What strange people." He flattened his white mane against his head with both hands, essentially petting himself. "Not the brightest, but interesting nonetheless. I feel for you. Trust me, I do. An errand boy with only a vague clue what his errand entails. Hired muscle without the muscle. You, my son, are a walking contradiction."

"If you're going to just sit there at your big table and insult me while playing with your hair all night, perhaps you could just hand over the money now and I'll be on my way. Do you guys do night trains on this rainy island?"

"Calm down. Stay. You've been traveling all day and the least I can do is put you up for the night. You do realize how much those sheets cost, don't you?" He motioned for me to stay in place even though I had not moved to get up. "Look, this really is none of my business as I said before. I have no personal stake in your organization other than to acquire this residence. Once this has been completed, I would be quite satisfied to never cross paths with your boss or yourself ever again. I must say, however, since beginning negotiations with your company, I have been quite shocked at the levels of disorganization and internal intrigue."

"Disorganization and intrigue are what Behr Properties was founded on."

"I see, I see." It was the first time I'd heard him laugh, his eyes gleaming in the moonlight filtered in through the stained glass. "Just based on what you were saying earlier, there are several things that do not add up. You are acting as if you are on a lone mission here, as if you've been sent in blind. And you very well may have, but keep in mind that I've been in touch with another of Behr's employees for many months and that this employee seemed to know all of the ins-and-outs surrounding this deal."

"What other employee?" I was in the midst of filling a glass of wine clear to the rim, drops sloshing over the side and onto the table. He motioned for me to top off his glass as well. "Behr doesn't have an army working for him. It's just me and Edward. Are you sure you aren't referring to the Oxford Man?"

AUGUST 5th

"The Oxford Man?" Perth was suddenly very interested, sitting up straight. "You mean Dr. Sneil?"

"Yes, Dr. Sneil. Is that who you've been dealing with?"

"It most certainly does ring a bell." He was stroking his chin, deep in thought. "Dr. Sneil… the Oxford Man. Brilliant! Apparently, you may know a little more than I had thought."

"So was it Sneil you were dealing with?"

"Dr. Sneil is the lone reason this deal is on the table." He tapped the tabletop dramatically. "I keep in contact with all professors of literature throughout this country, especially those who specialize in modern prose. They aren't exactly on my payroll, though they know I am willing to pay for any new information they should stumble upon concerning my passion."

"So Dr. Sneil found out about this illegal sublet that went down way back in the 40s? Wow. How much did you pay him for that? Why do you trust him? These professors could be feeding you bullshit for cash."

He held his glass out in a toast for some reason. I didn't raise mine.

"I've never taken bullshit for cash in my life. Every tip I get is investigated to the very core. Keep in mind that, unofficially, I am the foremost expert on the man. I know instantly if a tip is worth investigating. In this case, I knew that there was a hole in his residential pattern that summer. In the end, it checked out."

"How did Sneil come across this tip? Is he a Salanack freak too?"

This drew the second laugh of the evening from Perth, starting out as a snort before breaking into a controlled giggle that sounded vaguely sinister.

"Quite the opposite, actually. Many professors of serious literature tend to have a bee in their bonnet about Mr. Salanack. A pulp writer, they call him. A sensationalist coasting on shock value alone. Apparently, he is not boring enough for their tastes. But they do know about me, and they do know to come to me should anything cross their paths concerning this particular sensationalist. Money tends to slice through criticism."

Travels and Travails of Small Minds by Daniel Falatko

"You mean like when Rolling Stone gives Mick Jagger solo records five stars?"

"Dr. Sneil is no different," he ignored me. "It turns out a certain old American woman by the name of Ruth Gunnings lives in the same building as your boss's mother. Apparently, Ms. Gunnings spends her days wandering the halls of the building moaning about how she was friends with beatniks and used to sublet her apartment to Kerouac, how one time she even lent it to Burroughs when he was kicked out of his own apartment on the Lower East Side. It is like a mantra with this woman. 'I housed the beatniks. I housed the beatniks.' She moans the story to everyone she sees. She claims she never allowed Mr. Kerouac to sublet the place again after that summer, as Mr. Salanack had made quite a mess of the place. Thomas was not the most clean individual. Some say he wasn't potty trained. Let's just say he used her sink to soil more than just the dishes."

I remembered the woman, hunched over a walker with long red hair dangling to the middle of her back, moaning in the hallways of the mother's building. But I hadn't reported this back to Dr. Behr, who hadn't visited his mother in over a decade. So how did it end up reaching his ears?

"How convenient that it turns out Dr. Sneil's good friend Dr. Behr now owns the building in question." He rubbed his hands together excitedly. "Sometimes things simply fall into place. Ronald mentioned the woman and her ramblings to Dr. Sneil in a phone conversation, just as a simple aside, and Sneil brought it to my attention. The tip ended up checking out, and here we are!"

I realized that this was a celebratory evening for Mr. Perth, basking in the glow of his new acquisition. In his mind, he was the luckiest man alive.

"I noticed that you are to be placed on a train bound for the Sneil residence tomorrow morning," he said. "This leads me to believe Dr. Sneil will be getting a percentage of the payment for bringing this deal to fruition. Very interesting, though none of my business of course."

AUGUST 5th

I was wondering if Behr knew his good friend Dr. Sneil had already been paid for the tip. It was most likely a very handsome payment, and now he was being paid a percentage of the apartment fee as well. For the Oxford Man, payday had struck twice.

"The reason I was surprised to see you," he was slurring his words, perhaps revealing things he would not otherwise have espoused had he not been flat-out drunk. "Is that I had been dealing with Edward right from the very beginning, from the time Dr. Sneil first put me in touch with your boss. As a matter of fact, I have never dealt with your boss directly. It has always been through Edward."

A feeling I was not used to rushed over me at that moment, beginning in the pit of my stomach and spreading out as if running through my veins, right to the very tips of my fingers. A slump of the shoulders. A blush of the cheeks. It was shame. The shame of a fool.

"You dealt with Edward?"

"Right from the very beginning, as I said." He looked sorry for me, worried even. An arm snaked out, a hand on my shoulder. "To my knowledge, Edward is the one who related the beatnik ramblings of the old woman to your boss many years ago. Your boss, not being the most mentally together fellow in the world, had mentioned it in a casual conversation with Dr. Sneil only several months ago. Edward was the one who contacted me. We negotiated for months. Back-and-forth. He set up this whole deal."

My vision was swimming, images of Edward incensed over not being sent to England, of his seemingly genuine surprise at all of the twists and turns in the case. And yet he knew all along. Not only that, but he had set up the whole thing.

"Are you ok?" Perth was leaning toward me. "I'm not looking to cause any inter-office strife here. Just trying to clear up some things on my own end as well. I didn't mean to upset you."

Travels and Travails of Small Minds by Daniel Falatko

"It's ok," I told him, taking a deep breath. "I'll get to the bottom of it. Do you mind if I make a couple of phone calls?"

"Not a problem." His hair bounced with every syllable. "It is the least I can do."

Why had Edward lied to me? What was his stake in all this? I was not angry with him. I just wanted to know why. Perhaps he would tell me, now that he was quitting. Maybe he would put the whole situation in perspective.

"Perhaps I have said too much here," Perth could barely get up from the table, his head lolling about as if only loosely attached to his shoulders. "It is never my intention to cause conflict within an organization. This damned wine! This damned loose tongue!"

I thought he was going to start pummeling himself and was slightly disappointed when he didn't.

"We will now officially drop this subject." He nearly fell over, finally out of the chair. "This is a business relationship, a business dealing, and should not get bogged down in gossip and intrigue."

I rose to join him, fighting gravity in a much more graceful fashion.

"I am happy to let you know that the deed has checked out," noted Perth. "It is the official document, true to your boss's word."

"I'm so happy for you."

He winced, held a finger to his lips.

"This means I will be handing over the money to you tomorrow morning before you depart. American dollars. In cash." He coughed. "I am not so sure why this is a cash transaction. But once again, that is none of my business."

"For a deal that seems to be very much your business, you sure don't seem concerned with the finer details."

He had to put his hand on the back of the chair to keep steady.

"Finer details are very much overrated," said Perth.

I smiled and quietly dialed Edward, hoping to catch the lying scoundrel, despite the five hour time difference. "Edward, pick up. Edward, pick up. Edward, pick up," my mantra did not seem to be bringing him to the phone. "Pick up you lying motherfucker." His voicemail clicked on, cheerful and well-enunciated. I let it play until it reached the beep, hung up without leaving a message.

MIDNIGHT. There was a snooker room, of course, in the basement of the house. Mr. Perth and I had gotten into a second bottle of wine, then a third. He was beating me handily in our third or fourth straight game. We were smoking, lurching about the table not really knowing what we were doing anymore. We kept forgetting who was solids, who was stripes, eventually just whacking balls around the table with no strategy, just to hear them savagely click together.

At one point I dropped some ashes on the surface of the table and he told me to be careful. "This table we are playing on used to belong to the Slushhorn Tavern in the 1950s. Mr. Salanack, as well as other noted beatniks and poets, people such as Gary Snyder, have all played on this very table." He stumbled and nearly fell straight backwards while attempting to chalk his cue. "That cue you are holding was Mr. Salanack's favorite. He was 86'd from the Slushhorn for several months for attempting to steal it. He said it brought him good luck. They brought it to his funeral when he made the choice to leave this world." As we had misplaced the glasses some time before, we were swigging the wine straight from the bottle, passing it back-and-forth as we played. "Ah, just as Mr. Salanack and his fellow culturally groundbreaking cronies used to play!" Perth enthused.

"Indeed, Mr. Perth. You know, you're all right."

I went in to make a shot, lost my balance, and sent the cue flying across the table. It landed on the cement floor with a loud thwack, splintering into three pieces.

"Oops."

The Pash tries to explain to me where he had been, using his minimal English and acting skills, pretending to strangle himself and kicking an invisible man's head in, lifting his pant leg to reveal an oozing scab the size of a quarter just underneath his kneecap.

ONE YEAR LATER – PART FOUR

THE PASH IS BACK. His arrival is announced by a quarter-stick blast in the middle of the night, one of the same quarter-sticks he sells illegally from the back of the store, mostly to demolition crews. I do not hear the pounding at my door since I'm soundly into my 13th hour of sleep that night, the television glowing with white static in the darkened space.

 The dynamite explosion, directly outside my window, causes me to leap off the couch and sprawl immediately onto the floor. My heart beats against my ribcage with sickening force, the saliva gone from my mouth, on the verge of hyperventilation. A loud explosion in the middle of the night could mean a number of things in these parts. It could mean a car crash. The lack of stop signs and median lines on the street in front of the building often leads to collisions, especially after dark since most people are wasted at the wheel in beater cars with faulty headlights. It could mean an explosion, an occurrence which isn't all that unusual in this neck of the woods. Things explode all the time. Cars, sometimes with mid-level mafia members inside of them, go *KAPOW* on a fairly regular basis, as do the parked cars that the locals douse in gasoline for no particular reason. Sometimes whole houses explode, entire apartment buildings, from causes

Travels and Travails of Small Minds by Daniel Falatko

ranging from electrical malfunctions to bombs. Riots, which spark off on a fairly regular basis, are often brought to a halt with the bang of a strategically-placed *militsiya* flash bomb. But the scariest thing that could go bang in the night, the reason I hit the floor and nearly wet myself in fear, would be a random dude with a shotgun wildly firing into people's windows. Perhaps he mistakenly thought this was his girlfriend's boyfriend's apartment. Perhaps he knew I was an American. Perhaps he assumed (quite rightly) that I had many thousands of dollars hidden within a hollowed-out section of the wall behind a Gorky Park Poster, and many more in the toilet tank in the bathroom. Perhaps he was simply three bottles into his night and wanted to blast someone's head clear off.

Instead of a follow-up shot, this time through the window at the cowering foreigner lit up by the TV glow, there is laughter. The guttural, hearty laughter of The Pash. Uncovering my head, I look up at the window to see my landlord's bearded, beaming face. It is glorious to see him, a relief to hand over the rent I had owed him in his absence, to have him scoop me up into a massive bear hug. He tries to explain to me where he had been, using his minimal English and acting skills, pretending to strangle himself and kicking an invisible man's head in, lifting his pant leg to reveal an oozing scab the size of a quarter just underneath his kneecap. Clutching a bottle of beer the size of a liter soda and an unused quarter-stick, he settles in at my table as he had always done in the past, swigging and laughing and dealing out cards to a game we play that has no rules, no structure, no name. "You good, my little invalid."

On Tuesdays and Thursdays I am now put to work. My duties are minimal though thoroughly satisfying, and the structure is entirely welcomed. Not being able to show my face in the daylight hours, due to the *militsiya*'s habit of stopping by for their payoff bottles at morning and mid-day, proves to be a bit of a problem. Fortunately, there are ways I can be utilized. The Pash brings me boxes to unpack, generic cans of tomato and chicken

ONE YEAR LATER – PART FOUR

noodle soup, unlabeled bottles of bootleg vodka which I stamp with the high-end labels The Pash provides, unofficial DVDs and computer software and sick German porn magazines. The Pash or Mariska or one of the other workers will come to retrieve the goods throughout the day as needed.

One day The Pash shows up with two very thin junkies I recognize from the lines surrounding the heroin dealers down the block. A brand new refrigerator is wheeled in on a rickety hand. This is used to store overflow kiosk product. The smell from the hard boiled eggs and vats of cabbage soup is overwhelming, though I am permitted to purchase food from the fridge on an honor system. This relieves me of the difficult task of food shopping in the open-air markets full of pickpockets and strung-out children and the ever-scanning robot eyes of the *militsiya*.

On rare occasions I am permitted to stock the rickety shelves in the dark AM hours. The customers at this time are nearly always drunks, spending an inordinate amount of time scanning all of the bottles before inevitably settling on the very cheapest of the spirits. Often they will flirt with Mariska, some of them putting their dicks against the glass or getting down on their knees to propose marriage. Each is laughed off with the same dismissive wave of her hand.

On one occasion, when Mariska is waylaid due to one of the frequent whooping cough outbreaks in the area and the night boy is late for his shift, I am left in charge of the kiosk from 3 to 5 AM. It's the first bitter cold night of the year. Foot traffic is minimal. A total of two customers pass through during my reign. The language barrier proves to be a problem, though the first customer, a hunched-over old woman with a handmade walker apparatus fashioned from street sign poles, manages to indicate her purchase by pointing to the sticks of butter on display through the clear fridge window. I later find out that she short-changed me. The second, a thoroughly crazed teen with a shaved head and full camouflage garb, gets angry when I grab the wrong bottle of beer for the second time and unleashes

Travels and Travails of Small Minds by Daniel Falatko

a rather impressive roundhouse kick to the glass. Obviously underestimating the thickness of the barrier, his boot bounces off with merely a dull thud. Sprawling on the frozen mud, his eyes flash evil and he spits at me, the saliva streaking down the glass as he gets up and limps into the cold pre-dawn.

Appreciation for my help at the store is shown through a reduced rent rate, down almost 50 percent, which works to help retain the money stash. Oftentimes I wish I didn't even have the satchel of bills, as it tends to cause more paranoia than it does good. Every couple of days I become convinced that the local hooligans are onto the stash, causing me to find ever more elaborate hiding places within the tiny space, under mouse-gnawed floorboards, in a hollow space under the sink, slid under the plaster of the ceiling, until the bills have taken on a stained, moldy appearance. Eventually, it gets to the point where individual stacks are hidden separately at key points throughout the room. It would take your average robber many hours to find them all, which of course would be entirely possible since he would most likely kill me first and be able to take his sweet time, helping himself to boiled eggs and cabbage soup and large bottles of beer as he did so. But at least it wouldn't be easy for him.

Each night Mariska appears at my door to pick up goods from the fridge. On nights when the kiosk is slow she stays to watch the cheesy pop video hour. She knows each song, even the new ones, completely by heart. On some nights we just sit and watch, not saying anything to one another. On other nights, we dance. On one occasion The Pash stops by to find us flailing around the room. After admonishing Mariska and sending her pouting back to the kiosk, he winks at me while making a blowjob gesture with his giant hand.

AUGUST 6th

UPON THE TRAIN bound for Stiltonfordshire, sitting atop a stylish satchel containing three hundred thousand American dollars, I began delving deeper into the Salanack novel. Though the grandstanding, "check out how nihilistic I am" shtick of the first line did not necessarily let up as the paragraphs unwound, I managed to force myself on through sheer hung over boredom. The scenery was dull and drab outside the windows of the blue train, sparse fields giving way to shabby towns giving way to more sparse fields. The rain started twenty minutes into the ride, large drops pounding against the windows with surprising ferocity. Though the subject matter was obviously intended to shock, a value which had been diluted through years of intense decadence within mainstream culture, I did find myself gliding from line-to-line on what immediately struck me as a flawless and unorthodox sentence structure. Soon I was going back to the previous pages, which had merely been scanned through, with questions such as, "Wait, why is this handsome junkie so indebted to the one-armed amphetamine addict?" or "Did I miss the part where he was gangbanged by sailors?" Slowly, fighting against great inner resistance, the story began to ingrain itself in my thoughts.

Travels and Travails of Small Minds by Daniel Falatko

THOUGH I HAD BEEN FULLY PREPARED for the cash transaction, the handover of the light-brown leather satchel in Mr. Perth's ridiculously massive entranceway still proved something of a shock. So here it was, more money than I'd ever hope to see at any one time, cumbersome and heavy and digging into my shoulder as I shook hands with a clearly worse for wear Mr. Perth. His eyes were bleary and barely opened, the skin of his face alight with blotches the same color as the wine we had consumed the night before. He had apparently slept in his clothes, his white hair jutting out at odd angles as if under electric shock. He let me know that a car from a more reputable service was waiting for me outside.

"I will be billing Dr. Behr for the pool cue," he let me know before wrestling the heavy wooden door to a close behind me.

EVERY COUPLE OF PAGES I would attempt to phone Edward, making sure to hang up before his voicemail clicked on to avoid the long distance. I sent him several desperate text messages. Nobody was picking up at the office either, which was understandable since it was far too early for anyone to be there on a Monday morning. I tried Amy, instead, and she picked up on the fifth ring. I wasn't expecting her to do so and was caught a bit off guard, stammering while thinking of the astronomical costs associated with this call. She mentioned that it was four in the morning and that she had to work the next day. "If I hadn't broken up with you the other day, I would after this." After apologizing profusely, much to the amusement and intrigue

AUGUST 6th

of my fellow passengers, I let her know that I was on a train in England in the rain and that things were unraveling. "Everybody is working against everybody else," I told her. "I'm bouncing around between various conspiracies like a ping pong ball." Lowering my voice so none of the eavesdroppers could hear me. "I'm sitting on a bag containing three hundred grand."

She sighed, her voice dreamy and tinged with sleep. "All this over chump change?" Silence. Just the whoosh of the train and the rain upon the window. "Listen, I'll call you back when I'm awake. Be careful." She faded out and I assumed that she was gone, though her voice then returned over the static-laced line. "Oh, I saw your tweaked-out neighbor at Union Pool the other night. He told me to tell you he's using your apartment to start a tickle porn empire."

I WAS ONLY INTO THE SECOND HOUR of the train ride. The scenery remained uninteresting, the windows rain-lashed. At one point we blazed through what could pass for a city, its drab, puddled streets completely deserted, no shops in sight, just blocks of white houses with pointy roofs and porches with no railings that dropped off suddenly. I could imagine people walking right off of them if they weren't paying attention. Nobody came aboard at the stop, no cars in the parking lot. I could hear a man behind me say, "Auntie Ginny lives here."

The junkie protagonist of the Salanack novel had it bad. He was implicated in a murder, the vicious throat slicing of a gay hustler who walked around with a parrot named Mr. Casey on his shoulder (Mr. Casey got it too), that his friend the eunuch amphetamine addict had committed. Not wanting to withdraw in prison and equally unwilling to snitch on his friend, he was living in an abandoned warehouse by the docks and being

Travels and Travails of Small Minds by Daniel Falatko

repeatedly gang raped by the homosexual tramps who also inhabited the space, although he claimed to enjoy it and would score dope off the rapist tramps when they weren't buggering him repeatedly. A sticker on the back jacket read, "A searing and culturally groundbreaking account of a 1950s underworld left unseen by the legions in Eisenhower-age America. Salanack's prose explodes with a lacerating passion, a roving eye for the bizarre, and an all-encompassing desire to peel back the eyes of those who oppressed him." There were several passages that nearly made me stop reading, especially a scene in which the protagonist has his stash eaten by a stray dog and spends three days following the dog around eating its feces. But there was something about the way the paragraphs were put together, utilizing jump cuts and dips into the surreal while still managing to maintain some semblance of a story line, that continued to hold my interest nearly fifty pages in.

    A fellow passenger in his late teens with a mop of brown hair and large sunglasses, even though it was quite gloomy on the train, began dancing up and down the aisle for no particular reason, kicking out his legs and playing air maracas. After a couple of minutes, when it was clear that he wasn't going to stop, people began shouting threats. "Sit down, you poof!" "Don't make me kick ya' head in, then!" "Looka' him? Won't be dancin' after I smash his face in!" The kid danced on, oblivious, moving in a liquid motion and flailing his arms until a full can of Coke hurled from the front of the car clonked him on the head with a satisfying "ping." He lay sprawled in the aisle for some time as people turned back to their smartphones, finally rising to slump back to his seat rubbing his head, a dazed look on his face and his sunglasses knocked crooked.

    I was so enthralled with the book, re-reading a scene in which a sewer rat is speaking to the junkie in prophetic tongues, that I barely noticed the buzzing of my phone. Cally incoming. "Good morning."

AUGUST 6th

"Is it ok to be calling you? Where are you? How are things progressing? So sorry I didn't pick up last night. Things are hectic here too."

"I was being entertained by a man with pure white hair who lives on a hill and collects a dead man's syringes. It turned out to be an ok time. Food and drink. He was a prick, but what else is new with these people. Anyway, I miss you."

"I miss you too. Your trip sounds, um, interesting thus far."

The kid with the sunglasses appeared to be twitching in his seat, having some sort of seizure, but he was also laughing. Nobody paid him any mind.

"There are some strange fucking people in England," I let her know. "Listen, if a man by the name of Edward should contact you, an employee of Behr's, the same guy who first gave you the tour of that apartment, don't speak to him. I think he's plotting against me."

"Why would you think that? Your friend Edward? You may be on the verge of becoming too paranoid, my dear."

"No way," I was looking around while speaking, making sure that nobody was listening in. "The Salanack freak had too much to drink and let it slip. Hey, since you are calling me, do I have to pay roaming charges for this call?"

"How romantic," she fake-swooned. "No, no long distance. No worries. I don't think so, anyway. I'll go if you want."

I slapped myself on the forehead. What an asshole I was.

"Any charge is worth hearing your voice." This came out as more of a question than a stated fact, though it seemed to work since she breathed in deeply and didn't sound angry.

"Also watch out for Behr. Keep an eye out for people lingering around. He may be ready to intensify the harassment campaign since he thinks the cash will soon be in hand."

"I'll be on the lookout." She didn't sound as worried as I was. "Speaking of the deal going down, do you have a plan in place to make sure it doesn't go down?"

"I'm working on it," I said, even though I had no clue how it could be pulled off. "It turns out that our friend the Oxford Man is getting paid double. Money coming in from both sides. He was already paid a ridiculous amount for even turning the tip on the property in to the Salanack freak and is now supposed to collect thirty grand from the three hundred grand I'm currently sitting on top of. I'll be glad to make sure that doesn't happen."

Cally's end was silent.

"Oh, did I mention I'm sitting atop a satchel with threee hundred thousand dollars inside?" I whispered. "In cash?"

Still silence on Cally's end. I thought for a second that she was frightened. I told her it was all going to be fine. Maybe.

"It's not that," she said, seeming to choose her words carefully. "It's that you should let this Sneil guy have his money. He earned it. He made the whole deal go down. He isn't the one kicking me out of my apartment. Dr. Behr is."

Cally was now officially making things more complicated. Why did she suddenly care about the Oxford Man?

"You're making my head spin," I told her, laughing. "So what you're saying is that I should let Sneil take his 30 grand, but somehow not let the rest get deposited into Behr's account?"

She sounded relieved that I grasped this.

"That is exactly what I mean. Think about it…if Behr's deposit doesn't go through, then the apartment isn't sold. It'll still be Dr. Behr's. There is no need to interfere with the Oxford Man's cash. It's only Behr's cash that matters."

I thought about this. It did make sense on a certain level, but why did she seem so concerned with the Oxford Man receiving his money?

"The whole thing will break down. Behr and this Salanack guy will start fighting. The apartment will still be on Behr's roster and he'll have no reason to harass me out of the apartment. Hell, he'll probably just forget."

She was bringing up an interesting point. As a matter of fact, I was surprised Dr. Behr hadn't forgotten about the whole thing already. Usually his flights of fancy would come to an abrupt end

AUGUST 6th

with the late afternoon, day-ending Grunt. This one he seemed intent on carrying all the way through.

"Ok, Nathan, so is it agreed that you will let Dr. Sneil take his money and then somehow mess up the Behr transaction?"

"You're speaking as if you know him."

"Know who?"

"The Oxford Man."

"I can assure you I would know if I were acquainted with anyone named the Oxford Man," she told me in a soothing voice. "And it just isn't the case. But I do feel for him. He deserves his cut."

The knife twisting into my guts let up a little. She was simply sticking up for the middle man, as well as making it easier for me, as I would now only have to concentrate on what was necessary to foil Behr's plans.

"I get it," I purred to her, wishing she were with me on the train at that moment.

"You truly are the greatest," she purred back before her voice straightened out, became serious. "Have you had any ideas on how you'll mess this up? It seems like a sure thing no matter how you look at it. An elementary school student could pull off this assignment, it seems. How can something this easy possibly be blundered?"

The dancing guy had fallen asleep, snoring loudly until the woman in the seat next to him placed her hair clip on his nose. People laughed and snapped pictures with their phones as he slept on, the snores silenced, the hair clip causing the tip of his nose to turn red.

"Cally, I have absolutely no plan formulated. I have no ideas. I have nothing. Literally nothing. I could somehow try to play Sneil against Behr, but I already tried that with the Salanack freak, did everything I could to make him hate me. I scarfed his food. I broke his property. I openly insulted him. But he still handed over the money. It's been a tough mission to blow. But I'll blow it. Believe me."

She laughed, delighted.

"I think I just might love you," she told me.

"It's a little early," I let her know. "But I think I may be in the same place."

"It feels good to have you working for me, to have you on my side."

"Of course I'm working for you." I felt sad for her. She really did sound quite desperate, at loose ends. "And I'll figure out a way to make this whole thing work. Or in this case not work. Believe me, I can blow any mission. I can barely stuff envelopes. I'm not even trusted to file folders alphabetically. It took me an entire year of hanging up on people to finally master how to transfer a call. And now I'm trusted with a money handoff? Failure, in this case, will be a cake walk."

"Wow," she said before letting me know once again how much she missed me, before we hung up and the train once again plunged into silence. "I guess if anyone can fail on such a massive level, can blow such a simple mission, it would be you, Nathan. My eternal gratitude. I'll make it worth your while next time you're on Avenue B."

IT WASN'T UNTIL nearly an hour later, after switching to a red train at a stopover in the middle of an endless muddy field, when rain had ceased lashing the window and the sun was threatening but failing to break through the endless dull grey skies, that I noticed I was being watched.

There were two of them. Both in their thirties with wispy hair and angular features, occupying a seat near the bathrooms. I noticed the spies when heading for a piss, one with his left leg crossed and the other his right. There was nothing remarkable about them. Nothing outwardly suspicious. Just two ordinary blokes on a train. What did catch my attention was their eyes.

AUGUST 6th

While the other passengers didn't give the satchel a second glance, the two men seemed intensely interested. Catching their profiles as I ducked into the pisser, both had their heads facing forward but their eyes trained on me. I latched the door. I didn't panic. It was obvious they weren't there to rob me. They would be far more tightly-coiled had that been their purpose, their stares more menacing. No, these men were simply keeping watch. I wondered who they were working for. Most likely Mr. Perth, making sure his money reached its intended destination. The deed was in his hands, though Behr would most certainly make a fuss if the money didn't end up where it needed to be. There was, however, the slight chance that these were Behr's people, Behr and the Oxford Man making sure that I didn't get lost along the way. I had been whispering on the phone earlier so there was no way they had heard me unless they were equipped with Bond-like listening devices. *There is nothing to worry about*, I told myself.

Leaving the bathroom I gave the spies a glance. They hadn't moved, their heads in the same position, eyes trained on the bathroom door, legs crossed on opposite sides. Whistling the solo from "*Patience*" as I headed back to my seat, the satchel strap digging into my collarbone, I made a big show of sitting down, getting comfortable, even letting out a relaxing sigh before suddenly whirling around to face them. My eyes locked with the spy with his left leg crossed, his gaze stock-still and unblinking, mine frantic and twitching. This left leg spy seemed the most intense, focused on me with the unrelenting gaze of a robot or cop. The spy with his right leg crossed was a little more playful, his lips curling into a bemused grin at my challenge. I threw up my arms in surrender, letting them know they had made their point. I pointed to the satchel and gave a thumbs up. They were shaking their heads as I turned and slumped back into my seat.

It was difficult to concentrate on a story involving schizophrenic junkies digging suspected microchip implants out

Travels and Travails of Small Minds by Daniel Falatko

of their own heads with screwdrivers when I knew I was being spied upon. Every couple of paragraphs I would find that I hadn't been paying attention and would have to go back and re-read in order to find out why the junkie's ears were squirting blood or who this "Mr. Balls" character was and why had he suddenly taken over the narration duties. After a while I gave up, unable to shake the feeling of their eyes upon me. I pretended to read, flipping a page every now and again, furrowing my brow as if in full concentration. Instead, I thought about the day ahead. I wondered what awaited me at the Sneil residence. I wondered how I was going to blow the assignment while apparently being watched. I thought about Cally, about the way the locks of hair curled around her ears in a vaguely elfin fashion.

I was still thinking about this as the train pulled in Stiltonfordshire.

DR. SNEIL HAD GAINED WEIGHT since his faculty photo had been taken. Slightly hunched, in a black sweater with his belly hanging over the top of his trousers, he was the only individual waiting in the station's parking lot. The car he stood next to was so completely old and beaten down that I found it hard to believe he had driven it there. It was a black vehicle, small and tilting noticeably to the left, with half of the front bumper torn off and the other half tied on with a length of rope. I waved to him good naturedly while stepping off the train, hoisting the satchel and my other bag down the steep steps, deliberately moving slowly in order to annoy the other two passengers exiting at the stop, the two spies who had been watching me. One of the men who collected tickets in the aisles finally shouted "Let's fucking move!" and I hopped down onto the concrete, the spies moving to stand awkwardly behind me.

AUGUST 6th

From across the parking lot, where Dr. Sneil had parked even though the spaces right next to the tracks weren't taken, he indicated that he would pull around to pick me up. This ended up taking a full ten minutes, with Dr. Sneil struggling into the car, taking forever to get it running, finally firing up with a puff of black smoke, and taking forever to reach me in a drawn-out circular trajectory.

"The sun is out, huh?" The spies refused to answer. "Thought it was going to be a grey one with all that rain earlier, but now it's bright like yesterday. I was told to expect non-stop rain and gloom!"

They didn't move, standing at a safe distance, their eyes on the old car as it circled around. They too looked pained at the vehicle's slow motion pace.

"Looks like we'll be here awhile. Anybody up for a smoke?"

They didn't acknowledge the pack I held out to them, though I could tell the spy who had had his right leg crossed wanted one badly. When I waved it in front of their faces, they simply shook their heads.

"Man, this bag sure is heavy." I pointed at the satchel. The other spy, the one who had had his left leg crossed, was now paying attention. "Sure hope I don't lose it."

The spy smiled, his eyes gleaming. He was daring me.

There was no way these guys were too heavy. I could see if the satchel contained a million, but 300 grand? Chump change. They weren't even muscular or dressed in black. Taunting them was fun.

"Well, looks like my ride's here." I pointed at the beater as it finally jerked and putted to a stop next to us. "You guys want to help me load this in? Or are you union?"

The spies muttered and shook their heads. I opened the back door and motioned to the satchel. "Come on guys, this thing is heavy as all hell."

The left leg spy rolled his eyes, slapped the other on the shoulder. Sighing, right leg spy stepped forward and, groaning, hoisted the satchel onto the cluttered back seat of the car.

Travels and Travails of Small Minds by Daniel Falatko

"I'd tip you," I got into the front seat without saying hello to Dr. Sneil, indicating for him to hit the gas. "But it's not my money."

"Do you know those two?" I inquired of the Oxford Man as the car lurched out of the lot, watching as the two spies sat down on a bench, conferring animatedly with one another, crossing their legs in the same positions as they had on the train. "The one who crosses his left leg is kind of rude."

Heavy breathing from the driver's seat. He was concentrating hard on pulling out of the parking lot, his foot heavy on the brake, even though there wasn't another car in sight.

"I would assume they work for the Society, dear boy. Don't be alarmed. The man is simply looking after his investment."

That voice. Like shards of glass scraped over concrete. The same voice that had slashed apart my nerves over the phone line for the past two years, unfailingly polite but extremely rough on the eardrums.

"Why aren't they following us?" There were no cars on the road behind us, which was a good thing since we were traveling at barely 30 miles per hour. "They just wanted to make sure I got the cash to your car? How do they know we aren't planning to drive off into the sunset?"

He laughed at this, a guttural cackle from the depths of his raspy chest cavity.

"We would make an odd fugitive pair, would we not?" He was looking at me in a rearview so streaked with grime it made the word appear trapped behind a sooty screen door. A smile creased his cheeks.

"We certainly would," I agreed with him, finally offering my hand.

"It is nice to finally meet you, Edward."

We were passing through some seriously English countryside, like something off the cover of a Led Zeppelin album.

"It's nice to meet you too, Dr. Sneil." I didn't bother correcting him on my name. "This whole experience has been quite a trip thus far. Aren't you afraid of the spies?"

AUGUST 6th

"Spies?" He scoffed loudly, causing me to shield my ears. "Those aren't spies. Hired hands at best. Probably just some blokes from the local Wolfton watering hole. I'm sure they know where I live. They'll hang out for a bit until the transaction goes through and then be off. Probably drink up their pay within hours."

This made sense. Sneil's ability to put all that together without thinking too hard or suffering a minor freak-out was impressive.

"The man from Wolfton is smart." He tapped the side of his head. "Perhaps a bit eccentric in his methods, though that is nobody's issue but his own."

We drove for a while in silence. The car never passed 35 as we moved through what must have been the outskirts of Stiltonfordshire, emerging on the other side onto a wide road through thorny fields. We were moving toward a highway.

"Do you mind if I play music?" Sneil asked after turning on the tinny speakers. Brainy, progressive jazz spilled fluidly from the radio. He began humming along to the complicated sax lines, his ravaged vocal chords sagging under the strain.

"Don't you live in Stiltonfordshire?" I was nervous, paranoia running rampant through my synapses, imagining spies with opposite crossed legs in every bush, watching from every house window.

"I live 20 miles out," he assured me, bopping his grey head along to the jazz.

We were now on the highway. Thankfully, he sped up, the car shaking so hard once it hit 50 mph I thought for a second it might explode or come apart, spitting bursts of black smoke behind us like a charred dragon's tail.

"You're more together than Dr. Behr, aren't you?" I was thinking out loud, studying the heavy lines around his eyes and streaking across his cheeks.

"Why, yes, dear boy." He sounded sad. "I most certainly am."

Travels and Travails of Small Minds by Daniel Falatko

WE LEFT THE HIGHWAY at the first exit, and it wasn't long before we pulled into a driveway off a charming suburban road. A modest two-story affair, Dr. Sneil' house was adorned with neat-looking green windowpanes and tasteful shrubbery. I stood on the stoop for a long while as Sneil shut the car down, holding onto the satchel and watching tiny red birds dance around a feeder in the yard. Scanning the road for spies, I saw nothing to arouse any suspicion. A large field behind the house went on for miles, the highway snaking past in the distance. As a safehouse, this place was ideal. Anything that moved would be instantly out of place.

Inside the house we were greeted by Mrs. Sneil, a stooped, frail woman with a receding hairline and the most horrifying case of Rosacea I had ever witnessed, her entire face and neck one red blotch. She had a rolling pin in her hand which she promptly dropped when we entered. It rolled down the hallway and stopped at my feet. I picked it up and handed it to her.

"Roland, is this Edward?" she asked her husband as he stood awkwardly next to us in the hallway.

"It is he, dear."

I said hello, once again not bothering to correct them, and did a little wave.

"Tell him to make himself at home." She addressed Dr. Sneil, refusing to look at me, before heading back into the living room where a television was blaring. I was wondering why she had the rolling pin while watching television and also why she chose to speak to me through a third party. Looking to Dr. Sneil, he shrugged helplessly and led me to my room on the bottom floor.

The room was cramped but cozy, at the back of the house, with a bank of windows overlooking the field and the highway beyond. I wasn't sure if I should take the satchel out into the main house to give Sneil his cut right away, deciding to stash it behind some extra blankets in the closet. A gentle knock on the door, Sneil letting me know that I had a phone call. He shoved a black cordless into my hand and shut the door.

"This is Edward," I mimicked his voice the best I could. "How may I help you and stuff?"

Silence on the line, confused breathing, the light whistle of nose hairs. Dr. Behr was confused.

"Hello?" I knocked the phone against the wall three times. "Dr. Behr... Ronald, old chap, it's me, Nathan. You know... dear boy? On a mission here? Just kidding about the Edward thing."

He cleared his throat, the sound of phlegm competing with the static on the line.

"Ah, yes," he sounded far more befuddled than usual. "Edward has not arrived at work as of yet, and I was wondering what he would be doing in England on this fine morning."

"I guess one never knows with Behr Properties," I sighed.

Another round of silence. I didn't feel like breaking it, looking out over the field and checking for escape routes. The windows pushed outward and were easy to open. I wouldn't have to smash and jump if a quick escape was needed. The highway was about 2 miles off.

"Indeed, indeed." He was totally spaced. Edward probably hadn't been fetching him his Solid Ground. "How are things unfolding, dear boy?"

There were many things I was interested in asking. Did he have leg-crossing spies on me or were they under the employ of Mr. Perth? Did he know that his good friend Dr. Sneil was collecting money from both sides for his tip? And more importantly, why had he lied to me about being the perfect man for the mission when he had intended on sending Edward all along? Why did he have his tardy employee do all the legwork for this deal and then lead me to believe it had been handed to me cold? Even with such questions weighing heavily on my tongue, I decided not to confront him just yet. Perhaps having secret knowledge of these facts could work to my advantage down the line.

Travels and Travails of Small Minds by Daniel Falatko

"The dimensions are aligning nicely." I checked for shadows through the crack in the bottom of the door, making sure Sneil wasn't eavesdropping. "I fetched a bag full of stuff from that Salanack freak you sent me to. No problems. Now I'm safe and sound at your boy's place. Things are cool, though I must say Mrs. Sneil trips me out a little, wandering around the house with a rolling pin."

A relieved sigh. A shuffling of papers. I knew which papers he was handling, could picture him sitting there examining them, befuddled within the dust cloud.

"Excellent." A tinge of evil to his tone. "I knew you were the perfect man for the mission."

"I'm not even going to respond to that."

"Pardon?"

I bit my tongue, coughed.

"Well then, I have spoken to Dr. Sneil and everything appears to be arranged. You will be accompanying him to the bank for the first deposit on Wednesday. As I said before, you need to do very little. Just keep an eye out and make sure that the deposit gets made."

"And what about his cut?" I was thinking of Cally, still wondering why she was so concerned with the old chap getting his 30 grand. For a second I thought I saw the two spies lurking in the field. Upon closer inspection, they turned out to be two geese hovering in the oncoming dusk.

"You shall give it to him." Dr. Behr was speaking to me like one would a five-year-old boy. "The tip worked out. The money has exchanged hands. Dr. Sneil has done his part, Nathan."

I let him know that I would see to it he got his cash. The need to get off the phone was strong at that moment. I wanted to get in touch with Edward. I needed to think. I needed some time in that room with the door locked.

"I'll be in continuous touch."

"I'm sure you will."

I was pacing, inspecting the field, making sure the two geese didn't morph back into spies.

AUGUST 6th

"Oh, I forgot to mention," I sat down on the edge of the bed, finding it rock-hard and very cold. "You'll be receiving a bill from the Salanack freak for a damaged pool cue."

I clicked off, immediately phoned Edward using Sneil's line. No answer. Straight to voicemail. The second time yielded the same results. It took a great deal of self control not to throw the black phone through one of the windows. How was I going to pull this off? There were really several options. I could lose the money somehow, burn it or stage a theft after Sneil had taken his cut. But how does someone lose 270 grand? It doesn't just fall out of your pocket. They would accuse me of stealing it. The police would be involved. I'd end up in some English prison with a bunch of murderous soccer hooligans anxious to kick me to death for my accent alone. Staging a theft would also be a problem. This took a level of skill and cold-blooded calculation far beyond my abilities. What if I just lit it on fire? Right in Sneil's backyard? It would cost me my job and my flight home, but the money would not be deposited and the deal would fall through. Cally would most likely not be evicted. All I would have to do was make it back to her somehow. But who is to say the deal would fall through? What if the Salanack freak was crazy enough to dish out another payment? Perhaps send it with his spies this time, instead of some disrespectful American. Still, setting the money alight, preferably accidentally so I could have some hopes of retaining my job, seemed like the only option unless the Sneil Manor was to suddenly combust before Wednesday.

Another thought did cross my mind as I paced in Dr. Sneil's guest room that early evening. What if I were to just let the deposit be made? Just do my job and oversee the transaction, then go home? If Cally really loved me as much as she said she did, couldn't she understand that I had to do my job? Why would she want me to risk getting fired or arrested? She did, after all, have legal grounds to be there. Why couldn't she fight this through the proper channels? There seemed to be no foolproof option to blow this deal, no real way out of it minus handcuffs or heartbreak or the unemployment line. I was going to have to play things by ear, to coast on feeling alone.

THOUGH NOT NEARLY AS EXPANSIVE as Mr. Perth's dining room table, the Sneil eating station was nonetheless charming, with a tasteful set of candles in the center and plates of carefully sliced roast set strategically upon red placemats. Mrs. Sneil, her tiny head glowing red under the room's semi-harsh lighting, contemplatively nibbled her food and avoided eye contact with both her husband and I. Dr. Sneil, hunched over his plate as if guarding it, appeared slightly nervous, the food never reaching his mouth, running his fork to cut a trail across the plate, then another, forming jagged crisscross pattern, every now and then spearing a hunk of the meat and bringing it halfway to his lips before releasing it back to his food maze with a sigh.

"Lovely setup you have here, Mr. and Mrs. Sneil." The silence was beginning to bother me. Using my best Eddie Haskell voice, "And thank you very much for the meal."

Mrs. Sneil reacted to this as if I had just told her that her mother was ugly, frozen over her plate, wide eyes like cotton balls floating in a bowl of tomato soup. She was freaking me out. I looked to Mr. Sneil for help.

"We will be going to the bank on Wednesday," he rasped.

Nodding, I decided to concentrate on what was left of the meal.

Upon finishing my plate, the arthritic hand of Mrs. Sneil snaked in to snatch it. Dr. Sneil and I stared at one another uncomfortably until cups of tea we had not requested were placed before us.

"Well, I'll let you get on with it, then." Mrs. Sneil floated out of the room like a shifty, reddened cloud.

AUGUST 6th

"Get on with what?" I inquired of Dr. Sneil. He just shrugged and rolled his eyes at his departing wife.

"So, you spoke with Ronald?" The tea had a cinnamon taste to it which was highly unappealing. I set the cup back down with a sour smack of the lips.

"Indeed." His eyes drooped behind the glasses, blowing on his tea even though it wasn't very hot.

"So how long have you two known one another?"

He looked at me as if I were accusing him of something, his wrinkled cheeks shaking with his breaths like a turkey gizzard. He was spooked.

"We have known one another for a very long time," he said, sighing to indicate the years, the decades, the memories. "At one point we were colleagues, before I was stolen away by Oxford."

I let this resonate. There was an inner-gurgling from within his throat, a palpable sense of longing and dread. For a second I considered that they had been lovers, a thought that made me visibly shudder. Sneil was looking at me strangely.

"Tell me something about him," I nearly pleaded.

Sneil unfolded his hands, cocked his head. 'What would you like to know, dear boy?"

"What kind of person is he?" My voice cracked. "I only know him in the capacity of our quarters in New York. He doesn't say much."

The television was audible from the living room, some gardening show, a man's voice urging viewers to use a certain type of hand-held rake. Sneil's grey head hung low, he was silent for what seemed like a long while before finally looking at me. The heavy lines in his face seemed to have indented further in the time his head was down.

"At one point he was very sharp," he told me with a heavy frown.

"Interesting."

What's interesting," he rasped. "Is that it seems to be coming back."

Travels and Travails of Small Minds by Daniel Falatko

7 O'CLOCK ENGLISH TIME. Dead bored in the guest room with the door locked. The Salanack novel was unfolding into a nightmarish netherworld where harsh reality and cruel fantasy merged. Pagan gods, hallucinated in the midst of fever dreams, showed up in the protagonist's waking hours. Individuals and inanimate objects rooted in reality, chained to the daylight, found themselves trapped in dreams behind subconscious bars. All of this, of course, had something to do with heroin, although by now the plot was long forgotten and the novel seemed to be coasting on hellish surrealism alone. I had to stop reading when the lead protagonist, while escaping from a combination rehab center/psych-ward/dragon pit, began envisioning ghostly pterodactyls with diamond eyes closing in on him as he crossed a fog-shrouded field much like the one just beyond the Sneil backyard.

Eight o'clock now, pacing, no television in the room, nothing outside but dark and fog. I put on my shoes, unlatched the door, took a peak outside. Sneil was soundly unconscious, engulfed in a cushiony chair in the dark with flashes from the television spotlighting his grizzled nose and cheeks. In a separate chair, far across the room, Mrs. Sneil sat staring at me, looking horrified, her mouth open in an "O" shape like a black hole in the center of her bright-red face.

"Hello." I attempted a gentle wave, the movement thoroughly startling her. It looked like she was going to climb over the back of the chair. She attempted to say something, her breath audible with the effort, but all that came out was a dull croak.

"I think I'm going for a walk." I pointed out the window. "Out there. Out front. Not out back, through that field. I'm afraid of pterodactyls."

AUGUST 6th

If her head had exploded at that moment, skull fragments and brains showering myself and the sleeping Dr. Sneil, I would not have been surprised.

"Do you lock the doors? I shouldn't be long. I'll just ring the buzzer if it's locked when I get back."

She was nodding at me, seemingly in comprehension, her fingers digging into the side of the chair.

"I just need some fresh air." I began stammering due to her horrified expression. "I mean, not that the air in here isn't fresh... well... I just meant that... ok, bye."

THE ROAD IN FRONT OF THE HOUSE was deserted and foggy, the air refreshingly cool and moist against my face, walking on the grass of various lawns along the side of the road. Each house was nearly identical to the Sneil residence, small and tasteful with brightly-colored shutters, some red and others blue, some with the same shade of green as those which adorned the windows of the Sneil house. There were lights on in the living rooms and upstairs bedrooms, televisions flashing and laptops aglow. Dogs barked at me from windows and back yards, including a small Cocker Spaniel tied up on the front porch of the last house on the block. I offered my hand. She snapped at it. An old man in a train conductor's uniform stood on the edge of the last lawn on the block. "Don't mind Sadie," he motioned toward the Cocker Spaniel, inhaled on a cigarette. "She only bites Muslims." There was a bend in the road, just past where the houses stopped, a stretch of desolation with several lights visible a mile ahead. The fields on either side weren't as foggy as the one behind the Sneil manor. I would be able to see the pterodactyls if they were coming. I decided to brave it.

Travels and Travails of Small Minds by Daniel Falatko

THE LIGHTS TURNED OUT to be a small cluster of houses, seven or eight in total, situated around a crossroads with a streetlight in the center. At first glance, there was only one thing about this community that held my interest: the Regal Lion Pub dead center by the streetlight. The light from inside was yellow and welcoming. Three people loitered outside, smoking, two men in derby caps and a woman with large blond hair and stonewashed jeans rolled at the cuff as if it were 1987. They seemed startled to find me standing there.

"Well, ya' gonna' head on inside or just stare at us all night?" One of the men, clad in an Iron Maiden t-shirt, asked me. I headed inside. A little bell clinked on the door as I entered, the heads of the several people sitting at the bar turning, lingering for a second before looking back down at their drinks, one of them shaking his head. I ordered a Carlsberg, served to me frothy and thick in the largest mug I had ever seen. The bartendress, one of her forearms thicker than my thigh, grumbled at my credit card and fished out a dusty swiper from under a pile of papers behind the cash register. I was halfway finished with the beer by the time the transaction was finally settled, the other customers smirking, and retreated to a table in the back.

Joan Jett on the jukebox, lighting so dim it was nearly pitch dark, it felt good to be free from the bizarre houses this business trip had thus far confined me within. I didn't even care about the money anymore, could envision the satchel stashed under the guest bed free for anyone to take. But the comatose state of Dr. Sneil in front of the television and the cerebrally horrified state of his wife rendered the pair completely non-threatening. I could have left credit cards, my firstborn, a few bars of gold, and my entire life savings in cash sitting atop the living room table

AUGUST 6th

and they most likely wouldn't have even noticed it, just Dr. Sneil sound asleep and his wife switching between *BBC Gardening* and the *Inexpensive Antiquarian Roadshow*.

The plan had been to utilize the Regal Lion as a place to brood and think, to suss out the more complicated twists this business trip and the players within it had taken. In checking my phone earlier I had seen that Cally had phoned twice, though I didn't feel like contacting her back just yet. Not that night. There was something in her voice that bothered me when she had fought for Dr. Sneil to receive his money, a demanding quality disguised as empathy. Her dialog sounded rehearsed. Something about that conversation just wasn't right.

My plans for peaceful contemplation were shattered by Bilky. I hadn't noticed him, occupying a table in the corner underneath a Plyth Spartans banner with a man who appeared to be unconscious. Bilky was in his 50s, healthy-looking with a full head of long brown hair spilling over his shoulders. He wasn't getting much from his conversation with his passed-out friend, nudging him with his elbow every couple of minutes before giving up and coming over to talk to me.

Upon my saying "hello" Bilky exclaimed, "Fucking hell! He's an American!" Someone from the bar answered, "Who cares, ya' cunt?" But Bilky remained fascinated, demanding that I repeat back to him the lines he fed me, representing various American stereotypes. After each line he would roar with laughter, slamming an open palm on the table while the rest of the clientele rolled their eyes. "Ok, ok. One more!" He could barely contain himself. "Harold, did you read that fascinating article in *The New Yorker* on the death of urban farming?" I repeated it. "Oh my GOD!" He whacked me on the back." He turned around and nudged the unconscious man. "You getting this, Milly?" The man didn't move. He reached into Milly's jacket, pulled out a wad of crumpled pound notes. "How about a pint, mate? On me. Can't have ya' botherin' Rene with that damn credit card again. Comin' right up!"

I was going to like Bilky.

203

Travels and Travails of Small Minds by Daniel Falatko

OVER THE NEXT HOUR I learned that Bilky was out of work, having spent his career "workin' on the houses of these wankers round' here" until "they didn't have any more work to be done on em'." When I told him I was sorry to hear this, his face brightened. "No worries. My ex-coworker over there," he pointed to a snoring Milly. "was awarded a pension." I learned that he was a serious Super Tramp fan ("The most underrated fookin' rock band of the fookin' 70s") and was treated to *Give A Little Bit* on the jukebox, complete with Bilky's dancing and near-flawless lip-synching. One of the geezers at the bar became enraged when Bilky bumped into him during his dance, uttering vague threats of violence which served to wake up Milly. He rose to his feet, the geezer and I staring dumbfounded when we realized he was nearly seven feet tall and wider than the jukebox. The confrontation was over. "Which one of ya' ganked me fookin' bread, man?" He drawled in a menacing accent, half Manchester lout, half drunken hippie. Scared for a second, my fears of a stomping were eliminated when he laughed, exposing a row of broken and chipped upper teeth, and pretended to knock our heads together.

"Here, ya' giant fook'." Bilky tossed him the bundle. "Getcha' self a whiskey and sit her down right here. This one's an American. Crazy fuck wandered in here outta' nowhere waving credit cards around. He's a laugh fookin' riot! Go ahead! Repeat after me! 'Patrick, did you read that thought-provoking article on *HuffPo* about the rediscovery of Freddie Prinze Jr.?"

Apparently, bars in the English provinces shut down at ten, catching me off guard as I had just taken the last swig from another Milly-purchased pint. Rene began shouting, "Last call, you silly poofs! Get the fook' out!" Looking around, I realized we were the last people remaining in the Regal Lion. "What is a poof?" I inquired, inspiring another burst of laughter from Bilky and Milly, which was interrupted by Rene whacking our table with a long club, the loud crash finally budging us from our seats. Bilky tried to finish his pint as we were being chased out, Milly laughing as she swung the club at us, one of the swings knocking the glass out of Bilky's hand to smash on the floor.

"Til' tomorrow night, my dear," Bilky managed to sneak a kiss on her cheek as she closed the door on us.

Minutes later we were in Milly's van, with Milly tilting his head sideways to avoid hitting the rooftop, driving through a golf course as Bilky hung out the window snatching flags off the holes. He pulled a donut on one of the greens, wheels sending up huge clouds of shredded turf in their wake, before a man came running at the van from one of the maintenance houses wielding a rake and we tore off onto the road.

"Where ya' headed, ya' poof?" Bilky wanted to know. "Door-to-door service for our American friend."

"And all you have to do for it is repeat after me," Milly turned to me, his eyes joyous and sparkling. "Melissa, did you see Noah's post about new breakthroughs in meme therapy?"

IT TOOK AN EXCEEDINGLY LONG TIME to find the Sneil residence, zigzagging across dozens of back roads through fields similar to the one outside the Sneil guest room windows, but they never turned out to be the exact field. I couldn't remember the name of the road he lived on, though Bilky and Milly didn't seem to mind, having a grand old time as they plowed over mailboxes and paused to steal lawn ornaments with a teenage glee. I was drinking the warm cans of Carlsberg they kept pulling out from under the seats, straining my eyes to look for the Sneil manor. I had given up hope after Milly yelled, "Aw shite, we're on the fookin' highway! When did that fookin' happen?" But it wasn't long before we ended up driving by what I recognized as the

Travels and Travails of Small Minds by Daniel Falatko

foggy, pterodactyl-filled field I had seen from the guestroom windows. "Next exit! Next exit turn right!" I commanded. Milly responded by swerving into the right hand lane, almost crushing a tiny electric car which had to swerve onto the shoulder of the road in order to avoid its doom. Approaching the Sneil house, Milly was vomiting out the truck's window while Bilky took the wheel, swerving into the yard of their neighbors. The van nearly capsized, my beer flying and hitting the dashboard, covering the windshield in foam. Bilky managed to sidewind the out-of-control vehicle to a jerking halt in the middle of the Sneil yard, just feet short of crashing into the front of the house, the front bumper hitting the birdfeeder with an echoing "ding."

"Just as I said," Bilky grinned maniacally as the dry-heaving Milly got ready to retake the wheel. "Door-to-door service."

AUGUST 7th

AT TEN O'CLOCK the next morning I found myself handing the Oxford Man thirty thousand dollars in cash. The Sneil study, just off the main living room, boasted an impressive library, leather-bound editions that I felt an immediate urge to run my fingers across. From behind the medium-sized oak desk holding neat stacks of papers and no computer, Sneil appeared haggard but alert in the morning light.

Still halfway drunk, my vision slightly blurry, I could make out tire tracks on the lawn through the window. The birdfeeder was on its side and a patch of grass had been torn up, dirt splattered across the hedgerows. "Please don't turn around. Please don't turn around. Please don't turn around." This was my mantra. Earlier I had witnessed Mrs. Sneil exit the front door, a watering can in hand and sporting a large floppy hat. Her husband and I were just finishing our tea at that point and Dr. Sneil had, in a polite and almost hesitant manner, asked if I could retrieve his portion of the money and join him in the study. I fully expected Mrs. Sneil to burst in at any moment with news of the destruction outside, but she did not reappear. My head was throbbing so hard, at a pressure point just behind the eyes, that I decided to simply do as I was told. The previous evening, as I stumbled sideways through a front door that was thankfully left open into

Travels and Travails of Small Minds by Daniel Falatko

the silent, dark house, the Sneils asleep upstairs, I came to the vague conclusion that perhaps I should just allow the deal to go down. Perhaps fighting it was futile.

"The conversion rate will not be good for you."

He ignored this, gently patting the stacks of bills I had placed before him like petting a shelter cat he wasn't sure he wanted to adopt.

"Why does this whole thing have to be in cash? In American dollars? Those aren't worth much."

My voice was a little slurred. Sneil gave me a hard look, adjusting his glasses. He didn't count the money, giving it a "What the hell am I going to do with this?" look before carefully placing the bills into one of the desk drawers which I noticed he didn't lock.

Looking up I found him swiveling to gaze out the window. It was too late to stop him.

"What in the hell?" The words scraped at the sides of his throat like concrete on skin. "Some tosser has fucked through my yard!"

While he was occupied surveying the damage, muttering to himself and pressing his face against the window glass, I took the opportunity to steal a glance at a piece of notebook paper on his desk that had caught my attention. More specifically, it was the name written neatly on the Oxford University stationary that made my heart pound that morning. The name was "Cally." Right there on the first line. "Cally Braun." Next to it was a bank number, and next to that an amount, "15,000." I placed the paper back into position next to a pink bank deposit slip for 30 grand to the Sneil account and was back in my seat just as Sneil whirled to confront me.

"Do you have a vehicle here that we don't know about?" he demanded.

At this I laughed. "Wouldn't your spies know that?"

He grumbled at me, motioned for me to accompany him out of the room. I watched from the front door as he walked back-and-forth across the lawn inspecting the tracks, attempting to

AUGUST 7th

put the birdfeeder back in place, shaking his head at the deep grooves by the road, shouting at his wife in the garden, "How did you not see this?" I ducked back into the house and made a beeline for the guest bedroom, locking the door.

NO ANSWER FROM CALLY. I called a second time. Straight to voicemail. While leaving a seething message for her to call me right away, I realized it was six in the morning in America at that moment. The next two hours were spent pacing. There were no real thoughts or plans. Just a steady path between one wall and the other. Phoning her once more, I was in the midst of leaving another voicemail when I noticed the call-waiting beeping. Edward incoming. Another person I wanted to speak to.

"Hello, dear boy," he imitated the Oxford Man, speaking gruffly. "I figured I would check in before reporting to Behr duty. How are things on everyone's favorite rainy little island?"

"I'm not in Tasmania." I hissed. "I've got some serious things to ask you, Eddie."

An ominous pause. Edward let out a long, low whistle. "This isn't about Behr's whole dimensions thing, is it?"

Someone was knocking insistently on the door.

"Have you been working with the Salanack freak all along? Did you help negotiate this whole deal?"

The knocking was getting louder. I told the person on the other side that I would be out in a minute.

"Excuse me?" He gasped. "You really think I would go behind the back of my favorite straight boy? Wait... that sounded hot. Nevermind. You really think I would betray you? We're on the same side, you loser. Now what cretin is feeding you this bullshit?"

A key was jiggling in the lock. The door opened, the frazzled head of Dr. Sneil peeking through.

Travels and Travails of Small Minds by Daniel Falatko

"Join us for tea," he demanded.

I indicated that I was on the phone, would join him in a minute.

"Now."

Taken aback by the demanding rasp of Dr. Sneil' voice, I muttered, "The Salanack freak told me, Edward." And then, my voice sounding frightened, "I think I have to go now."

Sneil was grabbing for me. I jumped back to avoid him. Edward was shouting, "And you believe him? You're taking that freak at face value? The guy is a lunatic, Nathan! A fanatic! You have more sense than this!"

Sneil had now moved behind me and was shoving me hard toward the door with his fat, liver-spotted hands.

"Lay off, man!" He was pushing me out the door with surprising ferocity. "Edward, I'll talk to you later. I'm being assaulted."

SNEIL CONTINUED TO JAB AT MY BACK all the way down the hallway. I was forced into the dining room where cups of tea and Mrs. Sneil were waiting. Mrs. Sneil was still wearing the floppy gardening hat, her bright red chin peeking out the bottom. Her hands began shaking as I entered the room.

"I have phoned the police," Sneil let me know. "I'm sure they will have some questions for you. Do you take milk?"

"Questions about what?" I nodded to indicate that I did, in fact, take milk. "Shady Lower East Side real estate deals?"

Mrs. Sneil appeared bewildered at this exchange, not touching her tea, some sort of gardening instrument with a green handle sticking from her shirt pocket and an uprooted weed clutched in her fingers.

"All we know is that you arrived yesterday, left the house at an indecent hour last night, and now our yard has been demolished."

AUGUST 7th

The tea was better than it had been the day before, less cinnamon.

"Yum!" I held up the cup. "I would hardly call it demolished. A couple of tire tracks, perhaps. That birdfeeder cost what, 30 pounds?"

Dr. Sneil leaned in close.

"That yard means a great deal to me." His voice gurgled and grated in my ears. "You will understand when you get a little bit older. Your wife will begin to infuriate you with every movement. Your career will stagnate long before it is over. Your wishes to compose the definitive analytical biography of Hart Crane will crumble under the weight of your overly ambitious outline. When these things happen, and I can guarantee you that they will happen, the only thing that will matter to you is that inch-and-a-half of grass just beyond your doorstep."

My forehead had broken out in a cold sweat. It was hard to swallow.

"The police are coming to get you. I will make all of the necessary deposits without you. You are to have no contact with my wife or me ever again and are not to come within 10 miles of this house."

I nodded, half-expecting Mrs. Sneil's crimson head to start hemorrhaging at any moment.

It seemed wise to remain silent.

MRS. SNEIL AND I SAT IN SILENCE as her husband conferred with two Bobbies on the front lawn. I could see him gesturing wildly at the tire tracks, bemused grins on the Bobbies' faces. One of them kept shrugging. I caught Mrs. Sneil looking at me. I nodded and smiled politely. She then left the room. I had just finished my second cup of tea when the Bobbie who had been shrugging came to the door and shrugged for me to step outside.

Travels and Travails of Small Minds by Daniel Falatko

Dr. Sneil immediately launched into his accusations, explaining that I had left the house the night before and then, sometime between midnight and the morning, managed to wreak havoc on the front yard. The non-shrugging Bobbie, smirking, held up a hand to stop Sneil's stammering. "Come talk to us." He smiled at me, his teeth yellow. "Not you," he said when Sneil tried to tag along. We convened by the driveway.

"Look, we know you're the American who was drinkin' at the Regal Lion," the Bobbie shrugged. "We've heard all about ya'." The non-shrugging Bobbie slapped me on the back good naturedly. "We know ya' got a lift from Bilko and Mills."

They both started laughing, much to the displeasure of Dr. Sneil who was attempting to listen in.

"How was the ride?" The non-shrugging Bobbie's eyes were wide and comical.

Flashback to the lane-sweeping, the mailbox demolition derby, the golf course, the cans of beer that seemed to roll out of every nook and cranny of the van.

"It was terrifying."

This sent both Bobbies into hysterics, hanging onto one another for support. Dr. Sneil was demanding to know what was going on. The Bobbies, between laughs, told him to pipe down and take a step back.

"These tire tracks will grow out." The Bobbie shrugged. "And the birdfeeder is only a little dinged."

"The birds won't mind, will they?" the non-shrugging Bobbie pointed out.

"We'll have a talk with the boys, tell em' to keep outta' that van after the Regal."

They nodded toward the house.

"Why are you stayin' on with these old wankers, anyway?"

I looked back at Dr. Sneil, infuriated and pacing on the other end of the driveway.

"Business."

AUGUST 7th

After jotting a couple of notes on a pad, the Bobbies were gone, waving dismissively at Dr. Sneil as he shouted about charges and interrogations.

"I will be billing Ronald for the damages," he informed me before stalking back into the house.

"Join the club."

THERE WAS NO CHOICE but to head for my room and lodge a chair against the doorknob. I felt like a teenager in trouble with his parents. I texted Edward to call me, already planning on going delinquent on the next Verizon bill with all these international roaming charges, but no call was forthcoming. Cally hadn't phoned me back. I texted her as well, let her know I needed to speak with her as immediately as possible. It took me fifteen minutes to figure out how to abbreviate *immediately*, finally just typing out the whole word.

I sat on the bed, my feet resting atop the satchel now containing 270 grand, wondering when Sneil was going to demand it from me. I waited for five minutes, ten minutes, forty minutes. No phone calls coming through. It wasn't until then that I realized how tired I was, exhausted really, hung over and drained to the core.

MINUTES LATER I was cruelly shaken awake by the vibrations of the phone against my chest. Dr. Behr. "Why hello there." My voice, groggy and gravelly with sleep, sounded very much like Oxford Man's at that moment. "What have you got for me?"

Travels and Travails of Small Minds by Daniel Falatko

"What I've got are complaints." He sounded more direct than usual, which was refreshing, even though he was potentially about to fire me. "Complaints about damaged property from not one but two people. And the incoming bills to back them up. This windfall is designed to pay off the Con Ed bill, not to spawn more bills. Were you aware that the billiards instrument in question was valued at four thousand dollars?"

I found myself wondering what would happen if he did fire me. No plane ride home? Stranded forever within a foggy field with pterodactyls nipping at the top of my head? But then again, my feet did happen to be resting upon a very large sum of the man's ill-gotten gains. Surely he wouldn't take that risk.

"You are fast becoming a liability."

I said nothing.

"You are hereby relieved of your duties for this mission. I have spoken with Dr. Sneil and am fully confident he can handle the deposits on his own. Tomorrow you will be driven to an Inn and will remain there 12 days until your flight home. I expect no further troubles."

"You're locking me up. Getting me out of the way. I think I understand this new game plan."

"Good. And you will stick to it."

"Listen, man. The pool cue slipped out of my hands. I wasn't at the wheel of the van. Milly was puking and Bilky did what he had to do. It could have been a lot worse, let me tell you."

Silence on the line save the agitated whistling of nose hairs.

"It is like you are speaking another language." His voice rang low and hostile. "Dr. Sneil is a gentleman. He is not used to this type of treachery."

"Treachery?" I scoffed at him. "Did you know that your 'gentleman' got paid by Perth too?"

Dr. Behr said nothing for quite some time. I was watching as two birds landed on the windowsill, bickering, and then flew away in opposite directions.

"Who told you this?"

AUGUST 7th

Dr. Sneil may have been correct about Behr becoming sharper. There was a vitality to his voice that day.

"Perth the Salanack freak let it slip." One of the birds had returned and was looking at me through the window as if it expected something. I waved. "He gets a loose tongue when he's had some wine."

Behr scoffed at this, the sound of spittle hitting the receiver grossly audible.

"I am not sure if I would take what that man says at face value," he warned. "And I'm not sure what I will do with you when you get back. You've disappointed me more than slightly."

"Speaking of Edward..."

"We were not speaking of Edward."

"Oh, right. We weren't. Anyway, speaking of Edward, I wanted to ask you what his role was in this mission. Was it really true what you said about me, at that point at least, being the perfect man for the job and Edward having nothing to do with it?"

Behr sighed, centuries in his exhale.

"This is not the time for office politics and inner-bickering." He sounded suddenly distracted, a muffled voice in the background, wanting very much to get off the phone with me as quickly as possible. "Do not cause me any more trouble. And tell Dr. Sneil to phone me immediately."

THE OXFORD MAN did not look very pleased to see me when I relayed the message to please call his friend Dr. Behr. He was sitting at his desk working on a sketch of the front yard, a crime scene diagram, wincing and glowering at me from behind the huge, kaleidoscopic lenses of his glasses. I tried to stick to rooms that didn't contain any Sneils, though I twice frightened Mrs.

Travels and Travails of Small Minds by Daniel Falatko

Sneil as I lingered in the hallway. The second time, when she rounded the corner to find me inspecting an abstract painting on the hallway wall, she began hyperventilating and had to sit down in the kitchen. Her breathing got worse when I asked if she wanted some water. Eventually, I wound up sitting on the front stoop, bored to absolute death, watching the now-wobbly bird feeder pitch back and forth in the wind.

Salvation arrived, just as the boredom was threatening to deplete my pleasure centers and plunge me into a catatonic state, in the form of Milly's demolished-looking van. At first I thought they were going to take the yard route once again and ran out waving my hands to stop them. But the truck was moving at a civilized speed, coming to a halt on the road's shoulder. Bilky leaned his head out the window, a squashed derby cap upon his head.

"Why hello, our new American friend." He saluted me while Milly grinned dumbly. "Care to nip for a late lunch at the Regal?"

I was in the van within seconds.

IN BED THAT NIGHT I attempted to finish the Salanack book, barreling through entire sections devoted to electrodes and government microchips and bugs with gills that swim through human veins. I kept getting distracted by one thing: the bill that Dr. Behr had mentioned earlier. I had been hearing about this mythical bill ever since I had started at Behr Properties. Edward explained that there was a mix-up at some point with one of the buildings, potentially as far back as 1976, when the Con Ed bills had not been received for a period of time. This payment gap was not noticed until one giant bill arrived years later. Dr. Behr had refused to pay it. After the building was condemned it became a moot point. By the time I started working at Behr Properties, it was rumored the old bill had grown to $140,000 including penalty fees. "This may just be an urban legend," Edward had explained. "He mumbles about it from time-to-time, but I've never laid eyes on the bill itself." But a myth it was not. One day in my first year we had gone through the trouble of confirming the charges, navigating by phone through the complicated labyrinth that was the Con Edison customer service department, and found that there was indeed a $138,019.17 overdue charge to the Behr Properties account. I could clearly recall the defiant grunt Dr. Behr let out when we confronted him with this reality. "The day I pay that damn bill is the day I sell off all these damn buildings and goddamn retire."

"So why was he paying it now?" I had asked the non-shrugging Bobbie who was drinking with us earlier that evening at the Regal Lion.

"Sounds like he's getting ready to retire, then," he said. "Lucky bastard."

So was he? The amount being deposited over the coming days was indeed enough to cover the bill. He had mentioned "Con Ed" when scolding me earlier. So was that it? He would send the check to the fine folks of Con Edison so he could retire? It was about time, to be honest. Behr hadn't been firing on all cylinders for a good five years, according to Edward. Selling off all those buildings he would be sitting pretty, tens of millions. Condo companies would snatch those up without a second thought. So why did he need to pull off this whole caper just to pay off a measly 138 grand bill?

"Maybe he can't sell the buildings until the fookin' bill is paid," Bilky had suggested earlier, firing up a smoke even though Rene had told him the next time he lit up she would bash his brains in with her club. "Hell, if I owed that much quid, I'd have to pay it before sellin' anything. No geezer wants to inherit someone else's 'lectric company debt. Maybe they put a lien on him."

Travels and Travails of Small Minds by Daniel Falatko

Bilky had a point. It was entirely unlikely that Behr had 138 grand in ready cash. Most of his tenants were Chinese families under generations of rent control. Their monthly fees, judging by the state of Behr's buildings, were not quite enough to even keep up maintenance. Or perhaps he was just cheap. Maybe he did have the money for the bill but decided to pull off this caper just so that pesky 138 Gs wouldn't eat into his retirement cashout. Whatever the case, he was obviously looking to get out.

Perhaps this was why Edward was leaving. Maybe he knew that Behr Properties would not be in existence for much longer and had decided to get out while the getting was good.

"Maybe the bastard's in on it!" Milly had slammed his massive fist on the table in anger, startling the shrugging Bobbie momentarily from his drunken stupor. The Bobbie shrugged once more and went back to sleep. "How long you say he's been workin' for im'? Fifteen years? Hell, they're practically married! He's probably gettin' a cut of the action. He probably helped set up the whole fookin' thing, man."

Tremendous point, Milly. Had I not recently discovered that Edward arranged the whole Salanack deal? I sat straight up in the guest bed. Edward wasn't leaving to work at Michael's firm. He was helping Behr sell off the business, tie up loose ends, and would receive a piece of the action, possibly enough to retire right along with him. That is why I had been sent on this mission, a mission which could have been completed by a preschooler, a mission where my direct presence was barely even needed. Perth could have handed the cash over himself. He could have flown to New York or simply driven down to meet with Sneil and handed over the cash. I was currently in England because I would have been in the way around the office, and was being kept away for a further twelve days so they could shut down operations. I would be returning to a pile of dust.

"You're being left out in the cold, mate!" Bilky sounded infuriated on my behalf as Rene was tossing him out, pulling him by the ear.

AUGUST 7th

AS IF ON CUE, the phone started buzzing. Edward. "Why hello, dear friend." I greeted him, my voice sounding infected, poisoned.

"So Dr. Death is pissed at Oxford Man. He doesn't want to pay him anymore since you spilled the beans about his double-agent status. Why are you stirring things up, Nathan? Why are you making things hard? Behr says you've left a trail of damage across England. He's been a real bastard all day. Then you accuse me of working covertly against you. Have you lost your mind?"

"I already gave Oxford Man his money," I told him. "Behr can officially fuck off."

It was then that it finally hit home. Edward had been lying to me all along.

"I just wanted you to know, Edward, that I know, ok? Do what you will with this information. Sit on it. Tell Behr. Whatever. I just want you to know that I know."

Nothing on the line but Edward's confused breathing.

"Dr. Behr is right about the dimensions," he choked up, breathing hard. "There are many at play. Remember that."

I smiled in the cold of the guest room, not saying anything.

"What are you going to do?" He sounded scared. "Nathan?"

The fog was back, the field behind the house overtaken with billowing ghosts.

"I'll find a dimension I like and stay there."

I clicked off, held down the power button until the screen went dead, tossed the book aside and began pacing. There needed to be a streamlined plan, a laid-out course of action, though none was forthcoming. The fog was right up against the window now, tentacles of mist bowing forward to kiss the glass. I waited for it to swallow me, to envelope me within its white kingdom.

It was going to be a long night.

Nathan's British Buddies, The Hulking Milly and his Pal Bilky, help Nathan escape but an Unhappy Dr. Sneil follows them in his car.

AUGUST 8th

A SAGGING, GREY MORNING at the Sneil residence. My face in the bedroom mirror's reflection appeared older, lined at the mouth, ashen like the light outside the windows. I retrieved the satchel from underneath the bed. It was two hours until I would be driven to an inn.

While finishing the Salanack novel at the kitchen table, I kept topping off Mrs. Sneil's tea even though she didn't ask me to, just to see her face flinch at my movements. The last line seemed to set something off within me. "Following his eyeball onto the floor was a river like a blood red tide." I sighed and closed the book. "Good one," I slid the paperback to her across the table. "A gift. Enjoy it, my dear."

SNEIL BECKONED ME INTO HIS OFFICE, his voice like gravel churned through a blender. He demanded the satchel. I dropped it on the chair in front of his desk. From inside of a small leather pouch he withdrew a single deposit slip, placed it on top of the satchel.

Travels and Travails of Small Minds by Daniel Falatko

"So, how are things between you and your dear friend and colleague, Dr. Behr?"

He sneered, his eyes magnified by the lenses and so unrelentingly scornful I was sure he wouldn't mind if I were dead.

"I shall add the spreading of vicious rumors to the expanding list of treacheries you have committed under this roof."

I nodded. "Rumors that are true though, right?"

He held up his hand, indicating that this conversation would move no further.

"What is that, my dear," he called out even though I had not heard Mrs. Sneil say anything. He roughly grabbed my shoulder, his nails digging in, and dragged me slowly out of the room after him, placing me in the hallway. I snuck back into the office the second he walked into the kitchen to begin conversing with his wife. Taking a peak around the corner to make sure the coast was clear, I took a look at the deposit slip. The slip was for an international account belonging to "Roland Sneil." The deposit amount was $300,000.

A phone was ringing from within the house. Putting the slip back where it was, I headed back to the hallway and assumed position.

"Your boss is on the phone," Sneil rasped, appearing with the black cordless.

"Ronald! What is up?" I addressed my boss.

Dr. Behr let out an exasperated grunt that bore decades of confusion and dread.

"You are being driven to the inn today. Correct?"

"I will be safely confined at the hotel in less than an hour, no worries." I looked over my shoulder to find Sneil lingering in the hallway, shattering my opportunity to let Behr know that his dear old colleague the Oxford Man was not only being paid twice for his tip, but was now planning on stealing the rest.

"Make sure to cause no more problems." There was a desperate edge to his voice. "And don't damage anything at the inn."

AUGUST 8th

My eyes were locked with Sneil's, a staring contest. Did he suspect I had seen the slip?

"One other thing," Behr was still struggling on the other end. "I wanted to thank you. I've checked into what you told me yesterday and it sounds like it may be true. I take it you have already handed over Dr. Sneil's cut of the money?"

Sneil had finally blinked and looked away. I'd won the contest. He retreated into the kitchen, his shoulders slumping.

"I already gave it to him, just as you had ordered." I thought of the 30 grand sitting within the unlocked drawer. "And what about Cally's money? You're withdrawing her cut as well? That hardly seems fair."

"Excuse me?"

I didn't repeat it, allowed time for the words to sink into his old, soft brain.

"How do you know the tenant's name?"

His voice cracked, starting to lose it.

"I think I might know it all," I told him before clicking off. "The dimensions, as you said, are beginning to align."

HEADING BACK INTO THE OFFICE, I sat myself in Sneil's chair behind the desk, reveling in the comfort as I took the phone on the desk off its hook and whipped out my cell, waiting for Cally to call. No doubt Behr was phoning her at that moment, irate, wondering how I knew her name and demanding to know what she was up to.

Sneil came into the office, infuriated to find me there in his chair. He demanded that I stand, told me to get out. He came around the desk and starting to jab at me once again with his arthritic fists. "*Ouch*, dude!" The jabs hurt, like being repeatedly poked in the side by two knotty sticks, finally forcing me from the chair. "Whoa, whoa, whoa! Calm down!" He continued batting at me. I was laughing as my phone began to vibrate. "If you will excuse me, kind sir," I dodged one of his punches and ducked out the door. "I do need to take this."

IN MY ROOM with the chair back in place on the doorknob, I was getting my things together.

"Sorry about that. I was in the middle of being domestically abused... again... by an old man," I told Cally, who had not said a thing since I picked up the phone. "As a matter of fact, I think you might know him. Dr. Sneil? The infamous Oxford Man? Is this ringing any bells? Ornery old dude with a voice like churned glass? Seems to know karate?"

I could feel her spirit sag over the long distance connection.

"I really do love you, Nathan." Her voice was thin, tap-dancing on the border of tears.

"You knew me for less than a day," I stressed. "And I'm not sure how you talked me into blowing this deal for you."

"So you're still going to blow it?" She sounded hopeful, suddenly overjoyed.

"Oh, I'm going to blow it." I finished packing, zipped up the bag. "But not in the way you had planned."

Heavy breathing from Cally. Light sobs. "Don't do anything crazy," she said.

"Crazy?" I laughed. "You want to hear crazy? How about when you find out that some collector wants your apartment and you accept 15 grand to move out, but then you turn around and manipulate one of the realtor's lackeys into blowing the other half of the deal. You know that your 15 grand is coming from the Oxford Man's cut, so you tell the employee you've manipulated to allow that part of the deal to go through but to blow the other half, the part where the apartment is sold to the collector, so therefore the deal falls through and you still have your apartment and got paid 15 grand for absolutely nothing. And even crazier is the fact that you thought this would somehow all go smoothly, that they would what? Fucking forget they gave you 15 Gs to move out in the ensuing pandemonium? That you would somehow get away with it and be sitting pretty in your rent-controlled pad, 15 Gs richer? Now that, my dear, is fucking crazy."

She tried to say something but the words did not come through. She took a breath, tried a different angle.

"But you sought me out!" she exclaimed. "It wasn't some master plan! Catching you going through my mailbox, you stalking me, those things happened by chance!"

I slung the bag over my shoulder, preparing to venture out.

"So you came up with your plan on the spot." I shrugged. "That makes sense, in retrospect. You must admit it was pretty half-baked, Cally, my dear."

Her breathing pattern was out of control, punctuated by thin rasps and gulps.

"I just finally thought something good was going to happen." She let out a wounded sigh. "I've always struggled. I've always been in debt. I'm on first name terms with various credit agency chasers. I've never had a savings account. I have never, not once in my entire life, experienced a windfall, Nathan. Not once! Not a hundred bucks here. Not fifty bucks there. Nothing. So pardon me for going a little overboard the second a small windfall reared its head."

"A little overboard?"

I heard something, possibly a fridge door, slam in her background. Glasses rattled.

"Ok, a lot overboard. I didn't know what I was thinking. My head was spinning. I should have just taken the cash, moved out. But this place is important to me, ok? Pieces of my brother inhabit this space."

Travels and Travails of Small Minds by Daniel Falatko

I was halfway out the window, one leg dangling outside.

"Then don't sell his memories for a measly 15 grand."

I hopped down into the field, which was blanketed with a morning fog.

"No one has ever tossed me one thin dime." She was crying full-on now, utterly destroyed. "That's all I was after. Just one thin dime."

I had walked twenty yards out into the field and crouched down in the fog, keeping an eye on the house.

"That seems to be what all the players in this ridiculous saga are after, my dear." I held the phone in front of my face, whispering to her before ending the call. "But they aren't going to get it."

CLOAKED IN FOG and needing some quick advice, I realized there was only one person who wouldn't feel that my current situation was in any way bizarre.

"T Man." I could hear the sounds of police sirens in his background. "Look, I'm in a pterodactyl-infested field in England hiding from an assaultive, retired lit professor so I really can't be long."

There was static for a moment as he adjusted the phone. I heard sheets rustling.

"That all sounds perfectly logical," he drawled in a southern-tinged accent he had somehow picked up over the last three days. "It's just like you to call when I've finally gone to sleep after ten straight days awake. Here, let me hit a bump so I can fully understand you."

I rattled off the story as fast as I could. He stopped me several times, asked for me to repeat things. Not once did he sound incredulous or overwhelmed.

"So this Oxford Man is screwing Dr. Behr," he said as if answering a math question in class. "And probably Cally too

AUGUST 8th

since the chances of her cut finding its way into her account seem slim-to-none. Cally is, in turn, screwing you both figuratively and literally, as well as every single other person in this drama. Everyone else seems to be screwing you as well, Edward and Behr being the worst offenders, raping you from both ends, keeping you out of the country on a meaningless mission and having you return to an empty office. You're just getting gangbanged here, my friend, and all of your assailants... I mean every single one... are completely, unrelentingly, Syd Barrett-over-the-fucking-top-batshit-insane. None of their ploys would have even worked had they been pulled off! There is no way Cally could have kept the apartment and the money, just as there is no way this Oxford dude could just dump all the cash in his account and not have anyone notice, just as there is no way Behr could just pay off the Con Ed bill and pack everything up and retire to the tropics with Edward in tow. You've told me how he runs his business. There'd be loose ends for miles. When you think about it, the only upstanding person in this whole thing is the Salanack freak. And that's saying a lot. Man, that is one fucked up mess."

I agreed with him that it was.

"I think I know what I have to do," I told him. "But I think I need to hear it from someone else."

Terry was cackling, the fog swarming around me.

"All those people are just stabbing away at each other's backs like Manson Fam 1969, fighting for leverage, angling for position, believing themselves to hold some sort of trump card," he said, sounding excited. "So you, Nathan, need to get your ass out of that fog and trump them all."

THE FRONT DOOR OF THE HOUSE was, as usual, unlocked. My phone was buzzing in my pocket. I dismantled it in the hallway, pulling out the battery, dropping the pieces in the Sneil umbrella

Travels and Travails of Small Minds by Daniel Falatko

rack. Heading for the office, my path was blocked by Mrs. Sneil, her tiny head glowing bright red in the dim light of the hallway, clutching her rolling pin, her eyes burning with hate and fear. She raised the wooden utensil accusingly, moving her mouth as if she were speaking but all that came out was a pathetic squeak. "Hello, Mrs. Sneil. It sure is foggy out there. Ah, the charm of England. I just need to grab something from the office." I tried to slip past her but the little old woman advanced on me, practically growling while wielding the rolling pin like a baseball bat. She drew back and swung at my head, her movement so slow that I had seconds to kill before ducking the pin and running past her as she recovered from the swing. The last I saw her she was moving up the stairs, grim determination set in her red jaw, toward the sound of classical music and a running shower upstairs. "Roland! Roland!"

    The office was just as I had left it. Tossing the deposit slip aside, I grabbed the satchel and moved toward the desk, pulling open the drawer to find the stacks of hundreds still in place. While adding them to the satchel, I found myself humming the chorus melody from The Steve Miller Band's *Take the Money and Run*. I noticed that the piece of paper with Cally's account number had been crumpled up and thrown in the trash. The old shyster!

    Moving down the hallway I found myself on guard when passing doorways, fully expecting Mrs. Sneil to leap out at me ninja style with the rolling pin or, even worse, the green gardening tool. When I reached the front door, I heard footsteps on the stairs, turning around to find a naked and wet Dr. Sneil advancing like a sagging, liver-spotted fury. He began shouting when he saw me in the doorway with the satchel, a deep banshee wail which seemed to shred what was left of his vocal chords, his body covered with oddly located fat deposits. It was a horrifying sight. Not wanting to grapple with a soaked, naked old man, I turned tail and ran as fast as I could with the heavy satchel across the lawn, bumping into the bird feeder and knocking it over as I passed, its stem breaking in half on the ground.

AUGUST 8th

ONCE OUT ON THE ROAD I slowed to a trot, glancing over my shoulder, expecting to find a naked Dr. Sneil trailing me with his rolling pin-wielding wife in tow. Instead there was the sound of an engine gunning, the oncoming of wheels. I could tell it wasn't the Sneil vehicle since it wasn't backfiring every several seconds and leaving plumes of black smoke in its wake.

Stepping to the shoulder to allow the car to pass, it slowed to a halt next to me. Looking over, I found it occupied by the two spies from the train, the spy in the passenger seat scowling at me with his right leg crossed. He began to say something, his finger extended in warning, but I didn't hear it as I took off away from the car through someone's lawn. The right-leg crossing spy jumped out and gave chase while the car tore off toward the end of the block to cut me off should I somehow elude him. I could tell immediately that I was going to lose the foot chase, weighed down by the satchel with the spy gaining ground on me with a speed that indicated a massive amount of pent up aggression, as if he had been waiting for this chase all his life.

I circled around the back of a house that was identical to the Sneil exterior save the color of the shutters, light blue as opposed to green. A fence blocked my path. With much difficulty, nearly popping a joint in my shoulder, I managed to hoist the satchel over and made a running leap, using the ends of my pointy boots to scramble to the other side. Sadie, the Cocker Spaniel I had met the other night, was on the satchel in a flash, tearing at it with her teeth. I salvaged the *Rape World* 1st edition I had ganked from the Perth museum before abandoning my other bag entirely, putting the paperback in my back pocket. I hoisted the satchel, Sadie coming with it, and took off in a cumbersome fashion as the spy struggled over the fence, catching his right pant leg on the top chain link, buying me some time.

Travels and Travails of Small Minds by Daniel Falatko

My lungs burning, I weaved through some manicured bushes around the side of the house, a dwelling considerably shabbier than the rest of the houses along that road, hoping to make his path as difficult as possible. Sadie had let go of the satchel and was now on the ground nipping at my legs. Passing into the front yard of the last house before the fields started, Sadie ran into some sort of electrically-charged barrier and jerked back into her zone. Realizing that the spy's steps could no longer be heard behind me, I glanced back and found that he was no longer in pursuit.

The spy was standing in the middle of the overgrown back yard with his hands raised high in the air. I heard a double-click. The old geezer with the train conductor's uniform was pointing a quail-hunting rifle directly at the head of the spy. "If you move one more inch," the man said, clearly enjoying the moment. "I will blow your Muslim head off."

With one spy held at gunpoint and the other waiting at the end of the block, I ducked across the road and headed into the field toward the village. Thankfully, the fog was spreading toward the village as well, becoming increasingly thicker the further I walked, forming the perfect cloak to wear while crossing the otherwise exposed field. Not being able to see more than ten feet in front of me, I pushed on in what I hoped was the direction of the stoplight. A car could be heard on the road, gunning slow, its high beams attempting to illuminate the mist. The remaining spy, the left leg crosser, was having trouble locating me in the fog. When I reached the point where I felt the field should end, there was only more fog, mossy vegetation under my feet, and the satchel strap digging into my shoulder. The car had left the road now, bumping through the field in my general direction, headlights sweeping crazily and magnified through the mist. He had spotted me. Just as I became fearful that the car was going to run me down, I reached the first house of the village.

Moving onto the street, the fog cleared, the stoplight of the intersection visible ahead. The spy was forced to halt in order to avoid crashing into the house, but was no doubt circling back onto the road to pursue me into the village. True to form, Milly's van was parked sideways across the sidewalk in front of the Regal Lion. Bilky was passed out on the steps outside the pub's door. Someone had propped him up and had tilted his hat at an odd angle, an unlit cigarette jutting from his nose. I slapped him lightly to bring him to life. His eyes opened. He looked happy to see me. "Well, if it isn't Natey Boy," he greeted me. "Fucking hell! Guess I spent the night." I helped him up, let him know I needed their assistance.

Milly emerged with two pints as Bilky pulled the smoke from his nose and lit it up. "Top of the mornin' to ya'!" Milly shouted. "I came to pick up this one." He sipped his brew like someone would sip their morning coffee, handing the other to his clearly hurting friend.

"I'll give you a thousand American dollars to give me a ride to the train station."

They started laughing, stopping only when they realized I was dead serious.

OUT ON THE ROAD, bearing down toward the freeway, there were empty bottles all over the van's floor, clanging off of one another at every turn. I was riding shotgun with Bilky lying down on the floor in the back, moaning. In the filthy side mirror I saw the left leg crossing spy gunning down on us, smirking and shaking his head at the state of the vehicle he was chasing, his bony face set in determination. He was inching closer and closer to the back bumper of the van. "Who is this tosser?" Milly laughed, staring the spy down in his own mirror.

"He doesn't like me very much."

"Well, I know where to take him, then." Milly snorted.

Travels and Travails of Small Minds by Daniel Falatko

Swerving with absolutely no warning onto a country road instead of pushing forward toward the freeway, the spy car almost losing it on the unannounced turn, I watched a smile spread out across Milly's face.

"Oh my God, Mill!" Bilky was shouting from the back. "Not the bloody golf course!"

The spy car seemed to linger on the road, hesitant to follow, after Milly jumped the small hill and started tearing off across the course. Due to the fog, there weren't that many golfers on the links, though two men in a cart drinking gin and tonics had to swerve out of the way when the van came tearing out from behind a row of trees, roaring directly at them. The spy finally set out after us, half-heartedly at first, hanging fifteen yards behind us, unsure how to navigate the green terrain filled with sand traps and flags. Once we hit a long, flat link the spy car sped up, gaining confidence, catching up to us almost bumper-to-bumper.

"Why are you letting the bastard catch up?" Bilky was looking out the van's round back window. I clutched the satchel close, half-expecting the spy to utilize an expanding robot arm to reach into the vehicle and snatch it from me.

"You'll see." Milly grinned, rapidly approaching a bend around some perfectly manicured bushes.

Rounding the bend, a deep, long sand trap suddenly loomed in front of us, visible through a break in the fog, gleaming white and wet from that morning's mist. Both vehicles were traveling too fast to avoid it. There was a small hill in front of the trap. Milly's eyes grew wide. I held onto the satchel and ducked down as Bilky let out a frightened groan. Milly gunned it at the hill, bearing down fast. With two sickening thumps, the van's front and back tires hit the hill a split second apart. We were clumsily air-born, wobbling violently. Milly let out a warrior's shriek as the van came bashing down on what I hoped was the grass on the other side. The vehicle's shocks were not enough to absorb the hit. My teeth knocked together and my chin hit my chest, wrenching my neck as the bottom bounced off the ground

AUGUST 8th

with horrific force. Milly yanked hard on the wheel, throwing his considerable body weight behind it, managing to bring the rattling apparatus to a sideways halt. We had cleared the trap. Bilky had been hurled against the back door, on the floor with his white Reebok Classics sticking up from a pile of beer bottles. "I'm alright!" He held up his hand as if in surrender. "Think I'll stay down here for a while." The spy car had not been so lucky. He hadn't hit the jump at the full, fearless speed required to clear the trap, breaking at the last minute, plunging front-end-first into the wet sand, kernels rattling in the grill, front tires sunk deep in the crud while the back tires spun helplessly. The left leg crossing spy got out of the car, standing next to his now useless vehicle. He sat down in the sand, flipped us a two-finger salute and spit. A man, the same man who had chased us the other night, came running out of the utility shed wielding his rake.

"I'll leave them to sort this out." Milly aimed the shaking van toward the road as the man with the rake advanced upon the left leg crossing spy, swinging wildly as the spy crouched in a karate pose.

WE WERE ON A BACK ROAD which ran parallel to the freeway, a route Milly claimed was shorter and "more peaceful like." My teeth and neck still rung from the impact. Bilky had managed to pull himself from the floor. He was slung sideways across the back seat, his face pale and sweaty. Milly kept the van steady, only swerving slightly. Neither seemed the slightest bit interested as to why I had been chased by a lanky man in a rental car. We came upon a town, a real town unlike the one-stoplight settlement which boasted the Regal Lion, complete with side streets and a main strip. "Could you please stop at that Fed Ex store?" I told them I'd be right back, hopped out with the satchel.

Travels and Travails of Small Minds by Daniel Falatko

Stuffing the cash into a Fed Ex box and the **Rape World** 1st edition into a bubble-wrapped envelope, I waved to Rene who happened to be walking by the store carrying her club. She stuck out her tongue. The bubble-wrapped envelope I addressed to Terry, the box with 15 grand to Cally's on Avenue B. On one of the bills I scrawled, *One thin dime for you, my dear.*

BILKY SEEMED TO BE FEELING BETTER, talking rapid-fire as we moved out of the town about his seemingly genuine love for Selena Gomez and a turtle named Kirby he had owned as a child. "Ten minutes to the station," Milly announced. "Where ya' headed ya' silly sod? It doesn't go across the Atlantic, I hope you know." I asked them about the quickest way out of the country. "Go south," they both said in unison. We were stopped at a light on the edge of the town, before it broke off into more of the same misty fields. "Looka' that!" Milly pointed to the car across the street, stopped in the oncoming lane. I recognized the Oxford Man's car instantly, tiny and spitting black smoke, leaning to one side. He was behind the wheel, shirtless, with his hair standing straight in the air as if sprayed with Aqua Net, leaning forward over the steering wheel as he squinted at the van. He had recognized me, sitting wide-eyed in the passenger seat. I swear he smiled.

"Oh shit." The light turned green. I watched in the side mirror as Sneil pulled a slow U-turn in the empty intersection.

"What? That crazy fuck is after ya' too?" They both started laughing. Sneil began tailing us, not exactly giving chase, staying at a safe distance. I could see him in the mirror, his blinding white chest spotted and sagging, the little car spitting smoke as his glasses glowed demonically. "Jeez, this geezer's got liver spots the size of Milly," Bilky observed.

AUGUST 8th

"You have to lose him, Milly." Panic seethed through my vocal chords. "I knocked over his bird feeder. His wife has a head the size and color of a tomato. She tried to bash my brains in with a rolling pin. And that fucker," I pointed to the car tailing us. "He may be just shy of 80 and fond of day-long naps, but he has fists of fury."

The boys were in hysterics over my fear of this old kook and his Rosacea-ravaged wife. When Milly finally calmed down, his face red from laughing so hard and wiping a tear from his eye, he said, "Not a problem, my American friend." Whipping out a cell phone, he pushed a button and handed it back to Bilky. "Yes, hello. We seem to have a little problem on Cleidenshire Roadway. Yes, a follower. How long? Oh, good!" Bilky pretended to hand the phone back to Milly but slapped him instead. Milly turned around and attempted to slap him back, both of them laughing, the van swerving the length of the road before he brought it under control. Behind us, Dr. Sneil expertly mimicked the swerve. "That old man is really somethin'." Bilky found a full, warm can of Carlsberg amongst the backseat empties. He cracked it and toasted the Oxford Man through the rounded back window portal.

We drove up and down Cleidenshire Roadway several times, passing the train station and then doubling back, never breaking 50 miles per hour. Dr. Sneil kept his ground behind us, never taking his eyes off the van as we turned around in a petrol station lot and headed back up the road. Milly began playing games with him, swerving in complicated patterns, each of them echoed perfectly by the sagging, smoky car. Our rescue arrived in the form of a patrol car, the same car which had pulled up outside the Sneil residence the day previous to investigate the bird feeder damage, the shrugging Bobbie and his non-shrugging partner at the wheel. They passed us going in the other direction, smiled and waved cheerfully, then pulled an e-brake turn to fall in line behind the Oxford Man. Dr. Sneil did not respond at first to the flashing lights behind him, reluctant to lose our trail, his determined grin beginning to crack. The shrugging Bobbie pulled into the oncoming lane, right up next to him, the non-shrugging Bobbie shouting over the loudspeaker, "Pull over! You're half-naked!"

Dr. Sneil was gesturing wildly ahead at the van as he was forced to the side of Cleidenshire Road. We pulled over to watch. The Oxford Man was out of the car clad only in a pair of stretched-out white underwear, approaching the patrol car, liver spots like leopard print across his back and uneven clumps of white hair on his head swaying wildly in the breeze. He was pointing to the van, shouting about thieves and bird feeders. Bilky swung open the side door, stepped out with his beer. "He was flashin' his penis at us, officers." He gave Milly a sloppy kiss on the cheek through the rolled-down driver's side window. "My wife here was horrified!"

"Is that right, you old pervert?" Non-shrugging Bobbie barked at Sneil. His partner shrugged and ordered Sneil to turn around, pulling out a pair of handcuffs.

The Oxford Man's eyes looked as if they were going to burst out of his head, shouting at the sky in his garbled, gravelly voice, "They stole my money! Three hundred large!" He tried to run at the van but was held back easily by the shrugging Bobbie. "They destroyed my bird feeder!" He was shouting as they placed on the cuffs. By the time they got him into the back of the car, his shouting had morphed into a series of nonsensical shrieks.

"You're headed to a different kind of bird house, you old naked perv." Non-shrugging Bobbie knocked on the window, causing Sneil to lash out against the glass like a rabid dog. "Those losers ain't seen that much money in their lives. Likely story." Sneil spit against the window. "That'll cost im'." Shrugging Bobbie shrugged, smiling.

Bilky jumped back in the van as Milly fired it up with some difficulty.

"See you gents at the Regal. We need to drop our American friend at the station."

AUGUST 8th

I waved to shrugging Bobbie and his non-shrugging partner. They saluted as we drove off, the Oxford Man thrashing about in the back seat.

"Well, here we are." A train was idling at the station. Milly sounded sad. "I guess you'll be off then. Thanks for all the excitement, mate."

I fished out a grand from the satchel. They both waved it away.

"I'll tell you what," Bilky finished his beer, tossed the can onto the floor where it clinked against the pile of empty bottles and cans. "We'll waive your fee if you just give us just one last cunty American do-gooder whiteboy student question."

I stepped out of the van, took a deep breath.

"Martin, did you read the Op Ed on *Slate* about how Beyoncé was formed through an intricate combination of the genes of Mother Theresa, Ghandi, Jesus Christ, Aretha Franklin, and a touch of Allah?"

After a pause, they broke into violent laughter, punching the dashboard and seats.

"Americans, man. Too fucking much."

The van tore out of the station, black bits of rubber flapping from bald tires.

I DIDN'T EVEN LOOK at where the train was headed. "South?" I asked the man who swiped my credit card at the booth. "South," he confirmed. When he smiled, I noticed he had no teeth. I was one of only a few upon the train. A quick scan revealed no leg-crossing spies, no raging naked old men. Using the satchel as a pillow, I watched out the window as the train, after idling another ten minutes, finally rolled out into an early afternoon rain, passing hills and fog and circles of trees, dark clouds like

Travels and Travails of Small Minds by Daniel Falatko

dimensions overhead, restless and tangled, evolving and shifting in the winds until they were perfectly aligned.

DECEMBER 13TH

TRAINS. I had never enjoyed them previously, and still didn't even though they had temporarily become my existence. Unlike the few American trains I had graced, the shaky Amtrak cars or the filthy PATCO lines, the rickety stop/start NYC subways and pod-like airport bullets, European trains were set to glide. Even as I made my way into the Eastern zone, escaping the expenses and tourists of central Europe and moving into the cold monolith of the bloc states, all severe architecture and sharp angles, high-rise estates and long stretches of forest, the trains remained smooth with not a single bump or track shift as frost fused to the windows on cold mornings. The clothing of my fellow travelers became less chic, their cheeks chapped from frigid temperatures and general poverty, wordlessly smoking cigarettes on empty platforms in the middle of vast muddy fields. I learned to enjoy cabbage soup and home-brewed beer in plastic soda bottles.

Tearing through the Salanack novel I had purchased in Amsterdam, I found myself mesmerized as an average heroin addict named Steve mutated, over the course of nine hellish days, into a proton-radiating cyborg with a long metal penis that spit flames. A sentence in the third chapter, "Human voids walk amongst us, their souls sucked dry, their hands like splinters."

caused me to think fondly of Dr. Behr. Thumbing back to page one, I began reading again. Many of the passengers who would hop aboard the train in remote settlements, exiting several stops down into other remote settlements, resembled Mr. Salanack's author photo, bone-thin with yellow skin and those soulless insect eyes.

I HAD PURCHASED A CALLING CARD from a man who resembled a walrus at a long stop somewhere in what may have been Poland, phoning Amy one afternoon from a pay phone in the middle of a village of crumbling wooden houses with collapsed sheds, underneath a statue of a very tall bearded warrior. She told me she was looking for a new job, had attended several interviews, was on the verge of breaking free from the L.O.L. Empire. She told me that sometimes in the night she would wake up for a drink of water, fully expecting to find me staring at the still lifes in the dark. I couldn't tell her where I was because I didn't know. I couldn't tell her exactly what I was doing, what my plans were, since I didn't know these things either. Nor could I tell her exactly what had happened in England, what went wrong, just a blur of betrayal and instinctual decisions pulled off without much real analysis.

"You really have moved on," she told me, her voice full of awe.

The buzzer on the platform had sounded, indicating it was mere minutes before the train would clear out of the shabby, muddy station, away from the folks peddling smoked fish and vodka on the platform, leaving any passenger not aboard behind to wallow in the deteriorating wooden settlement. I slung the satchel over my shoulder, my eyes on the imposing, low-hanging skies.

"Progression is just regression in disguise," I told her.

ONE YEAR LATER - EPILOGUE

I AM NOW DEAF AND MUTE. Or at least this is what Mariska and The Pash tell the kiosk's customers in order to shield my status as an undocumented foreigner. My hours at The Pash's business have expanded into the full-time range, hauling crates of vodka and computer software and German coprophilia magazines from my apartment to be stocked on the shelves. An extension has been built onto the stand's structure serving as a soup station which proves massively popular as the winter fully clutches down. Eventually, I am placed in charge of this soup station, preparing the vats in my apartment on the new stove The Pash had installed not long after the spillover fridge. The customers give their orders to Mariska, who points to the proper soup for me to serve. With my thinned-out frame, hollow cheeks, and pale face, I am beginning to resemble your average Russian male. Most people, including the *militsiya* members, buy that I am deaf and dumb. The neighborhood teens buy it too, attempting to sneak up and mug or beat me on several occasions. Each time I secretly listen to their footsteps, their voices, advancing behind my back, waiting until the very last second before whirling around and swinging wildly upon the first advancer. They always retreat, not wanting to waste their

Travels and Travails of Small Minds by Daniel Falatko

time on potentially vital prey. A phrase that roughly translates as "The Retarded Ninja" has become my nickname amongst the teen terrors in the neighborhood.

My rent is now free. Due to the long hours at the soup station, I have not been able to keep up with the slimed teenagers or the Half-Crescent's new season, though from the lack of any major rioting I can assume that they are not doing as well as they had the previous year. My apartment is packed with The Pash's supplies, boxes of porn piled high and crates of bottles stacked to the popcorn ceilings. The bills from the satchel are now spread all over the flat, bundles hidden strategically in 105 separate locations. I could locate each bundle within seconds if necessary. I use the ten-pound bags of cheap kitty litter to sleep on, the most comfortable bed I have ever graced, molding perfectly to my body as the sound of street fights and wailing cats outside cradle me to sleep once again.

Mariska and I have developed our own language, a complex series of whistles and hums through which we communicate perfectly. She tells me of her father, who left when she was nine for a pack of smokes and never returned, and of a star she feels can only be seen from her block estate high rise. We still try to dance around amongst the stacked products in my apartment to the bad Eastern European pop videos, one time breaking several bottles of perfume and embarking on a complex (and ultimately successful) conspiracy, utilizing ground-up leaves and tap water, to hide the damage from The Pash. For Christmas I fashion for her a necklace using the cheap vodka bottle caps I was ordered to remove and replace with Stolichnaya and Skyy caps. On the slow, sub-zero nights of mid-winter we pelt one another with Twizzlers to stay awake. We have contests to see how many Pop Rocks we can hold in our mouths without vomiting.

It feels good to be working. Little-by-little, a crisp and streamlined feeling overtakes me, bold and severe like the cold, lending purpose to my movements and structure to my days. There is no urge to contact anyone, no need to circle back. There

ONE YEAR LATER – EPILOGUE

are people that I miss, though I know it is better to miss them than become entangled in their daily discourse once again. There are no hang-ups to trip me, no obstacles that I haven't created myself. For the first time since I made that run across the foggy field, I realize I am free.

One day, when the temperature soars above freezing, The Pash takes us on a picnic. We place a "Back in Ten Minutes" sign on the door to the store and drive through the provinces in his battered Lada, Mariska and I singing one of the pop songs we love, The Pash gunning the small car along some of the most forlorn and barren roadways I have ever seen. Twice the car hits black ice and nearly flips. The Pash is in a good mood, his beard swaying as he steers us into the forest. At one point he pulls a large butcher knife out from under the driver's seat, singing along with us, using the knife's handle as a mock-microphone. Mariska and I applaud his efforts.

We stop at a clearing in the forest, a snowy field littered with tires and bottles and burned-out car seats, a small, frozen pond in the center, its dirty ice glistening in the winter sun. Sitting on tires and a discarded bumper, we feast on kielbasa and deviled eggs from a wicker basket, our cheeks red, Mariska and I laughing when The Pash manages to get a full egg stuck in his beard. A hawk flies overhead. The Pash pretends to gun it down. The same with a rabbit who stops to watch us from the edge of the tree line. Mariska tosses it a hunk of meat. We relax in the snow for a long time, pointing out clouds, The Pash swigging from a bottle of Stoli while I share a Coke with Mariska. The Pash reaches into the pocket of his shiny, black leather jacket.

The papers in his hand are not in Russian, instead a strange language that appears even more complicated than the pagan-looking letters of the Russian alphabet. I recognize the word "Stockholm." Mariska and I inspect the document, a diagram of what appears to be a large, convenience-style store on the third page. From my past career I am able to recognize an application to place a down payment on a property. There is a map on the

Travels and Travails of Small Minds by Daniel Falatko

fifth page, the layout of Sweden, with a red dot just to the left of Stockholm. We now both know where The Pash had disappeared to for all those days. Mariska squeals and runs to him, The Pash clasping her in a one-armed bear hug while slapping me on the back. "What you say?" he asks me. "I get you papers." I laugh, the idea of staying with this makeshift family surprisingly comforting. The Pash points to the application and rolls his meaty fingers together in the universal sign for money needed. Thinking of the bills spread out over their 105 locations, I cannot think of a single better thing to use them for. An albatross I will be grateful to lose.

"Why the fuck not." I join them in the bear hug.

The picnic is now a celebration. Mariska launches summersaults in the snow, her blond hair a carnival-esque whirl, her nose red and breath steaming. The Pash attempts to bury me in a drift but I manage to break free by rubbing snow in his face. He retreats to his car, returning with a quarter-stick and a large foam Half-Crescents #1 hand, and walks to a safe distance near the pond, stumbling and falling several times, Mariska and I laughing at him. He places the quarter-stick inside the red hand and stands it in the snow near the edge of the frozen water. Setting fire to the hand, he lumbers back to join us, his massive shadow bobbing up-and-down upon the drifts, Stoli bottle clutched to his side. We watch the flames lick quickly over the foam, spreading out from the flashpoint under thin wisps of black smoke. Soon the hand is engulfed, a colorful burning blotch upon an otherwise drab terrain.

The explosion seems incidental, almost like an afterthought, a loud blast sending tufts of foam like confetti into the sky, floating gently down upon our shoulders and hair, settling over the pond like a blood red tide.

Made in the USA
Columbia, SC
08 October 2017